California Young Reader Medal
ALA Best Book for Young Adults
School Library Journal Best Book of the Year
ABA "Pick of the Lists"

"A transcendent story of love, loyalty, and courage . . . Superb plotting, extraordinary characters, and crackling narrative make this novel one to be devoured in a single unforgettable sitting."
—*Publishers Weekly* (starred review)

"A masterpiece."—*School Library Journal* (starred review)

"Pulse-pounding, on both visceral and intellectual levels—a wild, brutal ride."—*Kirkus Reviews* (pointered review)

"Crutcher possesses a novelist's greatest asset: an ability to create people who are real and believable and about whom the reader can care deeply."
—*Horn Book Magazine*

"Crutcher's darkest and most riveting work to date. . . . Older YA's are likely to read this in one sitting and then will be left thinking about it for weeks afterward."—*VOYA*

CHRIS CRUTCHER

STAYING FAT FOR SARAH BYRNES

GREENWILLOW BOOKS

An Imprint of HarperCollins Publishers

Staying Fat for Sarah Byrnes
Copyright © 1993 by Chris Crutcher
All rights reserved. No part of this book may be used or reproduced in any manner whatsoever without written permission except in the case of brief quotations embodied in critical articles and reviews. Printed in the United States of America. For information address HarperCollins Children's Books, a division of HarperCollins Publishers, 195 Broadway, New York, NY 10007.
www.epicreads.com
The text of this book is set in Maxime.

Library of Congress Cataloging-in-Publication Data
Crutcher, Chris.
Staying Fat for Sarah Byrnes / by Chris Crutcher.
p. cm.
"Greenwillow Books."
Summary: The daily class discussions about the nature of man, the existence of God, abortion, organized religion, suicide, and other contemporary issues serve as a backdrop for a high-school senior's attempt to answer a friend's dramatic cry for help.
ISBN 978-0-06-268774-6 (pbk.)
PZ7.C89s 1993   91-40097
CIP AC
First paperback edition, 2009. Revised paperback edition, 2018.
23 24 25 26 27 LBC 9 8 7 6 5

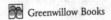 Greenwillow Books

For Molly and Hawk, in memory of Battle:
All true believers

STAYING FAT FOR
SARAH
BYRNES

CHAPTER
ONE

My dad left when I still had a month to go in the darkroom, and historically when people have tried to figure me out (as in, "What went wrong?"), they usually conclude that Mom spoiled me; gave me everything I wanted because I had no pappy. Truth is, Mom thinks I'm a whole lot better off without that particular pappy and has told me a thousand times she's glad I had the good sense to stay packed away until he split. They were young. My mother was my age now when I was born, and so was my dad.

I don't know very much about Dad, really. In eighteen years he's made no effort to contact me, and all I have is a picture. He's a college professor somewhere in the Midwest,

Mom thinks in Geology. She doesn't think Geology is in the Midwest, she thinks that's what he teaches. The fact that he's excited about rocks hasn't had much genetic influence on me as far as I can tell, but what I see in the picture of him has. My dad is a tub of lard. At least he was at eighteen. I'm not talking about a guy who should have gone light on the desserts and between-meal snacks. I'm talking about a guy who should have spread Super Glue on his lips before showing his face outside his bedroom each morning. My dad could have sold his extra chins for marble sacks.

And my mom is a fox. Really. Bona fide, hundred-thousand-dollar silver-pelt fox. She has dark brown hair and green eyes and this slinky, long, muscular body that she keeps in perfect working order, and I know for a fact half the kids who come to my house hope to catch her in shorts and a tank top. Christ, she's only thirty-six years old.

"Mom," I said one morning a couple of years ago, Dad's picture clutched tight in my beefy paw, "tell me something. Tell me why somebody who looks like you would fall for somebody who looks like *this*." I plopped the picture on the coffee table in front of her.

"Looks aren't everything, Eric," she said.

"His looks aren't *anything*," I said back. "And he left them for me."

She looked up and smiled. "You look a lot better than your dad," she said. "He was compulsive, ate all the time. You're big and solid. That's different."

"Big and solid as twelve pounds of mashed potatoes in an eight-pound bag," I said. "If you dressed me up in an orange-and-red sweater, you could ride me around the world in eighty days."

"And you have a much better sense of humor than your father," she said, probably remembering Dad's high regard for rocks. Mom was never one to let me dwell on the parts of me I didn't like.

My name is Eric Calhoune, and though I have spent hours in the weight room since that conversation, most folks call me Moby. My English teacher, Ms. Lemry, who is also my coach, sometimes calls me Eric the Well Read, because I'm pretty smart. She also calls me Double-E, for Eric Enigma. "I can't figure exactly how you're put together inside," she says. "You're a jock who doesn't compete in his best sport, a student who doesn't excel where his aptitude is highest, and you surround yourself with a supporting cast straight out of 'The Far Side.'"

"Tweech his own," I said, and pirouetted to tippy-toe out of the room, in keeping with my image as Double-E.

▼ ▼ ▼

If my belly button were a knothole it would certainly be more congruous with my keg-like body. I have chiseled away at my father's genetic code since I realized I was better equipped to roll to school than walk, but the bare-bones me is still more Raymond Burr than Arnold Schwarzenegger. All of which wouldn't matter, but for the amount of time that belly button is exposed, which approaches four hours a day. I'm a swimmer. I probably don't have to tell you the Speedo people don't employ William Conrad as a fashion designer, and I therefore do not step onto the starting blocks looking like a *Sports Illustrated* fashion plate.

Looks alone would be enough to keep most guys with my particular body design as far away from water as the Wicked Witch of the West, but swimming is a thinking man's sport and Ms. Lemry is a thinking man's coach. Besides, it keeps me far from the clutches of Coach Stone, who has been trying to get me to come out for wrestling since I was a frosh because he fancies me unbeatable as a heavyweight, which I very well might be. But the idea of a permanent gash across the bridge of my nose and mat burns on every pointed appendage does not appeal to me no matter how many trophies I might walk away with. I'm not a great swimmer, but I'm good—a lot better than you'd think looking at me—and I like the challenge of the clock, as well as the people involved. I also like the wake I create for the guy in the next lane.

We're eight thousand yards into the workout. Lemry's whistle blasts. "Let's wrap it up. Twenty-five yards. All out. Five breaths." Five breaths. No sweat.

"Twenty-five yards," she yells two laps later as we pull ourselves onto the deck at the far end. "All out. *Three* breaths." The oxygen bill is in the mail.

"Twenty-five yards. All out. *Two* breaths." Serious oxygen debt begins.

"Twenty-five yards. Did I say all out? One breath." The whistle.

"Twenty-five yards. Anyone hear me say all out? No breaths. Come on, ladies and gentlemen, we're almost there." The whistle. Oxygen debt approaches bankruptcy.

"Twenty-five yards. No breaths. Flip your turn and come back as far as you can. Last one, people. If darkness closes in or you hear the voice of God, come up." We hyperventilate so hard we can barely hear her instructions, though any of the twenty of us could recite them rote.

I hit the water almost full bore, backed off enough to keep from thrashing. At fifteen yards I feel the tightness in my lungs, and I back off the cadence maybe a half-beat, swallowing to give my body the illusion of breathing. I reach the far wall, tucking tight for maximum pushoff, blowing out only enough air to keep a chlorinated flash flood out of my sinuses, and go for it. In three years, no one on the team has outdistanced me at this drill. Mark Brittain says it's because I have a blowhole, but Mark is often intentionally unkind. It's because I *know* how to be mean to myself. I swim distance freestyle.

I'm within three strokes of the wall when my head pops out of the water like a marker buoy and a reverberation erupts out of me that would normally bring paramedics. Darkness crowds the edges of my peripheral vision, but I clutch the lane rope and suck air like an industrial-strength shop vac. Someday I'll make the full fifty yards. I can do it easily fresh, but not at the end of a three-hour workout.

"Good job, Mobe," Coach hollers from across the pool. "You'll never be extinct with that attitude."

I stand in front of the huge double doors at the entrance to Sacred Heart Hospital and breathe deep, my frozen hair hugging my head like a bicycle helmet and my breath shooting from my mouth like exhaust from a truck. I wear only a light jacket; my internal heating system boils for hours after workout. Coach forever tells me to cover up when I go outside, but when I cover up I sweat like a walrus in a sauna. I threaten Coach with my laundry.

Sarah Byrnes is inside. Eighth floor. Child and Adolescent

Psychiatric Unit. I've put this off, thought she'd be out in a couple of days, but it's been a full week. Sarah Byrnes. Toughest kid I know, and she just slipped away.

I don't want to go inside. I was here once about four years ago when my third cousin got drunk and attempted suicide. Not much of an attempt, really. He OD'd on Flintstone vitamins, but he was wigged out so bad they stuck him in for seventy-two-hour observation. What they observed was extremely yellow pee. I hated visiting him. The place itself was nice—thick carpeting and comfortable chairs, plenty of books to read and games to play. It felt safe in a strange way, not for me, but for the people in there. But they all had a look, as if something important had been peeled away. And you got the feeling it could happen to you.

Now Sarah Byrnes is here. My best friend. I stayed fat a whole year for her.

I push through the double-door entrance, passing the information desk on my left, following the carpeted corridors to the bank of elevators, where one stands open and empty. I push eight and turn to lean against the back wall when I hear "Hold!" and see a familiar face—a nameless kid from school—pushing a cart of linens toward me. I lunge for the row of buttons on the wall, intentionally pushing CLOSE DOOR, but appearing for all the world as if I'm trying to hold it open. "Oops," I say as the doors come together. I don't want company; don't want to explain who I'm here to see, or what happened to her.

After checking in, I spot Sarah Byrnes sitting on an overstuffed couch, gazing at that space-out spot three or four inches in front of her nose.

I say hi to no response and sit, lightly touching her forearm. Without her spirit behind her eyes, Sarah Byrnes is truly one of the ugliest human beings outside the circus. When she was three, as she tells it, she pulled a pot of boiling spaghetti off the stove onto herself, leaving horrible burn scars covering her face and hands. Her father, maybe the cruelest and certainly the most insensitive man I have had the misfortune to know, allowed only the medical attention required to keep her out of danger. Almost nothing reconstructive was done. He said it would serve as a good lesson to her in the future.

A woman approaches. "You must be Eric," she says.

I nod. "Is she going to be okay?"

"I'm Laurel," she says, extending her hand. "Sarah's counselor." She's a big woman, not fat, but strong and solid, maybe in her early thirties, with those earthy kind of features that require no makeup. She's not so much attractive as she is warm. "I don't know, to tell the truth," she says to my question. "She hasn't responded to much, though her doctor says she has all the proper physical reactions."

I study Sarah Byrnes's eyes while Sarah Byrnes studies the cosmos. "What should I say to her? I mean, can she understand me? "

"I don't know. Assume she can. Talk to her like you would if she were answering," Laurel says. "Make things as normal as possible."

I nod.

The nurse takes Sarah Byrnes's hand. "Sarah? Sarah. You have a visitor."

"If you want things to be normal," I say, "you have to call her by her whole name."

"What?"

"You have to call her by her whole name. Sarah Byrnes. She only answers to Sarah Byrnes."

Laurel stares at me blankly.

"When we were in junior high," I tell her, "Sarah Byrnes got sick of every new Einstein at school thinking he was the only genius in the world to figure out this great pun about her last name and her condition. She hated waiting for them to get it, so she made everyone call her Sarah Byrnes. If you just call her Sarah, she won't answer."

Laurel nods. "I'll tell the others. That's important. Is there anything else?"

"I don't think so."

"Well, I'll leave you two alone. Just talk with her about things that might jar her."

"Remember *Crispy Pork Rinds?*" I whisper into her ear when Laurel is out of sight. If anything should get a reaction, that should.

Sarah Byrnes stares ahead, while I remember.

I dropped onto the hard wooden chair outside Mr. Mautz's office, contemplating the conversation we were about to have. The chair creaked desperately under the pressure of my considerable bulk, the seat all but eclipsed by my beefy thighs. My mission, once that office door opened, was to not lie. I didn't want to tell the truth, exactly, I just wanted to not lie. There is a difference, I told myself. I was armed with information from Sarah Byrnes's report on the Bill of Rights that I would use if necessary.

Ms. Barker smiled from behind her secretary's desk, and I detected a hint of compassion. Ms. Barker had seen a lot of kids in this seat—probably none more than me—and knew well we needed all the compassion we could get, though it would be of little help once that door opened.

Her phone beeped and she spoke quietly into the handset, looked up and said, "You can go in now, Eric."

I grimaced, slowly lifting my carcass from the chair. Ms.

Barker smiled again. "Remember, it's against the law for him to do what he wants to do to you."

"Eric, have a seat," Mautz said, waving his hand toward another hard wooden chair, a twin to that in the outer office.

I sat, closing my eyes as I recognized the folded makeshift newspaper on his desk, forcing back the dread climbing through the top of my stomach and into my throat like a slow stream of burning lava. *Crispy Pork Rinds.* Rivulets of perspiration, a Calhounian trademark, began to run down my well-padded rib cage toward my belt. Soon my shirt would be soaked and Mautz, a true psychological mercenary, would have me. Think dry.

Mautz spread the paper deliberately across his expansive glass-covered desk surface. It looks at least as good as the regular school paper that comes out every two weeks, I thought. Maybe better.

Mautz glared at me, his light blue eyes penetrating my hopeless defenses like a laser through cotton candy, and I remember wondering if there's a graduate class principals take—Steely Gaze 501 or something—where they learn that.

"Have you lost some weight, Eric?" Mautz asked, his tone conversational, almost friendly.

I was not to be tricked. "No sir."

He squinted, cocking his head to one side. "Maybe you're just growing into your body."

"I doubt it, sir. I'll probably always be a fat kid."

"You shouldn't put yourself down, Eric," Mautz said. "It can't be good for your self-esteem."

Sarah Byrnes will be elected Miss America on the day Mautz cares one bit about my self-esteem. "I wasn't putting myself down, sir. I was just telling the truth." As was often the case under extreme pressure in those days, my mind ran nonsensically with his last words. Next to the steam room at my mom's fitness club was the self es-steem room. You go in after a hard workout and clouds of self es-steem roll out of the pipes to make you magically feel better. And if you used to stutter, you step forward from the watery mist, flawlessly booming out the Gettysburg Address, or if you had your face burned, like Sarah Byrnes, you emerge as a porcelain-skinned china doll. Or if you were fat . . .

Mautz jarred me back. "Well, be that as it may, I guess we're not here to talk about your weight, are we?"

"Probably not," I said.

"Probably not?" Mautz's eyebrows arched menacingly toward his crew cut.

"Well," I said nervously, the floodgates of my sweat glands creaking against the swelling reservoir, "I'm not exactly sure why you called me in here."

"Oh really?" Mautz picked up the paper, reading the headline. "*Crispy Pork Rinds.* Exactly what does that mean,

Mr. Calhoune? *Crispy Pork Rinds.*"

It was not a good sign that Mautz was calling me by my surname. "I'm not sure, sir. Isn't that like some kind of snack? Like Cheez Puffs or something?" The floodgates burst. Tributaries of sweat streamed south. I hoped the elastic on my undershorts was waterproof.

"It may very well be the name of a snack," Mautz said. "It is also the title on this so-called newspaper."

I nodded silently. "Oh."

"Oh," he mimicked. "Is that all you have to say?"

Gotta be careful here, I thought. Don't want to lie. I nodded.

"Do you know how I know this is your handiwork?" he asked.

No words were the best words.

"Because you're the only kid in this entire junior high who can write like this. You have a talent with language, Mr. Calhoune, but you're letting that talent work against you."

"Maybe someone from the high school wrote it," I offered. "You know, dropped it off right before school. Like maybe they're trying to get some kid here in trouble."

Mautz smiled. "Some kid here *is* in trouble. Every article in this piece of trash is about someone at this school." He sat forward in his plush, high-backed chair—the one Sarah

Byrnes called his throne—regarding me with the utterest contempt. "Now I'm going to say this once . . ."

Here comes, I thought. For my sake, Sarah Byrnes, this better work.

"Did you create this newspaper?"

I took a deep breath, my throat tightening over it. "I stand on the Fifth Amendment," I squeaked, "on the grounds that my answer may tend to incriminate me."

For the briefest of moments Mautz sat stunned.

I held my breath, wide-eyed.

"You what?" he said in a near whisper, his eyes slits.

"I stand on . . ."

"I HEARD YOU!"

I sank back as he quickly gathered what there was of his wits. "So you're going to lie."

"I'm not lying. I'm standing on the Fifth Amendment. That's this thing where . . ."

"I know what the Fifth Amendment is, Mr. Calhoune. It's used in a court of law, not in a principal's office."

"Sarah Byrnes's report on the Bill of Rights said it was a basic . . ."

"So Sarah Byrnes is in on this, too?"

"I didn't say that."

"And you didn't say she wasn't. Why don't you stand on

the Fifth Amendment?"

By now I was sweating so hard I began to slide across the seat. I said, "Okay. We stand on the Fifth Amendment."

"On the grounds that you may tend to incriminate yourselves."

I nodded. "Uh-huh."

Mautz stood. He was a full six feet five inches, weighing more than 235 pounds, carrying not one ounce of fat. His striped black-and-gray necktie spilled over his massive chest like a roller coaster track. His nearly black hair and dark beard served only to amplify the intensity of those unforgiving blue eyes. Mr. Mautz was one very scary dude. "Let me make something clear, Mr. Perry Mason," he said. "I'm willing to let you stand on the Fifth Amendment. One time. And I'm willing to let this *Crispy Pork Rinds* thing go. One time. But there will be no publications at this school without official approval, which means my approval. And if I see this again, I promise you I will make your life a living hell. Do you understand me?"

I can only nod.

"Very well. You may go."

I stood, turning to do just that, my pants plastered to the backs of my legs like wet cellophane and sweat pouring from my brow like rain.

"Eric," Mautz said as I reached the door.

"Huh?"

"You're perspiring. I take that as a sign you know you've made a big mistake."

In the outer office, Ms. Barker glanced up and smiled, searching for signs of the battle, finding them in my colorless face and soaked shirt. "Oh, Eric," she said, crinkling her nose. "Not so good, huh?"

"Not so good."

She reached into her center desk drawer, withdrawing a copy of *Crispy Pork Rinds*. "It's a little rough for a finished product," she whispered, smiling, "but I've seen worse. Why *Crispy Pork Rinds?*"

I looked to make sure Mautz's door remained closed. "Don't you get it? Sarah Byrnes is crispy, I'm a porker, and rinds are the part that's left—that no one pays attention to. We print the news the regular newspaper misses."

"Very clever," she said. "May I assume the first copy was the last?"

I looked toward the closed door, raised my eyebrows, and shrugged.

"So, how'd it go? You take the Fifth?" Sarah Byrnes asked in the hallway outside the math room.

I slapped a flat palm to my chest in a hopeless gesture to

quiet the jackhammer beating of my heart and breathed deep. "Yeah. I took the Fifth."

"And?"

"It must work better in court than here," I said. "And now he knows you're in on it because my brain went dead and I told him where I learned about the Fifth. I'm sorry, Sarah Byrnes. It just slipped out."

"I don't care if he knows I'm in on it," she said. "In fact, I hope he knows. I think we should get extra credit. This book I read says some of the best journalism in the whole 1960s came from underground newspapers."

"Well, Mautz says he's going to forget it this time, but if it comes out again he's going to make my life a living hell."

"Like this is heaven?" Sarah Byrnes said.

"Yeah." I looked down at my body, the target of every fat joke since Eve walked up behind Adam and grabbed his love handles. Like Sarah Byrnes, I wondered what Old Man Mautz could do to make things worse. "He could make me come to school without a shirt," I said out loud. "Or make me wear a bra, like the kids did in sixth grade."

Sarah Byrnes laughed. "He'd get fired. Your mom could sue the school for all the money it's worth, which can't be much. I say we get busy with *Crispy Pork Rinds Two*."

CHAPTER
TWO

"Okay, Mobe," Ms. Lemry is saying, "you dragged us off in this impossible direction, *you* tell us whether the world is a good place or a bad place." It's the first day of second semester. Thirteen of us have signed up for Lemry's baby, an elective class called Contemporary American Thought. To be enrolled, you must be a second semester senior willing to examine your beliefs. Through a magnifying glass. It's a Lemry class, so you'd best be serious.

"Considering the alternative," I say in answer to her query, "it's a good place." That gets a titter.

"All you're saying," she says back, "is that the known is better than the unknown. There's a strong case to be made for that belief being a core factor in keeping humans on their knees." She looks around the room, seeing mild interest. "I call this class Contemporary American Thought. That's so it will look good on your transcript. Its subtitle is Accountability, because you will be held accountable for everything you say. If Mr. Calhoune tells me the world is a good place to live given the alternative, he needs to define 'good' and he needs to convince us he knows the alternative. In other words, he's required to be *careful* when he opens his mouth. We need to put value back into words and ideas."

She scans the room again. Interest is picking up. I believe the prospect of talking about what we think in this class is exciting to most of us. Particularly when we're going to do it with one of the most exquisite human beings alive, for my money. Lemry is something else to look at, for one thing. She's petite and about as sexy as you can get without being a movie star or a belly dancer, with shoulder-length blond hair, dark brown eyes that look right through you, and big dangly earrings that push her face out at you. If you have impure thoughts about her, however, you better keep them to yourself, because she'll flat cut you up if you get disrespectful. Lemry is the women's rights poster girl. I mean poster person.

"So let's take a trial run," she says. "The subject's a

little broad, but go with it, Mobe. Is the world a good place or a bad place?"

I picture Sarah Byrnes up in Sacred Heart, as physically ugly as a person gets, staring into an empty pit. No one home. "It's a bad place," I say.

"Why?"

"Because you can't win," I say. "Not for long."

"Back yourself up, Mobe."

I look around the room, into expectant eyes. They want me to go first; see if I'm going to get eaten up. Send the pig to slaughter. It's a little scary because, though I have good friends here, I also have mortal enemies, and you don't want your enemies to know what you think. Or feel.

"I went to see Sarah Byrnes last night," I say.

"And?"

"It was bad."

"Make your point," Lemry says gently. "You're telling us why the world is a bad place to live."

"Well, I was thinking. Sarah Byrnes is up there just staring into space. She doesn't talk or respond to anything. When I looked at her close, when I saw her without her razor-sharp words and her fire—all the stuff she cuts us up with—she looked gone. And I thought, I don't blame you. I'd go away, too, because the world doesn't provide any place safe for her.

Every day when she gets up, she knows she has to bring her scarred-up face to school, knowing what everyone thinks and won't say. There's no place to hide and it never lets up. I'd call that a bad place to live." I look over to my good friend Ellerby for support, but he stares at his desk.

Lemry is quiet a second. "I'm not real comfortable talking about someone who isn't here," she says finally, "but I think this is worth pursuing. What does anyone else think?"

Kathy Gould sits forward. "That only makes the world a bad place for Sarah Byrnes."

"Yeah," I start, "but there are thousands of other people. . ."

"That still only makes it a bad place for them. Not all of us. The question is whether it's a good or bad place, period. If it's bad, it's bad for everybody. Or at least a majority." Kathy is a tall redhead, smarter than hell, with the sense of humor of a brussels sprout. It's hard for me to imagine her taking the side of the world in this one; depression has been her job—her way of life—since grade school.

I feel instant anger that I don't completely understand, and I want to hurt her some way, but Lemry reads my mind. "Tell you what," she says, "this is a good subject to get started with, broad as it is, but I'm really not comfortable letting it go too far without the person we're talking about being here and giving us permission. So what I need are examples a little farther from home for the time being, okay?"

I pull back while the rest of the class drags out examples from real life, newspapers, fiction, or wherever, pitting human joy against human pain. I realize I didn't want to talk about philosophy, I wanted to talk about Sarah Byrnes. She's my best friend and she's *dying*. We became friends when I was as fat as she is ugly, and I promised a long time ago that I would never turn away from her—told us both that my feelings for her weren't selfish, that I didn't like her only because we shared "terminal uglies," as she put it.

Actually, Dale Thornton provided the reason for *Crispy Pork Rinds*. By eighth grade, Dale should have been in his second year of the Army, as many times as he'd been held back. The guy had a driver's license, for Crissake. Teachers didn't know what to do with him because every year he was just that much bigger than the other kids in class and not one bit smarter. Every spring they tried to pass him on into high school and every spring his dad lumbered into the front office to say by dang Dale was gonna stay right there in eighth until he got it right and the only way he'd finally learn was to do it over and over and over. Then Mr. Thornton would say he'd hate to sue the school, but if they passed Dale on without his necessary life skills, well then he'd sure have to look into that. I don't know what kind of "necessary life skills" our school taught that Dale could have used in his life. The teachers all had license plates on their cars, and the parking lot was already paved.

And I'll tell you what. I'd seen Dale try to do his homework, and if old man Thornton thought he did anything over and over and over, he had another think coming, which, by the looks of him, he probably wouldn't use. Dale was so big that year he couldn't even get a good fight. We just rolled over like poodles in the path of a Doberman when we saw him coming. I'm telling you, Dale Thornton was pulling down a darn decent living from second-degree lunch money extortion alone, not to mention his protection racket.

But then he ran into Sarah Byrnes. When you live with a dad who has been rejected by the producers of the *Halloween* movies because he's too mean for the role, and your face has been burned beyond recognition for most of your memory, and you've been reminded every stinking day of your life with funny looks and nasty names, you don't get too excited when some two-bit would-be dropout sticks his fist in your face and wants your stuff. Sarah Byrnes has always used pretty rough language, so I won't say exactly what she said the first time Dale confronted her, but I will say she said it twice: once about Dale and once about his mother.

Now, probably half the people in our town knew Dale's mother ran off with his uncle, leaving Dale with his dad, who isn't exactly Andy Griffith, and Dale himself had said things about her that were five times worse than what Sarah Byrnes said. But he took immense offense, and he punched Sarah Byrnes square in the nose, or what's left of it, because Sarah Byrnes's nose is mostly scar tissue.

Sarah Byrnes's blond pigtails stood straight out on contact, and she hit the ground so hard the air rushed out of her lungs like a blown popcorn bag, but she sprang back like a plastic Rocky Balboa punching bag, swinging to kill.

"Just give me your money, Scarface," Dale said, "and I'll leave you alone."

She stuck her chin right in his face and said, "Take it," and he punched her again.

I don't think Sarah Byrnes got in one good lick. Dale was twice her size if he was a pound, and born to fight. But Sarah Byrnes kept getting up and getting up and pretty soon the bruising and swelling beneath the scars got to looking so bad it even scared Dale, so he said it one more time: "Just gimme your money. Gimme the money and I'll quit."

"When I'm dead you'll get my money," she said, her teeth clenched so tight I thought I heard them begin to crumble. Then she turned to me. "Eric Calhoune, if he kills me, you better make sure he doesn't get nothin' of mine," and I said okay, but if he really killed her I was pretty sure I'd be hard to find.

Dale glared at her again and dropped his fists. "You ain't worth it," he said. "You probably ain't got no money anyway. I'll just take it from your fat friend."

Well, my hands were into my pockets about up to the elbows when I heard Sarah Byrnes's voice. "You give him anything, I'll kill you," she said, and all of a sudden my choices were to get killed by Dale Thornton or get killed by Sarah Byrnes. Hanging or lethal injection. I figured just in case I only got crippled for life, I'd still need a friend to carry my stuff around, so I took my hands out of my pockets real slow like, and stood there, shaking like a jellyfish riding a jackhammer and sweating like I was going to melt.

Old Dale must have been plain worn out and frustrated from hammering on Sarah Byrnes so long with so little result, because instead of beating me into whimpering slime, he said "Forget it" and walked away—though not before I lost at least twelve pounds in nervous runoff. My knees felt so weak I dropped to my butt like a shotput right there on the ground and closed my eyes, but a shadow passed in front of them and they popped right back open. Two scarred hands grabbed my collar and yanked me to my feet, and I stood sucking air, inches from Sarah Byrnes's pummeled face. "You fat little dork!" she said. "You were going to give that juvenile delinquent money."

"He was going to kill me."

She pulled me closer and sneered. "Every time you let somebody take your stuff, or let them see you hurt, you get killed."

I already knew that, but the threat of her decking me had not completely passed. I changed the subject. "Hey, I thought we weren't going to call each other names. You called me a fat dork."

"You're right," she said, releasing my collar. "Remind me of that tomorrow, and if I'm not still so mad I want to skin you alive, I'll say I'm sorry."

Well, Sarah Byrnes never did say she was sorry, and I really didn't think she would, but it was the next day, when she really wasn't mad at me anymore, that we began plans for *Crispy Pork Rinds*. And on Friday of that week, right before first period, a copy appeared on the desk of every kid in eighth grade. The headline read:

SIXTEEN YEARS AGO IN HISTORY

Man with Brain the Size of Tic Tac Mates with Amoeba

Couple gives birth to giant adjusto; names him Dale

It didn't equal the level of *National Enquirer* journalism we planned to reach with a little practice, but it was a pretty good start.

The bell rings, jarring my mind back into CAT class, where my body has been filling up space. I drop my books into my backpack, and as I pass Lemry's desk, she stops me. "You zoned on me," she says. "Where'd you go?"

I say, "Away from Kathy Gould."

"Couldn't take the heat?"

"Not today. You got a minute?"

"Just about. You want to talk about Sarah Byrnes?"

"I don't know. Yeah. She just sits. It scares me, Coach, seeing her with everything stripped away. She looked like a beat-up old container or something. She looked dead."

"Did you talk to anyone?"

"A counselor. She, said to keep coming and act normal and talk about things we'd talk about if Sarah Byrnes were answering me."

Lemry puts an arm on my shoulder. "That must have been hard."

I smile. "And not just because I look like some kind of unconscious cretin holding a half-hour conversation with someone who doesn't give out answer number one, either. Sarah Byrnes is really important to me and . . . I need to be important to her, too. But I'm not right now. Nothin' is. God, back before there was swimming or you or Ellerby or anything, there was me and Sarah Byrnes."

Lemry starts gathering her books. "You need to remember what's going on with her right now isn't about you. You were right, Mobe. We forget she has to get up every day and face herself. This could be her way of taking a vacation."

"What if she never comes back?"

Lemry raises her eyebrows and grimaces. "I don't know. I'm not a shrink."

CHAPTER
THREE

Ellerby slides to a stop in the packed snow in front of my house in the Christian Cruiser and blasts the horn, which plays a sort of sick tuba rendition of "The Old Rugged Cross," then jumps out and starts up our ice-covered sidewalk. He nearly falls on his butt twice and calls to my mother to come skate couples with him. Mom opens the kitchen window to tell him to get that monstrosity away from her house before she calls a local Christian terrorist group, but Ellerby only smiles and says, "Hi, Mrs. Moby," and drops dramatically to his hands and knees to crawl safely to the kitchen door.

The Cruiser would be a true eyesore even in a nation of atheists. It's a pale blue 1973 Pontiac station wagon with airbrushed clouds billowing from hood to tailgate. Bold black old English script, stretching from the front to the rear fender, announces THE WAGES OF SIN IS A BUCK FIFTY. A MIGHTY FORTRESS IS OUR DOG, in identical script, screams at innocent bystanders from the driver's side, a testament to Ellerby's lifelong commitment to his family's Rottweiler, Dick. (He sometimes threatens to give the dog to me just so it could be called Moby's Dick.) And if you happen to be chasing Ellerby down in a police helicopter, a not altogether unfathomable possibility, you will be treated to ORAL ROBERTS TAKES ASPIRIN, an old Rodney Dangerfield line from the days when Oral healed all comers over Sunday morning television. Ellerby is a dedicated student of the history of Christian broadcasting. His car has been the target of more vandalism than the Berlin Wall in the two years since he unveiled it, but Steve is an excellent body and fender man, and he just drags it down to his uncle's shop, pounds out the dents, and repaints it. It looks brand new.

Ellerby whisks past my mother standing over the kitchen sink, patting her lightly on the butt. She has long since quit threatening to send his teeth home in a paper bag for that. "Call me a throwback," he says, a wistful glint in his eye, "but when I see a teenage butt on a thirty-six-year-old woman, well, I just *have* to attend to it."

In my room he plops onto the chair next to my bed,

where I lie staring straight up at the insides of my eyelids, listening to the Byrds full blast in my headphones from the CD player mounted on my headboard. Mom keeps me supplied with the finest in musical electronic hardware as long as I agree to buy one CD of songs recorded between the years 1956 and 1975 for every contemporary one. I'm hooked and I don't even know what's on MTV anymore, because I'm busy with Bob Dylan and Buddy Holly and the Byrds and the Rolling Stones and the Dave Clark Five and Turtles who are neither mutant nor ninja.

So I'm lying here, lost in a world in which "for every thing there is a season," and Ellerby's hand on my foot almost launches me clear through winter.

He picks *The Best of Buddy Holly* from the pile. "Half these people are dead."

I look at my watch. "Jesus, is it time already?"

"Past time," he says. "Our scales are crackin' and peelin'."

Yesterday's meet with South Central was the only one on this week's schedule, so we have a free Saturday. When that happens, Lemry puts it to us to be sure we don't peak too early in the season. She wants every kid at his or her fastest when it counts—for Regionals and State. Everything else is practice.

Today's workout is to be particularly dreaded because there is an asterisk beside it on the bulletin board, tabbing it as "special," which in real terms means torturous. "Special" means "How much can you take?" and is freshly dredged from the very bottom of the barrel of Lemry's fiendish mind. Today's will be a hundred—count 'em, a *hundred*—timed one-hundred yard swims, starting at two-minute intervals. If you make it in a minute, you have a minute to rest. If you make it in a minute fifty-nine seconds, you have a second to rest. But that ain't all. To remain in the workout, you must hit your time standard or faster, which is figured at ten to fifteen seconds slower than your best time in a meet, depending on who you are and what you swim. Miss your standard, swim no more. Also, every fifteenth hundred is butterfly, and like Walker Dupree in a book called *Stotan!* my idea of hell is swimming butterfly down a one-lane pool into infinity.

A sane person would miss his time standard after about twenty and call it a day, but no true swimmer fits that description even loosely. There's something about shared pain that keeps you going when you might back off on your own. And I would cram my tongue into a beehive and wiggle it wildly before letting her hear this, but when somebody puts as much into us as Lemry does, I'd die before wimping out on her. That goes for most of the rest of the team, too.

Ellerby and I whip the Cruiser through the snowy back streets of Spokane, Mahalia Jackson wailing "The Lord's

Prayer" through the speaker mounted on the roof. I crouch low in the seat, my stocking cap pulled low in hopes I won't be arrested as an accomplice to desanctifying the word of God.

The Cruiser has caused a bit of a crack in the solidarity of our team—maybe even a chasm. Make that an abyss. Last year, Mark Brittain, who has brothers named Matthew, Luke, and John and a sister named Mary—need I say more?—beseeched Lemry to prohibit Ellerby from driving it to meets, including those at our own school, and to put a major squelch on his sacrilegious antics whenever he is any way representing the school or the team. Lemry told Mark to read the U.S. Constitution. Instead, Mark logged fifty more hours watching the Trinity Network, then took his complaint to the administration—with a petition signed by twenty-five or thirty of his faithful followers—requesting not only that Ellerby be banned from representing the school in his loathsome powder blue monstrosity, but that it also be outlawed in the student parking lot now and forever more, world without end, amen. Brittain had a friend in high places, because Mautz is the vice-principal here at MacArthur now, and Ellerby is about an ear hair above me and Sarah Byrnes on his list of primary candidates for live organ donors. Luckily for all us backers of western democracy, Mr. Patterson, our principal, is a man of justice and vision and knows—though he would never say it—that Mautz is a wart on the butt of humanity. Anyway, Patterson keeps Mautz from turning MacArthur into a prison camp, and that means the Christian Cruiser rolls on past the scorn of Mark Brittain and his disciples.

I should probably also mention that Ellerby's dad is a preacher. He's the white, stiff-round-collar man at St. Mark's Episcopal church, where Ellerby wears a robe and lights the candles every week. And they call *me* an enigma.

My best hundred freestyle—a freak performance, actually— took me a little under 52 seconds to complete, so my time standard is 1.02. Lemry's kind and rounds her numbers *up*. I'm best at long distances, the five hundred and 1650 freestyles, so time standards are probably easier for me to hit. Ellerby is a flyer—so much a flyer that his best hundred fly time is almost the same as his best hundred free, which is the fastest on the team. That gives him an advantage over me in this workout, because the fly requirement every fifteenth hundred makes me consider suicide, while it recharges him. I may have said— there's something seriously wrong with Ellerby.

The time span on this workout is more than three hours, but probably only five or six of us will go the distance. When someone misses a standard, they remain and cheer the others on, and afterward Lemry will provide pizza, delivered hot and fresh from Pizza Maria's, and several billion gallons of Coca-

Cola. We have ten boys and ten girls on the team, so it's a nice little party, but there's very little chance of it getting too intimate after that kind of workout. In my own case, I should say to keep the record straight, Las Vegas bookmakers get migraine headaches even considering the odds.

"You up for this?" Mark Brittain leads the circle pattern in the lane next to mine, a tribute to Lemry's genius. Either of us would willingly belly flop from the three-meter board onto punji sticks dipped in dead animal rot before letting the other outlast us. Brittain can outsprint me any day at a hundred or two hundred yards, but repeat time standards are my game. He might touch ahead of me on the first twenty, but he can't afford to beat me by far or he'll waste himself for the stretch. We're about equal in the butterfly, so he has no advantage there, and though there's really no doubt he's a more talented swimmer, he doesn't have the guts of a man with eight years' verbal abuse from Sarah Byrnes. I have those guts.

"Yeah, I'm up for this," I say back. "How 'bout you?"

"Don't know. Been torn down a little lately. I'll give it my best shot." A cheap attempt at a psych job. Get me thinking he's barely holding on at first, and then come after me. Even though the real competition is against the dock, it's hard to ignore the guy in the next lane when he's Mark Brittain. Sorry, Mark. This is a hundred hundreds. I own you.

Ours is a regulation six-lane, twenty-five-yard pool. Ellerby, Brittain, and I lead circle patterns in adjacent lanes so we can see each other—another stroke of Lemry's genius which seems to keep our competitive juices flowing. My group and Brittain's have four swimmers each and Ellerby's and the rest have three. Fastest swimmer goes first, with the others leaving at three-second intervals, swimming on the right, just like on the highway. Pass down the middle, and if you catch the person in front of you on one repeat, you go first on the next.

The shrill blast of Lemry's whistle ricochets around the high walls, and the swimmers in Brittain's lane each drop to one knee, clasp hands, and bow their heads. Brittain leads them in a quick prayer asking God to let each do his or her best. On the far side, Ellerby drops to both knees, throwing his head back as he stretches his arms wide, and loudly begs Jesus to come swim the laps for him. When there's no answer, he opens one eye to a squint and asks if John the Baptist is home. "Damn," he says in the face of no response. It's old stuff and Brittain's squad doesn't react. Lemry sighs and shakes her head. Any conflict will keep us going. She knows we'll need every bit of love and hate we can muster to get through this.

The first ten repeats go down easy for everyone. At fifteen, the first of six flys, we get a hint of how this will end. Seven people drop out after forty-five—the third fly—six of them boys. The girls would gloat, but by now the idea of using even one calorie for oral communication is unthinkable. At sixty we lose two girls. At sixty-one, when the first of Brittain's group succumbs, Ellerby breaks the code of silence to ask Brittain's Lord why he has forsaken them, but after that the only sounds to be heard are the constant churning of the water interrupted by the slap of feet and calves on each flip turn, the shrill blast of Lemry's whistle, and the urgent whine of eleven wheezing, oxygen-deprived idiots sucking every last molecule of breathable air out of the chlorine-filled atmosphere.

At eighty-five, seven of us remain, and I'm holding less than a half-second under my time standard, cursing myself for my one miraculous hundred-yard freestyle during the second meet of the year—which was within two-tenths of Brittain's best, giving us both the same standard. I'm touching ahead of him now, have been since about thirty-five, but not by much. I feel at a disadvantage setting the pace, because he knows I won't miss. That means I have to think and swim when all he has to do is swim. Mostly I'm just looking for reasons to hate him because he's such a pompous turd, and the power of that particular emotion will get me through this.

At ninety, we swim our last fly. There's no time standard on the flys, but butterfly is butterfly and at this point a slow one is just as hard as a fast one, and the important thing is the recovery time between repeats. Brittain and I finish in a dead heat at about a minute forty—Ellerby beats us by an easy ten seconds—and for the first time I think I might not be there for the final ten; twenty seconds' rest just might not do it. Ellerby gives me the high sign—he's alone in his lane by now—indicating he'll set the pace for this one. If I can hit the next two, I'll recover.

We hit the water on the whistle and the surge of power I normally feel through the first lap is absent. I see Ellerby coming out of the turn a half body length ahead of me and know I have to pick it up on two and three to have a chance. Brittain is hanging with me, continuing to let me work the strategy so if I miss, at least he won't have done any worse than I did. That pisses me off, and I have a good second lap and feel a little power gathering when I flip into number three. At the end of three I'm out of gas and running on the simple knowledge that if I give it up to pain and go all out, I'll have a minute to catch up, and I grit my teeth and sprint for the finish, touching a tenth of a second under my standard, in a dead heat with Brittain. Ellerby is a half body length ahead.

Nine more.

Ninety-two is a carbon copy of ninety-one, and now I know I'll make it. Only three boys remain; four girls. The rest of the team is revived sufficiently to urge us on loudly, chanting our names on starts and finishes.

Before the whistle on ninety-five, I look past Brittain to Ellerby and nod, raising my eyebrows. Ellerby nods back. We're greedy. We want to make it, want Brittain to fold.

Ellerby holds up two fingers—the number of seconds we're going to take this one under the standard—and I nod. If we can pull it off, Brittain won't know what hit him; he expects us to cut the time standard by a razor's edge.

When Lemry's whistle blasts, we hit the water and I reach to the bottom of my reserves for a *strong* first lap. Ellerby does the same, and of course Brittain goes with us. Ellerby and I wring tenths of a second out on laps two and three, then kick all out on four. Brittain goes with us. We finish a second and a half under our standard.

Astonished realization passes over Mark's face when he sees the clock. He's not a distance man, and for him the jig is up. I smile and gasp, "Good swim." He misses ninety-six by a full second, and he's gone. Ellerby and I and two of the remaining girls finish the last three and Pizza Maria is banging on the door.

Mark Brittain is pissed.

The devil made us do it.

The euphoria of our conquest drives me through the

subsequent feeding frenzy in high gear, but within minutes of devouring my last slice whole, I begin to slip. Deep heat radiates from every muscle, and as that warmth consumes me I could fall asleep on the bare deck, but I still have to visit Sarah Byrnes, so I slap high fives all around and get Ellerby to shower with me and swing me home low in his sweet chariot.

"Guess we did a dance on Brittain," Ellerby says, settling behind the wheel.

"Guess so," I say back, sliding down in the seat.

"It's hard to resist. He's so damn righteous; such a dumb, plastic God Squadder. Sometimes I wish I could have religion their way. You know, no responsibilities in life but to cut down people who don't think the way you do." He waves a hand. "Aaahh. It's not worth talking about. But we burned him, didn't we? I knew we could get him. He's such a leech he couldn't check out his own body to figure out we were doin' him in." He pounded the steering wheel. "God, I love justice." He looks over at me. "Goin' up to see your friend?"

I nod.

"You like her." It isn't a question.

I nod again.

He starts to say more, but doesn't, and we ride over the silent snow-covered streets to my house, chuckling every once in a while when one or the other of us pictures Brittain's face the moment he realized he'd been duped.

At home, I grab Mom's car to negotiate the icy streets across the South Hill to Sacred Heart, thinking of those days long ago when I held onto Sarah Byrnes like the only life raft in truly tempestuous, treacherous seas. She pushed her scars directly into our tormentors' faces, while I disappeared into my cottage cheese carcass like a scared turtle in a soft shell, watching her wage our war of the outcasts alone. It's really hard to imagine how afraid I was then; how I pulled the covers over my head at night and prayed to hurry up and get older so I wouldn't care so much. It's also hard to imagine how I ate as much as I did.

The population of the Child and Adolescent unit is down on weekends. There are no classes and no therapy groups going, and a few older kids sit reading while others quietly play games. Younger kids trail nurses and counselors like pull toys from spot to spot.

Sarah Byrnes sits on the same spot on the same couch where I left her. Laurel isn't here, but a big, young guy named Sam is taking her place, and he approaches as I sit making conversation with myself in hopes Sarah Byrnes will latch on to something she wants to talk about.

He says, "You must be Eric."

I nod, shaking his extended hand. "Anything different?

Has she been on this couch since yesterday?"

Sam smiles and shakes his head. "No. She sits in on all the activities. She just isn't talking, that's all. We know she hears and understands because she does whatever we're doing."

"She eating okay?"

Sam nods. "Weight is good. She doesn't eat a lot, but then she's not burning a lot of energy." He squats beside us next to the couch. "Was there an event that set this off?"

"Not that I know of. She was sitting in American Government class and just tripped out. When the bell rang, she didn't move. It couldn't have been in response to anything we were talking about because we were answering the questions at the end of the chapter."

Sam nods, then grimaces. "Well, if you think of something, or if you know anyone who might shed some light on this, let us know. I'm told you're her best friend. You should know the more you come and talk, the better chance she has of coming out. Talk about old times, you know, familiar things." He pauses. "What do you know about her father?"

I look sideways at Sarah Byrnes and say, "I've known Sarah Byrnes since grade school, but she's only invited me to her house three times, and her dad was never home. He's mean, though, I'll tell you that. Mean big time. I know for a fact he wouldn't let them repair her face when she first got burned. He seems awful proud of how tough she is."

"What does she say about him?"

I remember her threatening me with her fists when I tried to talk about her father in junior high. "Not much."

Sam scratches his head. "That fits what we've seen. He's come up twice—didn't stay more than ten minutes either time. Does she have any other close friends? Anyone who might know something about her, or push her a little?"

"Well," I say. "There was this one guy back in junior high. His name's Dale Thornton. He was kind of a friend and kind of an enemy. He dropped out after eighth grade, though. Think he could help?"

"Depends on how much a friend and how much an enemy he was."

"More friend than enemy," I say. "At least at the end."

Old Dale was not having his best day. Though few of us would dare taunt him alone, there was safety in numbers and he'd already heard his name far more times than he would have expected. "Hey, Dale, I see you made the front page," greeted him as he stepped onto school property that morning, followed by several variations even before the first period bell rang. At first, Dale just smiled and waved in the direction of the voice. By the third time he heard it, however, he had seen

Crispy Pork Rinds, and though he didn't read all that well, understood clearly his role as the target of Sarah Byrnes's and my incisive journalistic focus.

In the hallway at the end of third period Dale caught up with Norm Nickerson, a blond, blue-eyed, bookwormish kid who spent our elementary years as the kid most likely to be beat up by someone from a lower grade. Dale clamped Norm's cheek hard between his thumb and forefinger. "Norman, my boy," he said with a sneer. "Let's you and me go to the can for a smoke—maybe have a little talk."

Norman mounted a weak protest, but Dale squeezed so hard Norm's lip began to numb.

I was hiding out in a stall with my paranoia, my feet pulled up onto the toilet seat, waiting for the fourth period bell, in the event Dale figured me for senior editor of our underground gazette and came for his pound of flesh. I peeked out the crack in the door, breathing soft as a man passing a township of killer bees in the night.

Dale offered Norman the pack.

"No thanks," Norman said, "I just had one." In fact, Norman Nickerson had never even puffed a cigarette, but at eighty-three pounds and well under five feet, he wasn't about to chance angering the man to whom most of us paid three-quarters of our weekly allowance—for protection from Dale Thornton.

"That's okay," Dale said, "I only got one left anyway." Norman reached into his pocket, but Dale raised a hand. "Got a deal for you," he said, and Norm was all ears. "I'll let you go today."

Norm waited.

Dale glared.

Still Norm waited.

Still Dale glared.

"That's not a deal," Norman offered finally. "What do *you* get?"

"Oh, yeah," Dale said, waving his cigarette in the air. "I almost forgot." He handed Norm a crumpled copy of *Crispy Pork Rinds*. "Read this."

Norm took the paper reluctantly. He glanced nervously at Dale, then down to the paper. He had thought it was pretty funny earlier in the morning. It was less funny now with Dale Thornton looming over him. Norman shot Dale another uneasy glance, and began to read silently.

Dale slapped the side of his head so hard Norman must have thought the phone rang. "Out loud, you dip!" he yelled. "Read it out loud!" and Norman realized Dale couldn't read well enough to get through the article. Holding his hot, reddened ear tenderly with his left hand, he opened his mouth to read.

"I'd read it myself," Dale said, "but a man of my statue hires his gruntwork done. Read."

I think Norman started to tell Dale that's *stature,* but thought better and adjusted his glasses. He began with the headline.

"I read that part," Dale warned. "Just gimme the small print." Norm skipped to the text, reading in his high shaky voice.

"A man described by authorities as one evolutionary step above a banana slug has recently admitted to having been locked in the Sacajawea Junior High biology lab over a long weekend nearly sixteen years ago when he fell asleep and was mistaken as a cadaver. Though the man is incapable of human speech, he was able, over a period of weeks, to chisel out his story in hieroglyphics on the bathroom wall of the insane asylum where he now resides. He claims that toward the end of the second day of his accidental captivity, he got downright lonely and sought companionship at his own intellectual level. He found that companionship in a petri dish."

Norman glanced up at Dale. He had to be terrified because Dale was famous for confusing the message with the messenger. If that happened, Norman knew his nose would soon be pressing hard against the bottom of the toilet, where it is extremely hard to breathe.

"Keep readin'," Dale said. "That ain't all of it. I seen it. It's longer than that."

Norman drew a deep breath.

"According to the man, who identified himself as Morton Thornton, the night got real long and by midnight, he was darn well wed to one of the lovelier inhabitants of the dish, a comely middle-aged amoeba of unknown parentage named Rita. When he was rescued on the morning of the following day, Morton plumb forgot about his single-celled nuptials and went back to his daytime job tasting the contents of open pop bottles for backwash and cigarette butts. Only sixteen years later, when a brilliant Sacajawea Junior High roving reporter— who shall remain nameless—discovered the product of this union lurking among us right here at Sac Junior High, was Morton's long-held secret discovered.

"This intrepid reporter was present three weeks into Dale Thornton's third try at seventh grade, when the young Einstein bet this reporter and several other members of the class that he could keep a wad of chewing tobacco in his mouth from the beginning of fifth period Social Studies until the bell. The dumb jerk only lasted twenty minutes, after which he sprinted from the room, not to be seen for the rest of the day. When he returned on the following morning, he told Mr. Getz he had suddenly become ill and had to go home, but without a written excuse (he probably didn't have a rock big enough for his dad to chisel it on) he was sent to the office. The principal, whose intellectual capacities lie only fractions of an IQ point above Dale's, believed his lame story, and Dale was readmitted to class. Our dauntless reporter, however, smelled a larger story, recognizing that for a person to attempt this in the first place, even his *genes* would have to be dumber than dirt. With a zeal rivaled only by Alex Haley's relentless search for Kunta Kinte, he dived into Dale's seamy background, where he discovered the above story to be absolutely true and correct. Further developments will appear in this newspaper as they unfold."

Norman folded the paper slowly. I breathed through my pores in order not to be discovered.

"That it?" Dale asked quietly.

Norman raised his eyebrows. "That's it," he squeaked.

"All that there story says is I'm pretty dumb, don't it? Me an' my dad," Dale said.

Norman winced and nodded. "Uh-huh. It's not necessarily true though. I mean it's not a real newspaper. I was there the day you did the tobacco. Really, it was pretty neat. Nobody else would have had the guts. . . ."

"How'd they know my old man's name is Morton?" Dale said. "Everybody calls my old man Butch. He finds out about this, he'll skin *my* hide, 'cause he'll think I told."

Norm was quiet. He lived with his family on a farm. He knew better than to mess with a wounded animal.

"How'd they know?" Dale was insistent.

"I don't know," Norman squeaked. "Really, I was there. The day with the tobacco. I mean . . ."

"Better shut up," Dale warned, then paused a minute. "Better give me your money, too."

"I thought you said . . ."

"Yeah, well, you was wrong. You gonna give me the money or you wanna go swimmin'?" Dale nodded toward the toilet stall, where I sat. Give him the money, Norman.

Norman Nickerson dug deep.

By fifth period, word was out that Dale Thornton was looking for Eric Calhoune, and a high-stakes gambling pool had been set up in an inconspicuous corner of the student lounge. Bets were running three to one that I wouldn't make it home with all my body parts. Dale had been seen in the hard chair in the outer office before the lunch bell, and rumor said he spent the entire lunch period in the office with Mautz discussing the relative merits of smokeless tobacco in the classroom. His only words upon release were: "Where's that fat ass Calhoune? He's a dead man."

"He'll have to go through me first," Sarah Byrnes said in an effort to get me out of my study hall desk.

"Oh, *that'll* take him all of about fifteen seconds," I said. "The only hurt you put on him in that fight was on his knuckles. God, I'm dead. I'm a dead man." I sat staring at the desk, considering. "Get Ms. Simmons in here right now. She'll win a Nobel prize if she gets me on video. I'm a biological miracle: a living dead man." A short, high-pitched laugh escaped me. "I could make the next issue of *Crispy Pork Rinds*. Oh, God, *Crispy Pork Rinds*. What a great idea."

"Come on," Sarah Byrnes said. "It isn't that bad. Let's go to science class. He's not going to beat you up in the hall."

"Oh yeah? What makes you think that?"

"Because he'd get in trouble."

"Right. By who? Mautz? Why should he care? He's already in trouble with Mautz. I'll bet Mautz told him who wrote the paper. That's *it*!" I screamed, realizing the truth. "See, this is like a big city gang war. The cops don't *really* care when one bunch of bad guys knocks off another bunch of bad guys. They're getting their job done for them. Mautz hates Dale Thornton, but he hates me, too. He wastes no bullets. I can see it now. He'll get to the scene right after I choke to death on my own blood, call my mom and tell her how sorry he is. 'If I just could've gotten there quicker. I'm awful darn sorry, Mrs. Calhoune. Maybe you could have another kid. A better one.' I don't see why . . ."

"*Eric!*" Sarah Byrnes said, "just calm down, will you? Dale Thornton isn't going to get you in the hall because he's never *in* the hall. He's out smoking somewhere. Now let's go to science. We can plan your getaway."

I slid out of my desk to follow Sarah Byrnes. What the heck did it matter where a dead man went?

"It's important that you get away," Sarah Byrnes said in the hall. "I've got a lot of money riding on you."

CHAPTER
FOUR

"Did you see Sarah Byrnes?" Mom asks as I walk in looking rode hard and put up wet, thanks to our three-hour workout earlier. She wears a green-and-blue Gore-Tex running suit over her sweats, and her hair is pulled back into a ponytail, bangs plastered wet against her forehead. Mom's been running.

I nod. I almost fell asleep sitting on the couch beside Sarah Byrnes thinking of new things to say to her brick wall self. "Yeah."

"And?"

"Would have been a good time to do my homework."

"Still no response, huh? What did the counselor say?"

"Same old thing. Told me to talk about things that might

jar her back. Remember *Crispy Pork Rinds*?"

Mom laughs. She spent more time up at school than I did during that corrupt chapter in my life. She provided the paper and the printer, though Mautz still doesn't know that. "Yes, dear, I remember *Crispy Pork Rinds*. Is that what you've been talking to Sarah Byrnes about? No wonder she won't talk to you."

"No way, man. She loved that rag right up till the final word of the final sordid exposé. If it hadn't been for trouble within the ranks she'd have brought it right on into high school with us. Hell, we brought Mautz." I pull a half-full quart of Gatorade from the refrigerator and drain it like a college kid sucking down a Bud, placing the empty bottle back on the rack.

"Prepare to die," Mom says, and I come to my senses, grabbing the bottle before the door can close and flipping it across the kitchen into the garbage can on survival reflex. Of all my dysfunctional behaviors, she hates me putting empty containers back where they don't belong. "I don't care if you weigh seven hundred pounds the rest of your life and don't stop picking your nose till you're forty," she told me once, "but if you put one more empty container anywhere but in the garbage, I'll have you put to sleep."

"You remember Dale Thornton?" I ask.

"The kid that used to come over here and bully you out of your junk food?"

"Yeah."

"Sure, I remember him. Pretty rough customer. Why?"

"One of the counselors up at Sacred Heart—his name's Sam—asked if Sarah Byrnes had any other friends. Dale was the only one I could think of. Man, that's shitty. Her only other friend than me she hasn't seen for more than three years."

"That is shitty," Mom says. "Did the counselor think Dale Thornton could do some good?"

"Didn't know. I think he was just fishin'."

"Is Dale still around?"

I laugh. "I don't know. If I were going to hunt him down, I'd probably start at the state pen. But you know, when I was driving home I remembered something he said once."

"What was that?"

"He got really pissed off at Sarah Byrnes one day when she was ragging on his family and told her he didn't believe her story about the pot of spaghetti."

"About how she was burned?"

"Yeah. At the time I thought he was just trying to get her goat. Man, he got the whole herd. Anyway, I've wondered about it sometimes. It was a pretty strong reaction if it wasn't true; she like to ripped him a new one."

The conversation dies because Mom has to get ready to go out. Her latest boyfriend, a guy named Carver Middleton, on whom the jury is still out, is taking her to the recreational vehicle show at the trade center. Now there's my idea of an exciting night on the town.

I think it's safe to say Dale Thornton took exception to his personal profile in *Crispy Pork Rinds*. He wasn't the publicity hound we might have expected. And let me say it was one thing to have him rough you up when you didn't have enough lunch money to keep him happy, but it was something else altogether to get him really mad. I feel truly fortunate not to have been the first in a succession of Dale Thornton serial murders.

By the end of that day of our first edition, I really did consider locking myself in the school furnace room until Dale was about a month into his first three-to-five for first degree assault on some other kid. But Sarah Byrnes thought she could get me out under cover. I actually thought there was a chance because Sarah Byrnes was—and is—one tightfisted kid with a buck, and she had three of them bet that I would get home that day with all my blood in its original container.

I hung around school talking with Mr. Webb, who was

one of the few teachers I liked—and who liked me, I think. Mr. Webb was one of those small oases for those of us who spent most of our time scorched on the deserts of humiliation. Someday I've gotta stop over at the junior high and tell him thanks. Anyway, he knew Dale was after me and he offered Sarah Byrnes and me a ride home, but the bet was off if I rode in a car or if an adult helped get me to the bus.

I said, "Hey, what's more important, your bank account or my life?"

Sarah Byrnes looked at me like I'd turned yupster before her very eyes. "Man, you're lucky to have me around," she said. "If you start using adults to save you, Dale will just wait till the one day there isn't one around. And waiting pisses him off. Then you not only get your butt kicked, but you worry every day till it happens. This way, the more times you outsmart him, the smarter you get—you know, like a forest animal. Pretty soon you'll be so good nobody will ever get you. You have to always think about survival, Eric. Trust me."

One of the reasons I hung out with Sarah Byrnes, besides that I was as fat as she was ugly, was her brains. I've always been considered pretty smart (a genius, if you ask me) but I consistently play Watson to Sarah Byrnes's Sherlock Holmes, and from where I stood at the time—petrified by fear—her thinking seemed sound. Looking back, however, I think she said it more to win the money than to turn me into some kind of environmentally wise escape artist. I have to say in her defense, though, that just before I lost consciousness I heard her screaming at Dale that she wrote the newspaper with me.

No help. Dale's last words were, "Mautz only said it was him."

To back up a bit, I was with Mr. Webb, refusing a ride home like a moron while Sarah Byrnes was down in the janitor's room getting an empty cardboard generator box and Mr. Otto's dolly truck. She told Mr. Otto she had to move this huge science project from the science room to the storage room so no one would mess with it until after the science fair. Sarah Byrnes was a stickler for detail when it came to telling a good lie. She even got Mr. Otto to write DANGER—FLAMMABLE on the side of the box in adult handwriting so it would look all official.

I was to get into the box so Sarah Byrnes could wheel me eight or ten blocks to the edge of the arboretum, where I would jump out and run through the trees like a bowling ball dodging pins. Dale Thornton would be lurking in the halls and out in the parking lot waiting for me to show, and I'd be scooting the back way toward my house and great riches for Sarah Byrnes, which she promised to share with me, though not fifty-fifty because I furnished only the body while she provided the brains.

So much for the difference between how smart Sarah Byrnes was and how dumb Dale Thornton was. He got one look at Sarah Byrnes wheeling a hundred-seventy-five-plus pounds of FLAMMABLE Eric Calhoune down the sidewalk, followed her out of yelling range from school, and made his move like the true thumb crusher I believed he would grow up to be.

I was bouncing along inside the absolute darkness of this box, feeling like a bat in an earthquake down in Carlsbad Caverns or someplace and thinking how Sarah Byrnes and I ought to go to Southeast Asia and see if Chuck Norris had missed any MIAs that we could spring, when I heard, "Uh-oh."

"What?" I whispered.

"Shhhh."

I shhhhed.

"Don't breathe," she said, as if I were.

Now give me a little fear and a small enclosure back then and I'd heat it up like a steam room, pronto. Give me a lot of fear and a small enclosure and I'd combust spontaneously.

I closed my eyes (which didn't help because it was already darker than a tomb) held my breath, and listened.

"Hey, Scarface."

Sarah Byrnes didn't answer and we kept rolling along.

"Scarface!" Closer. Still we rolled. Then I felt us stop. "What's in the box?"

"None of your stupid business," Sarah Byrnes said. "It's my science project. I'm taking it home."

"Lemme see."

"Get away from me."

"Just lemme look in there. I wanna see your science project."

"You wouldn't know a science project from a box of fish guts," Sarah Byrnes said. "I'm warning you, Dale Thornton, you better leave me alone."

"Flame-able, huh?"

"See what I mean? It's flammable," she said, pronouncing it correctly.

"Either way. That means it starts on fire easy, right?"

"That means it explodes easy. You better not mess with it."

I hear a *click*, then the sound of a stalled cigarette lighter. "Let's see," Dale said. "Let's just see if it explodes."

"You better stop that!"

"Know what I think, Scarface?"

"I don't think you think."

"I think if this thing really exploded it would look like when they blow up one of them whales that swims up on the beach sometimes. You know, like down in California? I think you got a big ol' fat-ass whale in there."

"That's just what I'd expect you to think," Sarah Byrnes said. "God, you're just so stupid."

"Oh yeah? Tell you what. I'm gonna just go ahead and light this thing. If what you got in there doesn't come out all cooked up with an apple in his mouth, I'll let you go." I heard the lighter again, pictured myself as Box-O-Bar-B-Q, and was suddenly wailing and battering at the lid and sides like a box of cats headed for the river. Once free, my running escape lasted all of three steps.

That's when I discovered Dale Thornton's true reaction to humiliation.

It should have ended there, right? Unconsciousness. Threat of serious injury. No more *Crispy Pork Rinds*, right? Right?

Wrong.

"So we can put this bad boy to bed?" I said, nodding at a copy of the underground newspaper as I tore the cellophane from another package of Nutter Butter cookies, bought to soothe the pain pulsating through the left side of my face. Sarah Byrnes and I were holed up safely in my attic.

She shook her head defiantly. "No way. They turn up the

heat on us, we turn up the heat on them."

I said, "Great. We hurt their feelings, they hurt our faces. It's a good thing we're so smart, Sarah Byrnes."

"What's the matter with you, Eric? I thought you were tough. You get roughed up a little by some two-bit bully and you crumple. Don't you know the price in human lives our forefathers paid for freedom of the press?" Then, more seriously, "Don't you get it that words are the only way people like us can fight back?"

I extended the Nutter Butters toward her, but she batted them away. I said, "They died for it so we wouldn't have to. Besides, our paper was supposed to be anonymous. It's no good if it's not. If they know who we are, anyone we write about can pound us into mush."

Sarah Byrnes stared at the bare bulb above and to the right behind my head to let me know my words were falling on deaf ears.

"Listen, Sarah Byrnes," I said. "It was a good idea. But it's only good if we're not getting killed." I moved closer and touched her knee. "Man, I was scared. I thought Dale Thornton was going to really kill me. Toward the end I could hear him hitting me, but I quit feeling it. Like I was already part dead."

"You learned a good lesson about pain," she said back.

"When you can't take it anymore, your body stops feeling for you. That was just your body being your friend."

"If my body were my friend, it would have run faster."

"But you're right," Sarah Byrnes went on. "If they know who we are, it's not good. They'll just treat *Crispy Pork Rinds* the same way they treat us." She scooted over and took the Nutter Butters out of my hand and said, "Listen, who's the real enemy here?"

I felt my eye. The entire left side of my face was dark purple and sore and soft as a sack of dead birds. "That's easy," I said. "Look at your face, Sarah Byrnes, and then look at *mine*. Dale Thornton's the enemy."

"I used to stay with my aunt—my dad's sister who's not alive anymore—for a couple of weeks every summer. You know what my aunt used to do when she was mad at me?" She didn't wait for an answer. "She told my cousin I used his bike or ate his candy bar or told some bad secret about him."

"So?"

"So do you know why? Because it got us after *each other*. We tried to kill each other, and she could give us any punishment she wanted because there was a rule against fighting. My dad isn't the only person in our family who treats people like shit. His whole family is like that."

"So our enemy is your dad's family?" I asked facetiously.

Sarah Byrnes rolled her eyes. "Humanity's enemy is my dad's family, but that's not the point. Who told Dale Thornton you wrote *Crispy Pork Rinds*?"

"Mautz."

"Who told you *Crispy Pork Rinds* was a piece of trash?"

"Mautz." I was getting the idea.

"Bingo. He tells you it's a piece of trash, but he uses the piece of trash to get the goods on Dale Thornton for the chewing tobacco. Dale gets punished at school for skipping, then probably gets hammered at home. Then Dale puts it to you after school because Mautz tells him who wrote the trash about him. Mautz sits back and lights a cigar. He's got all the people he hates on different sides. Now. Who's the enemy?"

It was my theory about how the police secretly like warring street gangs. "Mautz," I said.

"Right."

"So what do we do about it?"

Sarah Byrnes shook her head. "Boy, are you limited. I *long* for my intellectual equal and I get you. For twenty dollars in the Second World War category: Who fought on the side of right in World War II?" We had recently studied WWII in social studies.

"Easy," I said. "The good old US of A."

"Correct for twenty dollars. For forty dollars in the same category, who did the good old US of A fight against?"

"Germany and Japan. And Italy, I think."

"Correct again for forty dollars. Now for Double Jeopardy, Final Jeopardy, and all the Daily Doubles on the board, who fought *with* the good old US of A?"

"England."

"Who else?"

"Russia."

"Right for a million dollars and the right to put out a dozen more issues of *Crispy Pork Rinds*. Russia. Until 1991 our very worst enemy in the world. The Evil Empire. Why do you think we were fighting *on the same side* as the commies in World War II?"

"Maybe they were different then. Maybe they weren't commies. That was a long time ago."

"*Zooooooonk!* Back to zero. Your consolation prize is three days and two lovely nights locked in a room with my dad. They were just the same. They fought on our side because we had a *common enemy*. If that common enemy won, Russia *and* the USA were hamburger. Now, Final, Final, No-More-Last-Chance Jeopardy. For all your money back and the chance to be my friend long enough to put out another issue, *our* new friend is going to be . . ."

"Oh, Jeez," I said as the bulb above my head flashed bright.

"Close enough!"

I froze. We were going to make friends with Dale Thornton.

On their return from the R.V. show, Carver and my mother find a perfect indentation of my body in the couch, and I'm in it. I know it's after midnight because there's major skin all over the screen, in living color. Always the best on HBO.

Mom sees the woman in the flick touching herself in a full-length mirror and elbows Carver in the ribs. Carver is obviously embarrassed—probably because of his uncertain position with me—but he needn't be, because Mom has always been completely open about sexual stuff with me, so I don't react like a lot of my friends would if they saw their moms getting itchy.

But I decide to make him squirm a little anyway. "I've got the safe sex video here, Mom. Want me to slip it in?"

The woman on the screen has turned from the mirror, approaching the guy on the bed, who looks to have the IQ of a cucumber. He also looks to have a cucumber. "I better get your blindfold," Mom says. "Carver will call Child Protection Services on me for letting you watch this."

Carver eeps out an embarrassed laugh and says, "What's that number again?" It's a feeble attempt.

"What happens behind my eyelids is a lot hotter than that," I say.

Carver retires to the bathroom.

"When he comes out," Mom whispers, "you *can* it, okay? No more. Carver's a little modest for this family."

"I know topless exotic dancers who are a little modest for this family," I say. "Carver's too modest for a Barry Manilow concert. God, Mom, get a life."

We hear the toilet flush. "*You* get some manners," she says, "or you're going to be doing your own cooking and cleaning."

"Yes, Mommy Dearest."

CHAPTER
FIVE

My mother is a writer. A real one, not just somebody with a manuscript in a desk drawer that she'll finish someday when her kid finally gets arrested or goes to college. She writes a regular column in the local newspaper about women in sports and has had three articles published in *Sports Illustrated.* Two of them were space fillers, but one was a feature on a teenage girl who swam the English Channel. They sent her to the girl's house in Southern California and even put her up in a motel with a telephone in the bathroom. I know, she called me from there.

Mom has always had primo word processing equipment, including the latest in laser printers so sophisticated they double as weapons guidance systems, which is why Sarah Byrnes and I were able to bring to our readers such a high-quality rag from the information underground. Mom taught me to use her fancy electronic gadgetry clear back in grade school when she encouraged me to keep a journal, but even though she taught me to hide it in the computer so even she couldn't get to it without the code, I'm smarter than to put my thoughts about myself and others down in writing, where somebody might chance onto them and have me put to death.

Anyway, Sarah Byrnes and I had decided to lay off Dale Thornton for a while—at least until our wounds healed—and concentrate on an exposé about Mautz's two-headed son, the outcome of his clandestine sexual foray with a group of particularly brutal aliens one night several years back when he was wigged out on cocaine. According to our meticulously researched story, whenever Mautz came up short on new ways to treat kids astonishingly, he consulted with Huey-Dewey (one name for each head), whom he kept locked in an earth cellar behind his house.

I was revising the part where Huey-Dewey got into an argument with itself regarding the relative value of humiliating a kid in front of the class versus the three-holed paddle, and began banging its heads together in violent confrontation, when my doorbell rang. I looked out the window to see whether I wanted to answer the door, and standing right there beside Sarah Byrnes, looking almost as if he had come above ground to live full-time, was Dale Thornton. Sarah Byrnes was bringing a future freeway sniper into my home.

Oh, God, I promise never to shoplift again or touch myself without my clothes on if you'll please, just please let me live through this day.

I stared across our attic room at Dale Thornton, who, unlike Sarah Byrnes, had not refused my offer of Oreos and was, in fact, finishing up the package. Feeling invaded, I wondered if General Eisenhower let the Russians come to his house when he invited them to be on his side in World War II. If he did, I'll bet Mamie—that was Ike's wife—didn't use the good silverware.

"So this is where you freakos hang out," Dale said through a mouth full of dark brown crumbs and frosting. He was sunk into a bean-bag chair, scanning the room, gripping the sack of cookies as if it were a flotation device on the Titanic and the captain had just yelled, "Save the women and children first!" A home-crafted tattoo sporting BORN TO RASE HELL on a banner across a very poor excuse for a Harley-Davidson insignia graced his right forearm. He wore blue jeans, more hole than jean, and a black Twisted Sister T-shirt—the complementary pack of cigarettes rolled up in the sleeve—which also showed serious signs of aging. His curly brown hair clung matted to his forehead, and my olfactory senses said without question it was closing in on the time of month when the Thorntons should consider emptying the moonshine out of the bathtub.

Sarah Byrnes followed Dale's suspicious eyes around our attic hideaway. "Pretty nice, huh?" she said.

"Been in nicer."

"Maybe till you heard the sirens coming," Sarah Byrnes said, and I closed my eyes and held my breath. "I been by your place, Dale Thornton. You got a bunch of old wrecked cars in your yard, and I'd live in any one of them before I'd live in that house. And there's gotta be a skinny old dog factory out back somewhere. I don't care if you wanna live like a pig, nobody can help what their family's like, but don't you go saying, 'Been in nicer' like you live in some castle."

"You guys invite me down here to polish off these cookies, or you got something you wanna talk about?"

I looked to Sarah Byrnes. This was her idea.

She said, "What happened when you got home the other night after school? Old Man Mautz call your dad and tell him about the chewing tobacco?"

"None a your damn business," Dale snapped. "He didn't do nothin'."

"That right?" Sarah Byrnes challenged. "That why you didn't show up to school for three days and why you wore that stupid-lookin' turtleneck sweater for three days?"

"My brother gimme that sweater, Scarface!"

"Doesn't mean you have to wear it."

Just offer him a deal, I pleaded in my head, unable for the life of me to understand why Sarah Byrnes wanted to stir him up. Someone could get hurt, and I was farthest from the door.

"So what did your daddy do? Really."

"Same thing your daddy woulda done." He nodded toward me. "Or Fat Boy's. He kicked my ass. Whaddaya care?"

"Just wondered."

I started to tell Dale I didn't have a dad and my mom has never raised a hand in violence toward me, if you don't count when I was three and peed down the heat register during a week-long siege of below-zero weather, but I thought better. If Dale Thornton has a need to believe I get a regular ass-kicking, think away, Dale Thornton. I have recuperative work to do before I mess with you again.

"So I got places to go," Dale said. "I don't got all day to sit around and talk to a couple of freakos. What do you guys want? Got anything else to eat?"

Out of self-preservation, I went behind the dusty overstuffed couch at the far end of the attic, returning with a giant bag of corn chips. "Yeah!" Dale said, tearing them out of my hand before I could sit down, scattering perfectly good and unbroken chips across the hardwood floor. "Damn. They make these bags so you can't hardly get 'em open."

"The point is," Sarah Byrnes said as Dale stuffed his face with my corn chips, "that Mautz singed Eric's butt for producing a paper he said was trash, but he used the information in it to singe your butt. And speaking of butts, who do you think got the biggest bang out of you kicking Eric's?"

"Me?" Dale said, smiling, nodding toward me, salty crumbs sticking to his lower lip and chin.

Sarah Byrnes shook her head. "Couldn't have been much of a big deal for you, unless you're the biggest wuss since Mr. Rogers." She cast a semidisgusted look at me. "You could've got a better fight out of Norman Nickerson. Mautz, that's who really got off on it. He got Eric good and didn't have to lift a finger because he had a goon do it for him."

Dale achieved a passable imitation of thinking. "Maybe you're right," he said finally. "So what?"

"So we want to keep printing the paper and we don't want to get killed doing it. We have a deal to make with you."

"Make it."

"You protect us, and your name is never seen in *Crispy Pork Rinds* again, unless it's for receiving a Congressional

Medal of Honor. You can be on the staff. Every week we'll let you pick one thing to write about and we'll do all the grunt work. It'll be like you're literate."

Dale didn't pick up on the last comment, but the rest must have sounded good, though he didn't make any promises. Sarah Byrnes said after he was gone that we were free to go right on pleading the Fifth and cranking out our weekly rag.

It is nearly impossible for me to admit to people, be they friend or foe, what is important to me. A counselor friend of Mom's once said that's merely a function of adolescence—that teenagers are into separating from our parents and others in authority in order to establish our independence. To do that effectively we have to believe ourselves as immortal and are therefore incapable of facing our emotional truths.

Well, let me make something perfectly clear (as Richard Nixon says on those old news clips about the Watergate scandal, right before he's about to fill the room with fog) I am not immortal. I've spent more than ten hours in the psych ward with Sarah Byrnes—really and truly the toughest person in our solar system—and I'll tell you what, if life can shoot Sarah Byrnes out of the sky, it can nail me blindfolded.

In truth, the only reason I don't allow people up close and personal with my emotional self is that I hate to be embarrassed.

I can't afford it. I spent *years* being embarrassed because I was fat and clumsy and afraid. I wanted to be tough like Sarah Byrnes, to stand straight and tall, oblivious to my gut eclipsing my belt buckle, and say, "Up yours!" But I was paralyzed, so I developed this pretty credible comedy act—I'm the I-Don't-Care-Kid—which is what I assume most other kids do. But I'm not stupid; I believe there is important shit to be dealt with.

That's why I like Lemry's Contemporary American Thought class, which we call CAT for short. Lemry makes it safe to give any idea consideration, and she is ferocious in protecting the sensibilities of anyone willing to take a risk. You can celebrate or slam any idea you want, but you can't slam people. It's the most important class I have, and I'm glad both my friends and enemies are signed up.

Ellerby is there, and so is Mark Brittain.

And so is Jody Mueller.

I almost bowl Brittain over beating the bell into CAT. He's standing just inside the doorway talking with his girlfriend—who should be mine but doesn't know it—Jody Mueller, the classiest-looking girl in our school and maybe the Milky Way.

"Hey, Mobe, take it easy." Brittain acts as if he likes me, but after Ellerby, I would be the first on his secret ballot for candidates to be buried in a shallow grave with a small air pipe pushing up into a bus garage.

I say, "Sorry." I'm not, but until Jody understands that beauty is only skin deep, I want to appear civil in her eyes.

Brittain puts out his hand. "You guys sure got me the other day."

I don't know what he's talking about.

"At workout. It was a good move."

I smile and raise my eyebrows. It *was* a good move. I turn for my seat as the bell rings, but Mark catches me softly by the shoulder. "Could I ask you something?" Jody stands silently beside him.

"Sure."

"Why did you guys do it?"

"What do you mean?"

"You and Ellerby must really hate me. I hit ninety-seven repeats with you, and you sucked me into losing out on the last three. I can't imagine ever doing that to either of you."

I can. My stare drifts to Jody. I'm guessing she believes Brittain was victimized by a couple of insensitive pagan mermen.

"We were just being ornery," I say slowly, hoping to avoid alienating my future wife, "but you were on a free ride. I'd set the pace and you'd hang in. Ellerby would set the pace and you'd hang in. You never set the pace."

"All you'd have had to do was ask," he says. Then, "It wasn't a very Christian thing to do, that's all."

You don't get very far into a conversation with Mark Brittain without hearing that word. It irritates me because what he really means is, "You're wrong and I'm right and God knows it." I want to tell him I'm not a Christian, but that won't likely put me in better standing with Jody, who goes to Mark's church, so I just look away.

"You could be a little more compassionate, Calhoune. You know, you guys run around in that car, making fun of important things and blaspheming, and you don't have much consideration for the people you may hurt."

I'm caught. I mean, I can't take a guy seriously when he's using words like "blaspheming," but I'm over a barrel if I don't want to look like the worst kind of heretic in front of Jody. What I'd like to do is make Brittain horizontal, but that would only put me another rung lower on Jacob's ladder in Jody's eyes. It's a close call, though. I'm pretty embarrassed, and if Brittain says much more I might at least have to do verbal surgery on him.

Brittain looks wounded; my portrait as an ogre is complete. I make a note that he will not finish ahead of me on even one repeat today in workout. He and Jody walk off to their seats as I tell her, "Nice blouse." Great moves, Mobe.

"Park it," Lemry says, scanning her attendance book.

She moves to the front of her desk, hoisting herself up. "At the end of last class I asked each of you to be ready with a subject for your class presentation—something that addresses a contemporary social or psychological or spiritual dilemma. I asked that it be something with particular meaning to your life. Now. Today. I gave you possibilities such as war, world hunger, abortion, the homeless, children's rights, spiritual beliefs, political ideologies, et cetera. All I require is that you be willing to look at your subject from a personal perspective, that is, how the dilemma affects you." She glances quickly around the room. "Anybody want to step up and save those who didn't believe I meant what I said?"

Ellerby's hand shoots up. That's a surprise. "To the rescue," he says. "I want to talk about religion."

"As long as you don't try to lead us in prayer. It's against the law. "

"Rest assured," Ellerby says, "I won't lead us in prayer. I'll leave that to Brittain."

"And no personal remarks," Lemry warns.

Ellerby nods assent. "I brought a tape," he says. "I want to play it."

Lemry has audio and video equipment available because she has encouraged us to bring in outside stimuli to promote discussion.

"It's a song," Ellerby says. "Everybody's recording it these days, but this was the first person I ever heard." He pops in the cassette and passes out a sheet of lyrics, some of which are underlined, along with a color reproduction of the NASA photo of the earth taken from the moon. The song is "From a Distance" by Julie Gold, and it's sung by a country singer named Nancy Griffith.

Nancy's nasal twang brings a few guffaws from the heavy metal set, but we settle in on the lyrics, which talk about how "from a distance"—like maybe out in space—the world looks good. The air appears crisp and blue, mountains are capped with a pure, clean, snow frosting, and there's no scum floating where the ocean meets the shore. From that distance you can't tell the good guys from the bad guys, and when that's true, there's no reason to fight. You can't see germs and people dying from diseases; it's just all one big whole thing that needs to be taken care of by everyone, like a beautiful house and yard. Then, in the last verse, Nancy says that's where God watches us from: from a distance.

It's a good song. A great song.

"There's a stroke of real genius," Brittain says immediately. "Wouldn't you just expect some theological prodigy driving a blasphemous Pontiac station wagon to bring us his religious view packaged in a country-western song."

"If thine enemy offend thee, Reverend Swaggart," Ellerby says back, "meet him out behind the gym after school."

Lemry looks around the room in mock exaggeration. "Did anyone hear me say 'No personal remarks'?" Her eyebrows arc for the sky as she points one index finger at each. "Those are the rules. Don't make me enforce them at workout."

I see her point is well taken: *Mess up my class and I'll swim you so hard your arms will drift, unattached, to the bottom of the pool.*

Lemry says, "So make your point, Mr. Ellerby."

"My point is that God created a prototype for a reasonably sturdy carbon unit, gave us a perfectly usable place to live, some excellent advice, as in 'words to live by'—most of which are misunderstood by the least of my brethren—and stood back to see what we'd do with it."

I'm surprised. I didn't know Ellerby had any philosophical considerations. I thought he just drove his Christian Cruiser through the world seeing whose nose he could get up. And how far.

Lemry's eyes land on me. "Mobe?"

My hands shoot up in surrender. "I give a wide berth to all religious discussions. My plan is to get baptized late in the afternoon of the evening I die, so I don't have time to sin. A spot in heaven awaits me."

"Cute," she says. "And chicken. Jody?"

Shoot. I should have uttered something biblical.

Jody flashes a sideways glance at Mark, saying simply, "I guess I think God takes a closer look than that."

I could go either way on this. I don't have a quarrel with Christianity one way or the other. As near as I know, Mom doesn't have religious beliefs, so I wasn't brought up with any. I know some Bible stories from going to Sunday School with my friends when I was younger, but mostly they were just good stories. I see where getting religion quick here could work to my advantage with Jody, but I can't jump ship on my friend Ellerby. Steve has a reputation as a verbal troublemaker, and I would abandon him in a second for Jody alone, but not for Mark Brittain. So though I can once again see how the Russians and the Americans fought on the same side in WWII, I'm Switzerland. Good-bye, Jody, my love.

"Give us more information, Steve," Lemry says. "If you're right, what does it mean?"

"I'm not sure what all it means," he says. "But I'll tell you what made me bring it in. The other day when Mobe was trying to figure out whether the world was a good place or a bad place, and he used Sarah Byrnes for an example, I was ready to agree with him. No question, she's got a rough road to go down. But when I thought about it more, I realized the world is a good place for me, most of the time anyway, and that got me to thinking about fairness. If God is fair, how do you explain me and Sarah Byrnes on the same planet? And if he really rewards piousness and public prayer and all that, like Brittain seems to think, how come he lets me drive my car around without blowing out my tires, and how come he lets me kick Brittain's butt in the pool?"

Lemry says, "Watch it . . ."

"I had this Sunday School teacher," Ellerby goes on, "and every time I asked her a tough question—like 'How come nobody ever caught Jack the Ripper?' or 'Why did my big brother get killed when he got straight A's clear through college and was going into the seminary?'—she'd say the Lord works in strange and mysterious ways that we may not understand." Ellerby leans forward on his desk now, his intensity as visible as the pulse in his temple. "But I think there's nothing strange and mysterious about it. I figure if those things were in God's jurisdiction, he'd do something different about them. But they aren't. Those are in our jurisdiction."

I glance over to check Jody's reaction, but can't read a thing. Brittain, on the other hand, is having blood pressure difficulty, and explodes. "This is so much BS! People throw out this line of crap for one reason: so they can do whatever they darn well please. It's a bogus way of not having to be accountable to God."

Ellerby ignores him—I mean like Brittain isn't even in the room—and continues. "From a distance," he says, "my car looks like every other car on the freeway, and Sarah Byrnes looks just like the rest of us. And if she's going to get help, she'll get it from herself or she'll get it from us. Let me tell you why I brought this up. Because the other day when I saw how hard it was for Mobe to go to the hospital to see her, I was embarrassed that I didn't know her better, that I ever laughed at one joke about her. I was embarrassed that I let some kid go to school with me for twelve years and turned my back on pain that must be unbearable. I was embarrassed that I haven't found a way to include her somehow the way Mobe has."

Jesus. I feel tears welling up, and I see them running down Ellerby's cheeks. Lemry better get a handle on this class before it turns into some kind of therapy group.

"So," Lemry says quietly, "your subject will be the juxtaposition of man and God in the universe?"

Ellerby shakes his head. "My subject will be shame."

CHAPTER
SIX

From across the ward I watch Virgil Byrnes sitting next to Sarah Byrnes on the couch, his eyes burning into the side of her head, teeth clenched so tight it looks like there's a marble below his jawbone. He's talking, but his lips barely move. Dressed in his traditional black, angular as a hawk, he cuts a fearsome, dangerous profile. I can't see her eyes, but Sarah Byrnes's head moves not one iota, and I'm guessing she's locked onto her favorite spot. Mr. Byrnes sits back, breathing deep, then momentarily puts his mouth close to her ear and stands to leave.

Virgil Byrnes really is a scary dude. He's one of those shadowy people you can't imagine ever having been a kid;

the kind of man a dog circles warily, his hackles at attention. Mr. Byrnes doesn't talk much, but his glare makes Mautz look like Bambi. The most telling thing about him is how afraid he makes Sarah Byrnes. Sarah Byrnes isn't afraid of much, but your mention of her dad's name dramatically increases your chances of a black eye and a bloody nose.

I stand against the back desk, trying hard to fade into the background as he moves toward the exit, but he spots me and moves in my direction. His black, broad-brimmed hat rides low over his eyes, and a tattered black cotton sport coat pulls tight on his broad shoulders. His gray shirt is buttoned to the top, and his dark baggy pants complete the picture of Death, come calling at your door in the middle of a dark, rainy night. That may sound a bit dramatic, but I wanna tell you, Sarah Byrnes's pappy gives me maximum creeps. "You're Calhoune," he says, standing a few feet from me.

"Yes sir."

He glances back at Sarah Byrnes, then back to me. "She say anything to you?"

"No sir."

He's quiet another moment, staring hard at my eyes. I hold his gaze, vowing not to blink or look away, while sweat glands pop open like kernels of popcorn. "You let me know if she does."

"Yes sir."

The attendant stands patiently by the open door, keys dangling from her hand, and Mr. Byrnes disappears into the outer hallway.

I think I detect the fleeting shadow of a sneer across Sarah Byrnes's lip as I slip onto the seat beside her, but I know it must be my imagination, and I can't help thinking back to what Dale Thornton said that day.

"I think we oughta do a *ex*-pose on that little rat Elgin Greene," Dale said, pacing the wooden floor of our attic hideaway. "Little goofball's got some kinda bad news stink to him. We could chase it down, maybe find out it come from a giant comet turd landin' in his backyard or somethin'. You know, explodin' all over his whole family whenever it hit." Dale had definitely become comfortable with the content, if not the spirit of our biweekly rag.

I sat at the keyboard, chin propped in one hand, feeding myself nonstop Lorna Doones with the other, a major writer's block shrouding me like the stench around Elgin Greene.

Sarah Byrnes lay on the couch, heels planted firmly against the arm, absently drumming her hands on her stomach along with the Kingston Trio, one of whom was runnin' like a dog through the Everglades. "I've told you a thousand times, we don't pick on guys like Elgin Greene. He's one of us, only helpless."

"Ole Greene ain't helpless. Get downwind from that kid, he's a powerful mother." He laughed, nodding. "Yup. I think a *ex*-pose on Elgin Greene is right what we need."

"First of all, it's *ex-po-say*," Sarah Byrnes said. "Not *ex*-pose. Jesus, you could at least learn to say it right. And second, we pick on people who do us dirt. Picture us as good guys, Dale, hard as that may be for you. We're champions of the underdog. Underdogs call Elgin Greene an underdog. We're not giving him a hard time and that's it."

"So you come up with somethin'," Dale said. "You're so damn smart, got your brains all wrapped up in your ugly head by them scars." Dale was going for the throat; it didn't take much to wound him. Killing him was something else. . . . "That's the only reason you stay so smart. None of it gets out 'cause it's packed in there so good."

No half-witted remark about burn scars ever got a rise out of Sarah Byrnes—not since maybe first grade. "Oh, Dale," she said sarcastically, "you're just so darn clever. I bet all the girls swoon. Got lots of dates lined up for the weekend?"

"Up yours," he said. "You really ain't so damn smart. You think you got everybody fooled about them scars, but you ain't fooled me. Them scars didn't come from no pot of spaghetti. No way."

Sarah Byrnes was off the couch in a second, her teeth clenched like a sprung bear trap. "You better just shut up."

Dale laughed. "I'll shut up, okay, but that don't change the truth."

I said, "Why do you say stuff like that, Dale? Man, you got to be careful when you go slandering one of *us*. We're supposed to save that for the enemy."

"Ain't no slander. Just fact. I know it same way Sarah Byrnes knowed how my daddy kicked my ass when he found out about the chew. I seen her with her daddy. She got a shit family, just like me."

The fire in Sarah Byrnes's eyes blazed. "You're a Thornton. You wouldn't know the truth if it walked up behind you and bit your ass and stole your wallet." She sat back. "You know what? I'm kind of tired of this paper anyway. Maybe we should just quit. We've made our point."

I wanted to leap up and stop her, but I couldn't let Dale see us disagree without paying dearly after he was gone. We had published eight papers, in the course of which we had detailed each and every year of the sordid past of Mautz's illegitimate, twin-beaned alien son, including the two years he spent as Elvis's secret gay lover.

I certainly didn't want to halt the presses before we completed our four-part exposé, and this confrontation between Sarah Byrnes and Dale Thornton threatened to do just that. Though I was responsible for the word-smithery of about ninety percent of all written material, no way would I have had guts enough to continue without Sarah Byrnes's fierce resolve. Dale Thornton, I could have done without anytime.

Crispy Pork Rinds slid downhill from that moment. Sarah Byrnes said we needed to move on to other modes of terrorism and that Dale Thornton was as stupid as she had always thought and she didn't want him around us too much longer or our brain cells might start to melt. We printed only one more edition, in which I doubled up to complete reports on the Mautz family tree.

A few weeks later Dale Thornton was unceremoniously dumped as unassistant editor, and Sarah Byrnes and I began other kinds of tactical assaults on those who wronged us: a box of fish guts planted in a locker here at the beginning of a long weekend, analgesic balm spread lavishly there in someone's underpants while he was dressed down for PE. By year's end we had successfully distributed more than twenty hollow gumballs doctored with Tabasco sauce from a hypodermic syringe. All were single acts of vengeance requiring no protection from Dale Thornton. Sarah Byrnes and I were on a roll.

But that summer Lemry saw me swimming at a public pool and talked me into trying out for her AAU swim team, and Sarah Byrnes and I began drifting away from each other. She said it was me and I said it was her. For the first year, I ate like more of a pig than I am just to show her I wouldn't get svelte and handsome and popular so she'd have to hate me, but as workouts increased in length and intensity, my eating barrage couldn't stand up to my changing metabolism and I began to get occasional glimpses of my feet.

"Look," Sarah Byrnes said one day during our freshman year, after I'd been working out almost eleven months, "if you keep eating like a starving Biafran turned loose at the Food Circus just to prove me wrong about why we're friends, you'll die of a heart attack before you're fifteen. So stop already."

It was a relief, because I was actually starting to feel good about myself from swimming—at least better—and Lemry was ready to send me to "Ripley's Believe It or Not!" to find out why I was swimming four to six thousand yards a day and still puffing up like a blow-fish. "But what if I'm not fat?" I blurted in desperation. "Will you still be my friend?"

"God," Sarah Byrnes said. "You're such a lamebrain. It isn't me who'll go away, it's you. People will just look at you differently than they do now. Other people will like you, and you'll go to them. It's not a big deal, Eric. It's just the way things work."

For the thousandth time I protested, but she raised a scarred hand. "Don't worry. I've always known this. It doesn't even hurt."

Sarah Byrnes wasn't completely right, though she wasn't completely wrong, either. We did spend less time together, but mostly just because swimming takes a lot of time. I tried to get her to turn out with me, but she gave me a quick, graphic dermatology lesson on the effects of chlorine and intense sunlight on burn scars and that was that. I still saw her almost every day and we still did things together on a regular basis, but she struck up a cautious friendship with Dale Thornton, I think as a hedge against possible losses, and wasn't available as much of the time.

I made it my life's resolution to refuse any invitation that excluded Sarah Byrnes. Even though she rarely agreed to go anywhere with me, when I brought her name up, if one nose crinkled, I uninvited myself on the spot. That's how I stay fat for her now.

"Wanna have an adventure?" Ellerby and I navigate the Christian Cruiser through the dusky streets. It's Saturday night, about 7:30, and we're killing time before the dance over at the school gym.

"What'll it be?" he says. "Zero to thirteen miles an hour in the space of one short city block? Crank up the sound system and drive back and forth in front of Brittain's place?"

"Better," I said. "Let's take her down to the Edison district."

"You want to be an organ donor?" The Edison district has a tavern for approximately every three-point-five people over the age of six, and Spokane absolutely depends on it to keep our crime rate equal to or above other US cities of our relative size.

"There's somebody down there I need to talk to," I say. "We won't be there long."

"No," Ellerby says, flipping a U-ie, "we probably won't."

In the neighborhoods behind the Edison strip, most streetlights are broken, and twisted street signs point in directions where there aren't streets, so it takes us a while to find West Reardon. Ellerby drops the Cruiser to about ten miles per hour so I can read the numbers. I've only been to Dale Thornton's place once, and that was back in junior high when he made Sarah Byrnes and me prove we liked him by going there. I went, but I didn't like him.

"Here." Ellerby pulls up in front of a ramshackle cottage

with a tilted garage off to one side and several rusted-out cars and a truck on blocks in the front yard. "This has to be it—I remember that truck. Be careful. I think a dog lives in it."

Ellerby leaves the engine running, and I step onto a dirt road thinly coated with ice. A dim light shines from the living room, and I move cautiously up the sidewalk, eyeing the old truck from which I fully expect a saber-toothed junkyard mutt to spring, flashing yellow eyes locked on my jugular.

It doesn't happen. I take a deep breath and knock as Ellerby moves silently up the walk behind me. Canine thunder bursts forth from inside, followed by a deep, booming, "SHUT UP!" When the door opens, I'm staring at the three-day-stubbled face of Morton Thornton, aka Butch. I hope Dale never told him about the *Crispy Pork Rinds* story, or at least who wrote it. His beer-blurred eyes tell me he wouldn't remember anyway.

"Is Dale at home?"

He squints suspiciously. "Yeah. Out back. In the garage."

"Okay if we talk with him?"

"Okay with me," he says, "if it's okay with him. Go around and kick the door," and we hop off the side of the porch. "An' don't come knockin' on my door at night without no appointment."

"Right friendly part of town," Ellerby whispers as we

make our way through the pitch dark, over batteries and car hoods and enough spare parts to build a spaceship.

A bright light shines through the broken windowpane in the garage door, and I peer in to see a body bent over the engine of a station wagon that is the match of Ellerby's from a negative universe. A radio on the workbench blares pure country and Dale sings along, amazingly on key.

My hard knock brings no response, so I follow Mr. Thornton's advice and give it a kick, bringing Dale's head up hard under the sharp rim of the hood. He says, "Shit!" and turns down the radio.

I'm surprised at the neatness of his makeshift shop. Each tool hangs on the wall inside a meticulously drawn outline of that tool. The surface of the workbench is clean and the floor is swept. Dale stands, bright light shining in his eyes, holding his end wrench like a revolver recently fired, his legs spread like a gunslinger's. But he's so *small*. Dale Thornton hasn't grown one inch since junior high school. His tight, sleeveless T-shirt displays the same muscle definition, outlining his washboard stomach, but he's little.

"Dale?" I say.

He squints. "Who wants to know?"

"It's Eric. Eric Calhoune."

"Who?"

"Remember? From junior high? I wrote that newspaper with you and Sarah Byrnes."

He smiles a bit and steps forward. "Scarface?" he says. Then, "Oh, Fat Boy."

"Yeah. That's me."

He places the wrench carefully on the workbench, pulling a grease rag from his hip pocket. "What the hell you doin' here? Who's this?"

"This is Ellerby," I say, and Steve steps forward, offering his hand. Dale looks down at his own hand, still black with grease, smiles and shakes Ellerby's hand. Dale hasn't changed much.

"So, Fat Boy, what you doin' here? I ain't seen you in three years or so. Thought you hated my guts."

I smile sheepishly. "Naw," I say. "I never hated your guts. I was just scared of you, that's all."

Ellerby approaches the old Pontiac with reverence, circling slowly, touching the rough, dark gray primed doors and mirrors, peering in under the hood at the engine highlighted by the droplight. Dale's eyes follow him suspiciously, then dart back to me.

"So how is old Scarface?" he asks.

"Not so hot. She's in the hospital."

"Got herself sick or somethin', huh? Too bad. I kinda

liked her. She was a real hardass."

"Yeah, well," I say, "she's not sick like that. She's having head trouble. She just stopped talking one day. Wouldn't get out of her desk. They finally had some guys come and take her right from school."

Dale moves closer to Ellerby, as if to be certain he doesn't get away with any spare engine parts. "That right? That don't sound like her. I thought she'd end up kickin' somebody's ass. Like that prick Mautz."

I smile. "Quit talkin' before she could get around to that."

"So how come you come to see me?" He looks at Ellerby and can't stand it anymore. "What you lookin' at?" It's a challenge.

Ellerby looks up in surprise. "Nothing," he says. "I mean, I've got a car just like this, and I've been looking for somebody to work the engine. Dealer's too expensive. You know a lot about this thing?"

Dale puffs up. "I know ever'thing about this thing. You want anything did to it, I'm your man. Course you got to pay."

"Course," Ellerby says back. "Tell you what. I can do the body work on one of these babies, but I'm not much of an engine man. Maybe we can trade some labor."

"Maybe," Dale says, his defenses down a bit in the face of this common interest.

I answer his original question. "The reason I came to see you is I remember once you told Sarah Byrnes that she didn't get her scars from a boiling pot of spaghetti. Remember that?"

"Remember it? Shit, she liked to took my head off. That's how I knew I was right."

"You still think that?"

Dale smiles. "Never heard her come out an' deny it, did you? Why? What binness is it of yours?"

"The people at the hospital are just looking for reasons she might have quit talking."

Dale leans against the car door. "Well, there's a bunch of goddamn geniuses," he says. "One look'll give you all the reasons you want."

I agree. "Yeah, but they're looking for more. I mean, she's always looked like that, but she just stopped talking recently."

"Well, I don't know nothin' about talkin' or not talkin', but I'll tell you what. There wasn't no pot of spaghetti. You can count on that."

"Sarah Byrnes tell you that?"

"Hell no. Scarface didn't tell nobody nothin'. But I know. I seen her with her dad a couple a' times, an' I know."

"How . . ."

Dale stares as if I'm a dog turd on his plate. "You guys seen my old man? Think I can't tell when somebody's got a nasty pappy? Hell, I seen Sarah Byrnes with her daddy once even before I *knew* he was kickin' her ass regular an' I could tell right off."

"You think her dad burned her?"

Dale shrugs. "You figure it out." He looks a little closer at me. "Hey, Fat Boy, you lost some weight, huh? An' growed. I might have a hard time takin' all your shit from you these days." He laughs. "Guess I changed careers just in time."

"No, Dale," I say, "I think you wouldn't have any trouble taking all my shit even today."

Ellerby gets Dale's number for business purposes, and we're outta there.

"What do you think?" I ask Ellerby as we glide through the darkened streets away from Dale Thornton's house toward the freeway.

"I think Dale Thornton lives in a very scary part of town," he says. "And I think he knows about cars." Then he answers my real question. "I think guys like Dale Thornton don't lie."

"So you think Sarah Byrnes's dad did something to her, like to her face?"

"I don't know," he says, "but when I want to know about swimming, I ask Lemry. When I want to know about my teeth, I ask my dentist." He glances over. "Always go to the expert. If I wanted to know about hard times, I could do worse than to ask Dale Thornton."

I sit back. Ellerby's right, and I'm smart enough to have figured that out. But Sarah Byrnes is my friend. She was with me when nobody else was. In the days of my life when my body embarrassed and humiliated me every time anyone laid eyes on me, Sarah Byrnes—this person with fifty times my reason to be embarrassed and humiliated—walked with me, even ahead of me. I can't stand to imagine someone hurting her like that on purpose.

CHAPTER
SEVEN

I'm standing behind Brittain and Jody at Lemry's desk, minutes before the second bell. Because my ears are tuned in like a phone tap from the Nixon White House, I can't help but overhear the conversation.

"We're thinking of dropping the course," Brittain is saying to Lemry.

"We?" Lemry says, eyebrows raised.

"Jody and me."

"Too demanding?" Lemry asks. She doesn't mean it. Brittain is a straight-A student. The guy has a memory like a fax machine.

"No," he says. "I don't think the subject material is cut out for us."

You don't have to be an astrophysicist to know Brittain's speaking as if he has a turd in his back pocket is going as far up Lemry's feminist nose as is possible without the use of an exploratory probe. "I'm having pronoun trouble here," she says. "'*I*,' meaning *you* in the singular, 'don't think the subject material is cut out for *us*'?"

Brittain nods while Jody shifts nervously from foot to foot. I put my mouth close to her ear. "If you ever want a boyfriend who encourages freedom of expression," I whisper, "dial 1-800-FAT-BOY." I have decided over the past few days that passive admiration may not be the best way to get a girl. If it were, Jody'd have been mine long ago.

She smiles nervously and moves a step away from me.

"I just don't think it's healthy for us to sit by while people knock the Lord," Brittain says, ignoring Lemry's challenge to separate himself from Jody. "It's blasphemy, pure and simple."

"Then I would think the Lord would want you to stay and defend him." Lemry glances around Brittain to Jody. "Jody, is Mark talking for you?"

Jody nods. "Yes. I mean, I guess so. We decided to take our electives together this year."

Lemry nods. "Well, I hate to be the one to break up your little alliance, but I'm an educator, not a dating service, and in order to drop a class after five days you need my signature on your drop card. I'm willing to sign yours, Mark, on the grounds that you don't feel compelled to stand up for your convictions, and I don't want it to appear as if the school is challenging your religious beliefs. I won't, however, sign yours, Jody, because wanting to be with your boyfriend twenty-three hours a day does not constitute reason for a transfer. Of course, you're free to pursue the issue with the front office."

"No," Jody says without expression, "that's okay." She turns to walk to her seat.

I can feel myself falling out of love with Jody. It's like she's the Pillsbury Doughgirl. Doesn't this girl ever tell anybody to go to hell?

Brittain stands stiff before Lemry's desk, his neck and face reddening. "That isn't fair," he says, in the perfectly controlled tone that makes me want to cram a banana down his throat, then reach in and peel it. "You're persecuting us because of our beliefs."

"Mark," Lemry says patiently, "I said I was willing to sign your drop slip. A number of my beliefs may even match yours. Now the bell has rung. Either give me your card, or take your seat."

Brittain glances over at Jody, but she does not acknowledge him. Having forgotten why I was standing there in the first place, I walk toward the seat behind Jody, the one Brittain seems about to vacate. "Excuse me," I say, just loud enough for him to hear, "is this seat taken?"

Brittain crumples his card and walks briskly to his seat, and I willingly step away. Truth is, this class wouldn't be half the fun without his Jimmy Swaggart zeal. I return to my regular seat across the aisle to find a note folded neatly on the desk top. I open it and silently read: 1-800-FAT-BOY *doesn't have enough digits to be a real phone number. Please advise.*

Sarah Byrnes sits across from me in what has become our nightly standoff. It occurs to me that if she actually is understanding every word I say and choosing not to respond, it pisses me off. Today I'm going to try to find out.

"Brittain almost quit Lemry's class today," I say, in keeping with so-called normal conversation. "Lemry would have let him go, but he tried to take his girlfriend with him." I didn't mention Jody's note or my lustful imaginings about her. Sarah Byrnes has never been someone with whom I felt comfortable talking about my illusory love life. Since she can't imagine having one of her own, talking about it seems cruel.

I mention CAT class. "We even talked about you a little," I say. "About what it must be like to be burned and everything." I think I see a flicker, but that road has dead-ended before. "Actually, Lemry cut that short because you weren't there to give your permission or your input."

Nothing.

"Dale Thornton thinks your dad had something to do with you getting burned."

Sarah Byrnes's head jerks, and she penetrates far enough into my eyes for corneal surgery. Her jaw clamps tight; then, as quickly as she looked, she's glazed over.

"That's what I thought," I say. "You've been hearing me all along. You could talk if you wanted to, I'll bet. I thought you were too tough to just pull an el foldo."

Nothing.

"Anyway, I remembered what Dale said that day right before we closed shop on *Crispy Pork Rinds,* how you almost tore him a new one when he said you knew about bad dads the same way he did." But the shock effect is gone. I badger her a little longer, but this girl has a will of steel, and that's it for today.

I see the nurse headed our way and think better of mentioning Sarah Byrnes's response. If she's faking, there's a reason, and if I blow her cover she'll get even. And if you had your choice of having Saddam Hussein or Joseph Stalin or Adolf Hitler or Sarah Byrnes after you, you'd pick A, B, and C only, before you picked D. On the off chance she's not faking, if I just penetrated her catatonia for a second before it regained control, then nothing has changed. I'll try her out a few more times before I say anything to anyone. Shit, maybe I should grow up to be a psychologist.

I plop the note Jody left on my desk during Lemry's class three days ago on top of Ellerby's burger bun.

"What's this?" he asks as I snatch it back from between his greasy fingers.

"The legal document for my entry into heaven." I give him enough history to lend meaning to the strange message.

"No shit," he says, reading as I hold the note. "I didn't think Jody Mueller was real. I mean, I considered her Brittain's Stepford wife."

"Yeah, well, reconsider. The girl has hidden taste."

"Did you give her your number?"

"Not yet."

"Want me to ask the waitress to turn up the heat?"

"What?"

"Sounds like your feet are cold. She gave you that note three days ago. I'd have written my phone number in permanent marker on the back of Brittain's alligator shirt before the class was over if I was in your covetous state."

I laugh. "When the time's right. Listen, I been meaning to ask you about the other day in Lemry's class."

Ellerby chomps down on his burger. "Which day is that?"

"The day you talked about Sarah Byrnes. About shame."

"What's to tell?"

"Ellerby, I've known you since the first day I turned out for swimming. You haven't uttered a serious sentence in four years."

He smiles, paraphrasing the punch line from the old joke about the kid who went through his entire life without uttering a word. On his seventeenth birthday his mother brought out a beautiful angel food cake with a sweet rich buttery frosting. The boy blew out the candles and began to cut the cake, then stopped and put down the knife. He said, "Mother, I don't mean to be impolite, but I like chocolate frosting on my angel food cake." Well, of course, the whole family was astonished, and they gasped and then cheered and patted him on the back. When his mother finally asked why it took him so long to speak, he said, "Up till now, everything's been okay."

"Right," I say, watching Ellerby polish off the burger on the third bite.

"I just said what I believed, that's all," he says, swallowing.

"Yeah, I know. I heard you. It's just that I hadn't heard much about what you believe before that day. Or since."

Ellerby sits back in the booth. "Beliefs." He smiles. "You're talking to the son of a preacher man," he says. "You better set aside a few hours before you get me started on that.

I glance at my watch. "I ain't goin' nowhere. I've wondered

about you being a preacher's kid. Is that tough?" I've never heard Ellerby complain.

He shakes his head. "Not with my dad." He nods toward the window, in the direction of the Cruiser. "How do you think I get away with driving that beast?"

"I figured you must be as hard to handle at home as you are at school."

He smiles again. "Shit, man. If my dad said the word, I'd have it sanded down and primed by morning."

"I've never thought of your old man as scary."

"He isn't scary. I'd do it out of respect."

I'm aware I've known Ellerby almost four years and I know almost nothing about his family. In fact, often as not I think of him as an orphan that my mother feeds.

"When my brother died," Ellerby says, his eyes almost dreamy, "times were hard. My mother couldn't quit crying and my dad just lost himself in his work. I remember wishing for Sunday to hurry up because I knew I'd at least see him at church. Mom was so hurt she couldn't even talk to me, and after about six months I started thinking my brother was the only kid in the family worth being happy about. I got it in my head that it should have been me who died. When Dad finally started getting back to normal, he was so busy trying to take care of Mom and running the church and all, he seemed to have forgotten about me. I was just a little shit, but I packed my stuff in my brother's old gym bag and lit out for my uncle's.

"Only problem was, my uncle lives on the East Coast. Cops picked me up five blocks from home and called Dad. When he came down to the station I ran and buried my face in his chest and babbled how sorry I was, that I was sorry it was Johnny instead of me, and Dad dropped to his knees with me and held me tight and told me right there, on the cold concrete floor, how bad he'd screwed up. Since that day, I haven't had a better friend."

Ellerby's eyes are shiny and he continues quietly. "Beliefs. Man, I changed the face of God for my old man forever."

"What do you mean? How?"

"By making him explain to a nine-year-old kid why God would let a preacher's son die when he was going to grow up to be a preacher, too. I told him I thought God must be dumb, cheating them *both* out of a high draft pick like my brother. I said I thought if you were a preacher, God ought to give you a little extra protection. You know, like cops don't give each other tickets?"

"What'd he say?"

Ellerby smiles. "He said he thought so, too. That he was as surprised as I was when it happened. Anyway, that's when we sat down and tried to figure out God's job description. You heard a piece of it the other day in class."

"You were a real hit with Brittain."

"That stuff scares guys like Brittain. Guys like him don't want to be accountable for shit. They fall to their knees on the deck when they should concentrate on swimming hard. That's why I said what I said about your friend Sarah Byrnes. She's been around all my life and I've done nothing; stayed as far from her as I could because I don't like thinking about her pain. But that's chicken shit, because once a thing is known, it can't be *un*known." He sits back and folds his hands behind his head. "Dad and I sit around and watch the God network a couple of hours a week just to see what guys like Brittain are thinking. You know, keep up with the enemy."

Ellerby stands. "That, my friend, is about as much philosophical bullshit as I can take in one night. Let's crank up the Cruiser and spread the word."

The Cruiser slows to a stop in front of my house a few minutes before midnight. "Get some sleep," Ellerby says. "We've got a tough meet tomorrow." He squints into his side window. "Look, isn't that Dale Thornton's wagon?"

I cup my hands around my eyes to block the light from the dash. "Hard to imagine there's *three* of these things." As I say it, the door to the wagon swings open and Dale steps out. "Wonder what he wants. You didn't steal anything from his garage the other night, did you?"

We meet Dale in the middle of the street. "Hey, man," Ellerby says, "got her running, huh?"

Dale locks his fingers into his belt loops, a stance preceding the moment he used to kick my butt, or take my lunch money. He says, "Yeah. No sweat." He stands, eyes shifting from one to the other of us.

I'm on past conditioning. "You pissed, man?"

Dale smiles uneasily. "Naw. Why would I be pissed?"

"To tell the truth, Dale, up until the other night, I never saw you when you weren't. It was just a guess."

He looks at the ground. "I wasn't always pissed," he says. "I just needed to make sure all you guys were a-scared of me."

"It worked. What brings you out this late?"

"Got to thinkin'," he says. "The other night. You guys talkin' about Scarface."

"Yeah?"

"Yeah. She really laid up in the crazy house? Like you said?"

I nod. "Yup. Why?"

"Well," he says uneasily, "we was purty good friends there for a little bit. After that stupid newspaper, when she was kinda mad at you for goin' off to be a jock . . ."

"Yeah?"

"Yeah. Helped me out of some tough spots. You know, let

me talk without tellin', stuff like that."

I say, "Yeah."

"Thought I better tell you somethin' else. Told her I never would, but I don't wanna see her rot in some crazy house. I got a aunt there. . . ."

I wait, and Dale looks at the street again, kicking at a pebble. "You got to be careful what you do with this. I mean, who you tell."

"Okay."

"Can't just be tellin' anybody."

"Okay, I won't. Tell me."

"Reason I know them burns wasn't caused by no boilin' pot of spaghetti is she tol' me different."

"What'd she say?"

"Said her daddy pushed her face against a burnin' wood stove."

The hammer hits my stomach with such force that my knees turn to rubber. *"Jesus Christ.* Are you shitting me?"

Dale casts a sideward glance at Ellerby, then back at me. "You think I'd drive over to your house in the middle of the goddamn night to shit you?" To Dale the very worst thing in the world is to be called a liar. I need to remember that.

"No. I didn't mean that. I just meant . . . Jesus, Dale. Are you sure?"

"Yeah, I'm sure. Night she tol' me she was fixin' to kill herself."

God, I'd had no idea. "How'd you stop her?"

"Had to slap her around pretty good," he says. "That ain't no way, to go killin' yourself."

I glance over at Ellerby, who has just set a personal record for speechlessness. In the dim streetlight I see his face is drained of blood. He says, "Why didn't you tell someone?"

"She tol' me not to."

"Yeah," Ellerby says, "but. . ."

"Ain't no buts. I said I'd keep my mouth shut and that's what I done. Shit, who would I of told?"

"I don't know," Ellerby says. "Cops. Child protection people."

Dale snorts and spits on the ground. "Shit. When was you born, man? Those guys don't listen to jokers like me. I give my word to Scarface I'd keep my mouth shut, an' that's just what I done. 'Cept for now. Don't wanna see her rottin' in some crazy house, like I said. Maybe we ain't such good friends anymore, but we was once."

I put my hand on his shoulder, but he pulls away. "Listen," I say. "We'll figure out who to tell. We'll be careful. Thanks for coming here, man. Really. I owe you."

Dale laughs. "Gimme your lunch money."

CHAPTER
EIGHT

"A number of you have chosen abortion as your topic," Lemry says toward the end of class, studying a list in her hand. "Since there is such an interest, I'm setting aside several days for discussion to be sure everyone gets time." She steps around to the front of her desk, removing her reading glasses. "Let me warn you, this is a topic that can get out of hand. *Adults* don't handle it well. I'd be surprised if there weren't people in the room who have had experience with abortion, either directly or through friends. So I'm going to keep a tight rein on things. I will feel free to remove you from the discussion, or even the room, if you're disrespectful toward other people's views. That won't necessarily mean you're in trouble with the law, it'll just mean I think you need a break. As always, you're entitled to your opinion, but you're also accountable for decency."

She doesn't ask for agreement. We've had some pretty spirited discussions over the past three weeks, about child abuse and women's rights and racism, among other things, and what's becoming clear is that most tough problems in the world run into each other. We start talking about one and we end up talking about another and no one can figure how we got there. I think Lemry knows that.

I'm off my pace a bit. Jody's in the bleachers watching Brittain, and I can't take my mind off her note. I'm hitting my time standards, but when I should be bearing down in the stretch laps my mind wanders.

I've always tried to stay cool when it comes to matters of the heart. As a fat kid growing up I just assumed there would never be a girl for me. In junior high I watched the popular kids hang out playing boy-girl games, and I told myself they were stupid and wrote mean things about them in Sarah Byrnes's and my trashy newspaper, but truth is, sometimes it hurt so bad I wanted to die. I told myself the kind of friendship I had with Sarah Byrnes—the tough kind—was better. I think most of us tell ourselves we don't want what we think we can't have just to make life bearable.

When I started swimming and began to shed some of my outer insulation, things changed a bit. A few girls have even shown interest in me over the past couple of years; they just weren't the ones I was interested in. Don't think I didn't consider taking up with them anyway, just so I wouldn't look like a social adjusto, but I didn't.

So far, I've opted to laugh off my loneliness in that area, but I do know it's serious stuff and I'll have to deal with it someday. I wish my mother could be more help, but she treats love like an extracurricular activity. I think my dad hurt her a lot, though she's never said much about that, probably because I have as many of his genes in me as hers—twice as many visible ones—and she doesn't want me thinking there's something wrong with me because my dad was a jerk. Someday I'll have to sit her down and have a serious discussion.

And now there's Jody. Sure, she's in the bleachers watching Brittain, so maybe she's changed her mind since dropping me that note, but she's a possibility now. As Ellerby said, anything that's known can't be unknown, and I have that note locked away in the headboard above my bed. And believe me, it's known. In a biblical sense. I have consummated its existence, yes I have. Ellerby was right—I should have acted more quickly. The longer I wait the more reasons I can think of why it means something other than what I thought it meant when I first read it.

"Steamrollers," Lemry yells. "One hard, one easy; two hard, one easy, up to ten and back." My mind calculates; a total of 100 laps hard, 19 easy. Jesus, will I be glad in a month or so when we start to taper off for state. Being a distance man, I'm expected to come out on top of this.

Brittain and Ellerby go out in front. The first lap is a twenty-five yard sprint, then an easy twenty-five followed by a fifty-yard sprint. They're still pulling away from me at four hard—a hundred-yard sprint—but there I begin to close the gap. My easy laps are faster than theirs, and as we begin into six hard, then seven, stored blubber comes into play. By eight hard, we're even, and beyond that I'm pulling away with every stroke. At ten hard, they're in my dust—or my mud. God, this feels good. There is no place I feel more powerful or more in control than in the second half of a tough distance workout. I piss and moan with the best of them reading Lemry's workout on the bulletin board, but once I'm in it, I'm *in* it. Whoever beats me can't let up, because the older I get, and the longer the distance, the tougher I am. I figure I'll make the *Guinness Book of World Records* by swimming the Bering Strait some New Year's Eve after I turn ninety. I hope

Brittain's still around for me to hate by then, though he'll probably be secure in heaven, and out of everyone's hair.

I'm cooking in the decreasing laps, eight hard and less. Ellerby's pulling away from Brittain, but he's way back from me and I need a challenge, so I'm thinking it'd be a nice touch to double-lap old Mark, especially with Jody watching. It shouldn't bother him. Brittain's talent is speed, not tenacity; but I have survived my years as a fat kid by mastering the adolescent psyche, and I know he'd rather eat his own liver than have Jody see me standing in the shallow water looking for something to do while he finishes his last two laps. Hey, nobody ever called me sensitive.

Skullduggery is in order here. I'll have to push harder through the easy laps without his knowing, because if he discovers me, he can hold me off.

When I finish seven hard, we're at opposite ends of the pool and I'm due for one easy. Instead, I turn it on coming off the wall, back off when I swim into his view and pick up again once we've passed each other. I don't think he caught me, so I'll get another chance to make up a bundle after six hard. This is too easy. I hope Jody appreciates it.

"Abortion," Lemry says, pacing the perimeter of the room. "This is delicate stuff, so let me remind you once again to be careful. I've read some rough drafts, and it's clear that those of you who chose the topic have strong feelings. My guess is that others do also. For purposes of discussion, keep your passion to a minimum and make your points rationally."

I'm going to sit back, at least for the first round. I know for a fact that Brittain and two others in the room—Sally Eaton and Cynthia Parrish—have picketed the clinic up at Deaconess Hospital where women in this town go for abortions. And Jody has been up there at least once. Plus it's one thing to mess with Brittain's head in the pool, but when a subject bangs up against his religious beliefs, he gets *cranked,* and anyhow I don't even know what I think about this. I do believe women ought to have a choice, but that's because my mother has always been so vocal. Truth is, I don't have to worry about getting pregnant (a line Lemry better not hear unless I want to do push-ups in the aisle until the end of the period), and unless something in my life changes drastically, I won't be approaching an activity that will cause anyone else to become pregnant in the near future. Mr. Moby Calhoune has been voted the Closet Sex Maniac Most Likely to Become Pope three years running.

"Who wants to start?" Papers shuffle, eyes fix to desk tops. Lemry fingers through the rough drafts. "Ms. Eaton, you turned in an extensive draft. Could you give us a rough sketch of what you wrote?"

"Sure," Sally says. "The hard fact about abortion is that it is murder. A fetus has no capability to stand up for itself, and yet it is as alive as you or I. So-called prochoice activists say it isn't because it doesn't speak or communicate in any way we know. Yet if you look at the growth between conception and birth, which is greater than in any period between birth and death, no one can say in good conscience it isn't life. The taking of life is murder."

Whew. Lemry has to be impressed; I am.

"Mr. Brittain?"

"Couldn't have said it better," Mark says. "The truth is, potential mothers and people who conspire with potential mothers to allow abortion will pay for ever in the afterlife."

Lemry nods. "Let's keep this discussion a bit more immediate, okay? We'll discuss religion and belief systems in another segment."

"That's the problem," Brittain says back. "You can't separate this question from spiritual reality. That's the only way pro-choicers can make an argument. But there are laws far more powerful and absolute than human laws. You can't argue the question of abortion without including the laws of God."

"You make a good point," Lemry says, "but for our discussion we need limits, or the next thing you'll hear is Mr. Ellerby making a case for every self-proclaimed prophet and cult leader and tribal shaman and TV huckster, and your spiritual argument will get lost. You'll say once again that the Bible is the word of God and Ellerby will say tell that to twenty billion Moslems and Chinese, because Ellerby is prone to exaggeration. Then you'll bring in faith, and Ellerby will counter with biblical interpretation, which you will point out is nothing more than cheap rationalization in order to avoid being responsible to God. Both of you will feel right, nothing will be resolved, and the few members of the class who remain awake will hate both your guts." She said it all in one breath. Not bad. "So just let it be understood that your belief says anyone who participates in abortion will be punished in the afterlife and let it go at that."

Megan Buckman raises her hand. "Abortion is not murder," she says. "It's a decision."

"I agree it's a decision," Brittain says. "It's a decision to commit murder."

Megan talks right through him. "It's a decision not to have a baby. Calling it murder is just a way to ignite the issue; get emotions in the way of rational decisions."

"A fetus is a life," Sally says back. "Pure and simple. The

taking of a life is murder. There's nothing emotional about it."

Ellerby watches intently, holding back, which is unusual; nothing excites Ellerby more than a good fight. I'm also surprised we haven't heard from Jody.

Megan takes a deep breath. "There's some question among scholars about when life actually starts."

"Only among scholars who have a need for abortion to be okay," Sally says. "It doesn't take Albert Einstein to know that if something is growing and using nutrients, it's life. If they discovered it on Mars, they'd sure say it's life."

That's a good point.

Megan is unflappable. "By that reasoning, anything that can swim upstream and bang its head against the walls of a female egg until it crashes through is also life, which means every time one of these guys takes his love life into his own hand, that's murder, too. Willful destruction of sperms is mass murder, using that argument."

Ooh, Megan! Gettin' close to *home*.

Lemry has the hint of a smile on her face, but she says nothing. I guess she dropped her tight rein somewhere.

"It's not human life until the two are united," Sally says. "That's the beauty of two people being together."

Megan won't be moved. "But we're looking for the *line* here. The line between when there's life and when there's not. That means we have to look at capability. By your definition, knowingly killing a sperm would have to be murder, particularly if you know it could be put to good use—and every guy in this room has taken sex ed."

Christ. A minute ago I was just a big old husky bugger out there turning in most of my homework and getting from one end of the pool to the other in a hurry. All of a sudden I'm a Son of Sam. I hold world records in this field.

"Sally and Megan are taking this argument in the classic direction, though maybe a little far," Lemry says. "And I must say, ladies, you've done your homework. Anyone else have thoughts? If you don't, you'd better get some. This issue won't go away. What about you, Mobe?"

"I was just thinking of what to say when I turn myself in to the authorities," I say, staring at my desk. "'Yes sir, detective. I knew they could make a baby, but I gave them a home in my sock anyway.'" It gets a laugh, and even a few female shrieks.

"People who joke about something this serious," Sally says evenly, "are either poorly informed, or they're afraid to stand up for what they believe."

That embarrasses me a bit. "Look, Sally. The reason I haven't said anything is that Coach will ask for a solution, and I don't have one. If I took seriously what I've heard so far,

I could wind up thinking all the guys in the room are going to have to spend the bulk of their adult years in prison, to get out just in time to go straight to hell. And I guess there could be a case made for bringing charges against any girl who knowingly lets an egg drop without trying her best to get it fertilized, but by Brittain's standards she'd have to be married to do that, so everyone should be married by the time they're twelve just in case. In other words, it gets pretty ridiculous."

"The sperm and egg argument isn't mine," Sally says. "It's Megan's. And she used it to make a rational argument look silly."

I say, "Maybe. But even if you drop the sperm and egg argument, that still leaves room for some question about when human life begins. Yeah, from the moment of conception it could grow up to be a baby. But it ain't a baby. It doesn't have baby trappings. You know, arms, legs, eyes. They're coming, sure, but they ain't there yet." Actually, I'm remembering most of this from listening to my mother. I really don't have much feeling. I'm just reacting to Sally calling me down in front of the class.

"But once there's conception, it's all continuous; there's no way to draw the line," Sally says.

"Sure there is," Megan breaks in. "We draw the line wherever we want to draw it. Changing abortion law proves that."

Brittain explodes. "There's a law higher than that! Don't you understand? There is *higher law*! And it's not flexible!"

Lemry raises her hand. "Mark, take it easy. We've got a pretty orderly discussion going here, all things considered. Jody, what do you think?" Boy, there's a mischievous side to Lemry.

Jody glances sideways at Mark. "I'd like to agree with Mark," she says, and there's a strength in her voice I haven't heard, "but every time I think something is absolute, it turns out not to be. So I guess I don't know." If looks could kill, Jody would be meat.

Lemry scans the room. "Mr. Ellerby," she says, glancing at her watch, "I've never been in a room with you for more than five minutes without having to tell you to shut up. You're making me crazy."

Ellerby smiles. "All right! I knew you cared."

"You're wrong," Lemry says back. "It's just that if you're terminally ill and you drop dead in my classroom, I'll have to answer to the school board. I'm too close to retirement for that. Don't ever get it in your head that I care."

"Methinks she doth protest too much," Steve says to the class. "But now that you've sought my opinion . . ." He scans the room quickly. Ellerby loves an audience. "I think this 'When does life begin' argument is kind of cute, but it's dead end. If we let it go long enough somebody will get punched in the nose, or Brittain will have a coronary incident. No offense, Sally, but most of the right-to-lifers I know—and I know a lot of them because they call at our house pretty regularly to say how much they hate my dad—get all wrapped up with life in the womb, and life after death, for that matter, but they don't give a rip about life after *birth*. All you have to do is look around to see we've got big trouble in that area. People are starving to death all over the world. Their lives are spent trying to get something into their bellies, which they never get, and then they die. And to tell you the truth, the people who seem willing to fight to the death, or who are at least willing to carry a poster in front of the Deaconess clinic, are politically against *giving* them anything. The second they're born, they're on their own."

Ellerby shakes his head in exasperation. "Or take right here in this country. Take babies who aren't starving to death, but who nobody wants and are only going to make their mother's life impossible. I know this mom in my dad's church, she's had one baby who was permanently brain damaged because her boyfriend beat the kid when he was only four months old. No shit, broke his skull. She has another baby born with fetal alcohol syndrome, because she was drinking so much grieving the first baby that she marinated the second one. Now she's pregnant again. She doesn't want the baby, but she also knows if she has it, she won't adopt it out. She just can't. She just wants to not have it. She's in school and her life looks almost manageable, but she says this pregnancy will take her under. And let me tell you, I know this lady. If she says it'll take her under, believe it." He puts up his hands. "I just don't think you can have this argument without talking about *quality* of life. Not just life. Quality."

Sally is quiet, seems to be thinking about the woman Ellerby described. Lemry snatches control. "So where are we?"

"If we buy into Steve's BS," Brittain says through gritted teeth, "we're lost. The world is tough. There are strict rules. Ellerby's story is sad. But the rules here are clear. If you fornicate, you take the chance of pregnancy. If you get pregnant, you have the responsibility to have the baby. You have the *obligation* to have the baby. Ellerby said a lot about that woman, but he didn't say she didn't know how babies are made. She fornicated; she needs to step up and take the consequences."

If I could hold back, I'd just humiliate Brittain in the pool again, but we won't be in the water for several hours and I can't wait. Brittain's "Christian way" is so goddamn unforgiving. Maybe it's because I grew up fat, or maybe it's because I grew up with Sarah Byrnes, but when he gets righteous about people having hard times, I get hostile. But I have to be cool, or Lemry will step in.

"I don't think a baby who is born as a 'consequence' has much of a chance. Maybe an ingredient in the 'When does life begin?' argument ought to be *want*. Life begins when you have a sperm and an egg together with some *want*. Or maybe Ellerby's right, the 'When does life begin?' question should only be on game shows. But I know one thing. This religious argument, at least the way Mark Brittain presents it, is one cold damn argument, and it doesn't address human pain. And maybe this is more an argument about your particular religious view, Mark, but whether we're talking about Sarah Byrnes, or a baby with brain damage, or a mother who can't face another pregnancy, you are one heartless SOB."

Lemry cuts me off. "That's enough, Eric. That's personal. It has no place in this discussion."

"That may be," I say. "But Brittain argues in a way that isn't fair, either. He goes for people's open wounds, then brings God in with air support. You have to agree, there's a certain cowardice to that approach."

Lemry hoists herself up on the desk. "This might be a good place to stop for today," she says, but Brittain interrupts.

You can almost take his pulse from across the room, but he speaks in measured tones, looking at his watch. "Tell you what, Ms. Lemry. We've got fifteen minutes till the class ends. Let Moby and me have this out. Nobody calls me a coward."

"It's tempting, Mark. But we're trying to look at this from a scholarly perspective."

Mark's hands shoot up, palms out. Intensity thick enough to choke him gathers in his throat. "We'll keep it scholarly. Agreed, Mobe? No punches."

"No punches."

Lemry shrugs, looking, somewhat amused, around the room. "This is not mandatory," she says. "Anyone who doesn't want to participate may be excused. Just don't hang out in the hall."

No one moves a muscle.

I try to take away a little of Brittain's steam. "First of all, Mark, I didn't call you a coward. I called your approach cowardly."

"No difference," he says. "You can't separate me from my actions. A man is known by his works."

I shrug. "Have it your way."

He nods as if to say, I intend to. "Number one, your argument is the cowardly one, and you have to be a spiritual coward to make it. The rules that God made to govern the world are strict, but they're the same for everyone. They don't change because some female doesn't have the brains to stay out of situations that lead to fornication. They don't change because you got born into a family with no dad, or because your father is a misguided, permissive preacher who lets you drive around in a car that screams blasphemy. They don't even change if you're scarred all over your face and hands like your friend.

"We're all born into different situations, but the word of God is the word of God and everyone has to adhere to it. *Everyone.* If you choose to have an abortion, you're a killer. If you're a killer, you're going to have a tough time staying out of hell. It doesn't matter what kind of a hard time you give me, Calhoune. How many times you trick me in the pool or mock me in front of others. When the time comes for the real judgment, guys like you and Ellerby are going to have to stand up and face your actions." He raises his eyebrows. "*Then* we'll see how clever you are."

Brittain's tone has a Mautz ring to it: *Let me tell you something, young man, you're not as smart as you think you are.* I can tell he's scored because the old Calhounian sweat glands are creaking open. I have to be careful not to spin out of control. "Here's my problem with your argument, Mark. I'm not a big-time Christian. I haven't spent a bunch of time locked in my room with my Bible. But when I close my eyes and imagine God the way you paint him—and Jesus, too—I just can't buy it. They'd have to be a pair of horses' asses to treat people that way, with no consideration for their circumstances. Think of any king, any president, hell, any *mother or father*, who could treat people that way. One mistake and you're out of the ball game. That just doesn't make sense."

"And that's my point," Brittain says, more to the rest of the class than to me. "It doesn't make sense because Calhoune doesn't want it to make sense. If it makes sense, then he has to answer to it. He says he hasn't spent any time with the Bible. Then he shouldn't even be in this argument, because he hasn't gone to the one place where the answers about abortion are."

"Wait a minute," Ellerby breaks in, "I've spent a little time locked in my room with a Bible, and I think you're more full of shit than Moby does. Certainly I'm for birth control before abortion, but I'll tell you one thing, Brittain, if God kept as close an eye on us as you say he does, and if he felt the need to intervene in daily human problems, he'd put on his steel-toed holy boots and come down here and kick your butt for making him look like a mean-spirited, unforgiving ayatollah. I mean . . ."

Lemry breaks it off. "Listen, guys, I could watch you beat each other to death all day and never get enough, but the bell is about to ring." Ellerby opens his mouth to continue, but she hits him with a look that has knockout written all over it. "What you've seen in here today is not unusual when we deal with emotional issues. But it dramatizes something important in looking at any contemporary American thought. No issue is isolated. We started out talking about abortion, but the discussion quickly drifted to general beliefs. No amount of effort could have stopped that, because our *points of view*—the way we perceive things—are inextricably linked to our beliefs. If you don't leave with anything more than that today, leave with that. What I hope we can learn is to be aware of how our beliefs color what we see."

I wanted to tell Brittain that Lemry was trying to tell him that his own little view of the universe wasn't the only view possible; that if there's a heaven, decent people all over the world who have never even *heard* of Jesus Christ would get to go there. Even if they'd made mistakes. Even if they'd had abortions.

Headed for my locker, I pass Brittain and Jody in an animated exchange, probably discussing which level of hell Ellerby and Megan and I will inhabit.

As I dig through the primordial ooze for my Government book, a hand touches my shoulder. "You never answered my note."

I turn, speechless.

Jody says, "Could we talk?"

"Now?"

"Not right this minute. I have class. What about after school?"

"I have to swim."

"After that."

"Sure. How about we go get a burger? Five-thirty? I could pick you up."

We agree to meet at the Burger Barn, and after shyly asking me to keep our meeting to myself, at least for now, she's gone. And I stand dazed in front of my locker, having forgotten where my next class is, or what it is, for that matter.

CHAPTER
NINE

I push through the double doors of the Sacred Heart psych ward, spotting Sarah Byrnes in her now-familiar position on the end of the couch. The on-duty nurse waves to me as if I worked here. Several patients greet me by name. On my way out I'm going to ask for a white coat, or at least a stethoscope.

"How's it goin'?" There will be no response, no head movement, nary a twitch of the eye.

"I've been better," she says.

If my eyes popped as far out of my head as it seems, I'd have to dive to catch them.

"Don't be a jerk," she says in a whisper, lips glued to her teeth.

"Jesus, you're talking. You're coming out of it."

"I was never in it. Keep talking. Nurse. Don't you blow it."

"How's it going?" the approaching nurse asks, nodding at me.

"Same," I say back.

"Would you like some juice or something? It's snack time."

"Sure."

"Great. Be right back." She walks around behind the front desk to the kitchen.

"What the hell . . . ?"

"I needed some time off," Sarah Byrnes says.

"Yeah, but . . ."

"Listen. She'll be coming right back. I'm only going to say this once. Don't you go trying to put your head together with Dale Thornton to figure out what happened to me."

"Dale Thornton already knows, doesn't he?"

"Maybe he does and maybe he doesn't. But you leave it alone."

I want to tell her what I know, and I want to know the rest, but I promised.

"I don't know if I can still kick your ass, you lifting all those weights and swimming like there's gonna be another flood, but I'll sure give it a try."

I think a second. "I'll make you a deal. This has something to do with how you got up here, right?"

Her eyes slide sideways. "None of your business."

"Well, I'm making it my business. You probably can still kick my ass, but I've been learning to be more gracious about that over my lifetime. Here's the deal. You tell me why you're here, and you tell me what happened, how you got burned, and I'll keep my mouth shut."

"I don't have to tell you *nothin'*!"

"And I don't have to keep my mouth shut about whatever I think, or whatever I trick out of Dale Thornton."

Sarah Byrnes stares ahead, stone silent.

"Look, Sarah Byrnes. I've proved I'm your friend. I didn't go off after I lost weight and leave you behind. I've been up here every day, even when I thought you didn't understand a word I said. I'm still with you even though I feel like a fool, knowing you've understood every word I've said over the past few weeks. You're still the person who knows me best. But you coming up here scared me. It's been like you died. This friendship thing goes two ways. You *had* to know I was dying. That's chicken shit."

Sarah Byrnes waits as the nurse brings my juice, and a glass for Sarah Byrnes. She places a straw in each glass, then wanders back behind the desk.

"It might be chicken shit, but I haven't been *okay*. This has kept me alive. Friends aren't the same for me as they are for you, no matter how scared you were or how fat you used to be."

"What do you mean?"

"Look at my face, you cheeseball!" she spits, almost blowing her cover.

"I've seen your face," I say back, holding my own. "What's different about it now than ever?"

Sarah Byrnes's shoulders slump, and I briefly glimpse deeper into her, past that hard crust, past her inclination to double up her fist at the sound of the first syllable of the wrong word. "Every day I live with it is one more day I've lived with it; I'm a little fuller up. Nothing changes. I have to be tough or funny every minute. If I let up for a second, it gets me. It gets me when I'm half awake in the morning and forget who I am. After all these years, I still dream I'm okay once in a while. In fact, I dream it all the time." She glances sideways again. "Look, ask the nurse if we can go for a walk—outside. I'm tired of talking like Edgar Bergen." Sarah Byrnes knows Edgar Bergen from all the old television shows we watch on cable TV. He's like the granddaddy of ventriloquists. I know him because his daughter is Candice Bergen, who I would like to own.

I step over to the front desk to make my request, the nurse makes a couple of calls, and before I know it, Sarah Byrnes and I are in the elevator.

"Might as well trust a fat kid," she says, when we're definitely out of earshot of the hospital. At least two inches of snow covers the ground, and we crunch over the unshoveled walk, alone in the freezing afternoon. Frost stands on the bare branches of trees like white icing.

I say, "Fat kids give you more to trust."

"My dad burned me on purpose."

"What?"

"Spare me the surprise, okay?"

"Okay. Jesus, you mean he poured the spaghetti on you?" It's my last lie to Sarah Byrnes. My last lie to her ever. But I have to make her believe Dale didn't tell me anything. When I saw him in my neighborhood, standing next to his junky car looking all out of place—and like he *knew* it—I knew what a risk it was for him to be there. I'd rather have Sarah Byrnes think *I* was the liar than Dale.

"There was no spaghetti. I was only about three and a half, but I remember it like it happened this morning. My mom and dad were fighting. Real bad. Hitting, throwing things. It's the only time I ever remember my mother fighting back. Dad had her by the hair, and he was filling the kitchen sink to put her head in. I was sure he would kill her—that she'd be gone and then it'd be just him and me. I was so afraid of him.

"I was watching from this little cave underneath the stairs, where they couldn't see me. Then the sink was full. She was screaming, but it didn't sound as much like fear as rage. She kept threatening to kill him. Dad laughed and yelled, 'Oh, yeah?' over and over, and then he pushed her head down. She kicked and I heard the bubbles, and then I had to try to save her. I ran at him, screaming, and crashed into his legs. It knocked him off a little, and he loosened his grip and my mother got away. I swung at his legs as hard as I could, over and over, but all of a sudden I was in the air, almost over his head.

"Mom got a knife out of the drawer and came at him, but he held me in front of him and backed through the open hallway into the living room, laughing. Then he said, 'Here's your pretty little baby for you,' and I looked up and saw the wood stove coming right at my face. I put my hands out and . . ."

My stomach is in knots I believe will never unwind. God, I don't want to hear this.

"I don't remember him actually doing it," she says. "When I woke up, I was in the hospital with bandages covering my face and hands, and a nurse there said I had pulled a pot of spaghetti off the stove onto myself. I couldn't talk, or even move, but I wanted to tell her she was wrong, but all I did was lie there and drift off. The next thing I knew, Dad was leaning over me. He said Mom was gone and would never be back, and that if I told what happened he'd burn the rest of me. He said he didn't care what they did to him."

I sit hard on a cold cement bench, staring silently up at Sarah Byrnes's scarred face. Words would jeopardize the thread of trust, because they would sound fake. They would be fake. There aren't words for this.

She says, "That's it."

I put my hand on the side of her hip as she stands in front of me, and she doesn't knock it away. She stares straight ahead into the trees behind my head, looking so tough; and so fragile. "What happened to your mom?"

She shrugs. "Gone. I never heard anything from her again. Eric, I swear to God if you ever tell anyone this, I'll kill you, but I used to sit in my room and look out the window at the stars and the moon and stuff and imagine she was figuring a way to come get me; that one night there'd be a light tap on my window, and I'd just put some clothes in a bag and crawl out onto the limb of the big tree and slide down and be saved. I even thought she'd make me look pretty again. But my dad accomplished what he wanted when he ruined my face. Mom didn't want me anymore. I've thought maybe he killed her, but I guess I don't think so. I don't think she could have just disappeared without somebody checking. He told everyone she left."

"Jesus Christ."

She nods. "Yup. No shit."

We're quiet a second or two. "So why did you come to the hospital? I mean, why now?"

Sarah Byrnes closes her eyes. "Dad was getting crazy again. I started having dreams about the stove. He held my *face* against it, Eric. He's drinking more now, and he sees and hears things. I got the same feeling I had that day he burned me, and I decided if I had the feeling it was probably right."

"Jesus, Sarah Byrnes, why didn't you call the cops or something?"

Her soft edge instantly hardens. "What're they gonna do? Put him in jail until he dries out? Then what happens? Jesus, Eric, get an idea."

"You could tell them what really happened."

"Right. Why would I be telling it now? It's been fourteen years. They're sure gonna believe me. Besides, just after it happened some people tried to get the state to believe it couldn't have been from scalding water, but I was afraid to talk and that ended it."

"Yeah, but it ended because you didn't tell them."

The spell is broken, Sarah Byrnes's interior is closed for the day, and I'm angry because my need for revenge on her father is what closed it. "Look, Eric," she says impatiently. "Don't ask me a bunch of questions. I told you because you said you'd keep quiet. Don't make me regret it." She looks away. "Or *you* will. I came to the hospital to think. I needed to get away before something really bad happened. I'm old enough to get away now. I've always known I'd have to. It's just hard, looking like this. . . ."

"Yeah. Listen, Sarah Byrnes, what do you want me to do?"

"For right now, don't tell them I talked, but that you think the walk helped. That you want to do it some more. Then all you have to do is keep your mouth shut. I mean it, Eric. You can't tell your swimming friend, or your coach or your mother. Nobody. You said you wanted to prove how good a friend you are. This is your chance. You tell nobody."

"Okay." I know what Sarah Byrnes is doing. She has to have control because of how big this is. You don't let something this big out unless you have it on a leash. It would eat you alive.

It's after midnight. I'm in my room, staring at the ceiling, lost in the 1960s with the Lovin' Spoonful. Do I believe in magic? they want to know. We'll see. I've been thinking about what a huge risk it was for Sarah Byrnes to tell me her story; not about the story itself, which is certainly bad enough, but about how scary it must have been to let me see her like that. Scared. Vulnerable.

I wanted to get off by myself afterward, just to consider things, but I had my date with Jody, and only a natural catastrophe would have kept me from that.

This was a *strange* date. In the beginning Jody seemed as removed as ever, except she sat on my side of the booth and her hand touched my leg enough times to kick start me pretty good. Not that I'm complaining, but the Burger Barn is a local hangout and Brittain's friends could have easily seen us—that is, if they weren't joining hands in a circle at the Church of Jesus Christ of All The Good Guys, praying for me to drop fifty pounds the hard way: in a leper colony. But Jody didn't seem to mind whether anyone saw us, and believe me, if she didn't mind, I didn't mind.

"So," I said, after we had ordered, "what did you want to talk to me about?"

She smiled. "Get right down to business, huh?"

"I've been real curious all afternoon. I mean, I don't get invited out much."

She smiled again. "Did you have guesses?"

"Yeah," I said, running my hand over the back of my neck, "I guessed you'd developed a brain tumor. Then I guessed you were writing a research paper on Chunko Swimmers of the Western Hemisphere. Then I guessed . . ."

"You've been busy."

"I have been busy. Then I guessed those weren't good guesses, and decided to just come out and ask."

"Tell me what you think of Lemry's class."

I said, "I think it's the best class I've ever taken. It makes me think. Sometimes I hate that, but mostly I don't. Why?"

"I'll bet you think I hate it."

"If I had to bet a month's pay one way or the other, that's the way I'd go."

"I'll bet you think Mark Brittain and I think exactly alike about everything we've covered so far in that class."

Now I smiled. "That's crossed my mind, but I'm getting the feeling you're about to tell me how full of shit I am."

She smiled back. "You're so full of shit."

"That's what I thought. Exactly *how* full of shit am I?"

"I had an abortion."

Jesus.

"Surprised?"

"Naw. Girls are forever asking me out for a burger so they

can tell me about their abortions." I paused a minute. "Was it Brittain's?"

"Yeah. It was Mark's."

"Does he know? I mean, he knows, right?"

"He knows."

God, put *that* together. Mark Brittain. What a hero. Broke major blood vessels in his neck and eyes today in class preaching the evils of fornication and all the time he's been a fornicating fool.

"I almost spoke up in class today when he got so excited, but it's not something I want the world to know."

I swatted the thought of what all this meant about Jody and Mark out of my head like a mosquito off the back of my neck, because that could make me seriously depressed. Plus I found myself genuinely curious. "What does he say to you? I mean, after an attack of hysteria like he had today, what does he say? He has to know how chicken shit that is."

Jody smiled sadly and stared at the table as the waitress placed our burgers and fries in front of us. "Sure," she says. "But he says he's different, that when you have a mission, you can't let human errors stand in your way. You expect people to help you with that."

"Meaning you?"

"Meaning me. He says people as committed as he is get

special leeway in the Lord's eyes. It was my job to prevent it."

God's sliding scale. I bit into my burger. "Committed. That's a good word for what he ought to be." Then it occurred to me. "Why are you telling me this?"

"I've known all along—in fact, since I had the abortion—that Mark and I weren't going to make it. He's treated me like shit since then, at least when we're alone. One thing about Mark, he forgives himself a lot more easily than he forgives others."

"He gets forgiven for 'fornication,' but you don't."

"Something like that," she said. Suddenly tears welled in her eyes. "God, I've been so stupid. I didn't want to go to bed with him in the first place. Then I didn't want to have the abortion. Oh God, and then I got starry-eyed and lovey and wanted to get married and have a family with him. I didn't know what to do. I just felt so dirty I wanted to do *something* right."

I put my hand on hers and felt it tremble.

"But that threw a crank into his mission. I should have stopped seeing him before the abortion, I really should have. I still don't know how I'd have handled it if it hadn't been for Mark, but I'll tell you one thing."

"What's that?"

"You can't imagine the emptiness. There's a piece that

isn't getting talked about in class. Mark took me to the clinic, but he dropped me off two blocks away because he thought somebody might recognize him. When I came out, I was just *lost*. All Mark wanted to talk about was how we'd made the right choice and how his life was no longer ruined. I just wanted to cry and have somebody hold me."

This was a very different Jody than I'd imagined. God, nothing is as it appears. I placed my fingers on the cords running the length of her neck and massaged easily. They were strung like the high notes on a grand piano.

"All I could think was to get away from him, so I went home that night and laid down in my room and cried and hated his guts, and I was going to go to school the next day and tell him to go to hell."

"That would have been appropriate."

"Before I got a chance, he got me alone in the breezeway out by the gym and said how sorry he was he hadn't paid better attention to my feelings yesterday—said he'd been a senseless boob and that he'd make it up to me. I felt so bad about myself, so really desperately bad, that I went for it. I just wanted somebody around me who knew, and I couldn't bring myself to tell anyone else." She shook her head. "I marched in the picket line with him."

"I take it you couldn't tell your parents," I said, thinking how Mom is the first person I'd go to in that kind of a jam.

Jody looked at me as if I'd blown my nose on her burger. "They'd die. Right after they killed me." Enough said. "Anyway, I just wanted somebody to like me, and Mark was it. Later I saw he didn't really like me any better than I did, but I was convinced I'd done something so horrible that nobody would ever like me again. I thought people would be able to look at me and know." She touched the back of my hand. "My family goes to the same church Mark does. Ms. Lemry's class is really the first time in my life I ever heard an adult question anything I grew up believing to be a sin. At least an adult I respected. If my parents knew what goes on in there, they'd jerk me out so fast my seat would ignite."

I feel bad about what I said next, because I should have just been thinking of Jody, but I said this for me. "I wish you'd known me then. I don't think there's anything you could have done to make me treat you like Brittain."

She smiled and said thanks. "I knew that, I think. That's why I'm telling you now. I don't want you to do anything about it, I'm not hustling you. You just seem to know about . . ."

"Feeling like a piece of shit?"

She smiled. "Feeling like a piece of shit."

▌ ▌ ▌

So I'm lying here, thinking I may have a girlfriend or something. And you know what scares me? It's easy to sit back, like in Lemry's class, and take shots at guys like Brittain, but if Jody and I end up being together, I'll have to perform, and to tell you the truth, I've always been a better sniper than a true soldier. In my friendship with Sarah Byrnes I've just followed her lead, and up until recently my friendship with Ellerby has been a couple of guys loaded up on testosterone yukking it up. When the class is discussing abortion, I can't sit back with no real opinion if I have a girlfriend who's had one.

I need to have a serious talk with my mother before it's too late.

▼ ▼ ▼

CHAPTER
TEN

I find Lemry folding towels near the clothes dryer back behind the lockers.

"I thought that's what managers were for," I say, leaning on the long table next to the two industrial washing machines.

"It's therapy," she says back. "It's the one thing I do in life that gets results."

"Hey, you get results from me. And Ellerby."

She gawks, snorts, and walks over to the wall phone. "Could you send down more towels, please?" she says into the mouthpiece. "The wrestlers must have towels they need washed. What about basketball?"

I slap my chest. "I'm crushed."

She puts the handset back onto its cradle. "If only it were true. What do you want, Mobe?"

"World peace. An end to hunger. Homes for the homeless . . ."

"Very noble."

". . . a new car."

"That's closer to the truth. I meant why have you invaded my sanctuary? What do you want from me? Now."

"What would you think if I started taking out Brittain's girlfriend?"

She places the towel she's folding slowly on the top of the heap and stares up at me. "You mean Jody?"

"What would you think?"

"I'd think you and Mark would probably swim faster."

"Well, I think I'm going to do it."

"Jody have anything to say about this?"

"She asked me first."

Lemry returns to her towels.

"So what do you think? Really," I ask.

"I think it's none of my business. I don't know what's behind it, but I've watched your eyes glaze over in Jody Mueller's presence for three years. I just hope you're not doing it to get at Mark. I'd think something about *that*."

"That's a pretty good side benny, but it's not why."

Lemry puts down the towel she's folding. "Look, Moby, I don't care who you go out with, but I think you and Steve should both take it a little easier on Mark."

I shrug, a little embarrassed because it sounds like Lemry thinks I'm mean, and though I may be sometimes, I don't want her thinking it.

"He keeps himself on a pretty short leash," she says. "He has a lot of serious beliefs and almost no sense of humor. That's not a good combination."

"To tell the truth, Coach, if it weren't for the fact that he's a good swimmer, I'd think any leash long enough to let him out of his house was too long."

"I know that. I'm not asking you to go to church with him. Just don't push so hard. If you're going out with Jody Mueller, go out with her. Just do it without a lot of fanfare, okay?"

"No fanfare. Thanks, Coach." I take the steps back up to the hall three at a time.

Moments before the third period bell, I gaze down my row of lockers into the eyes of Mark Brittain. He shows no pretense of good cheer, and I figure he and Jody have talked. *It's not my fault*, I think, *I didn't start this.* How gallant. I dig into my locker, and a hand touches my shoulder. I turn slowly to face him. "What do you need?"

He says, "I think you know."

"Manners?"

"Jody told me she wants to start seeing other people."

"You must be proud."

"She wants to go out with you."

"Finally getting some taste, huh?" I say, staying casual. I don't want to have to prove I'm no fighter.

Mark says, "That's low, Calhoune. It's one thing to come after me in the pool. It's something else to go after my girl."

"I didn't go after your girl."

He sneers. "You've been sniffing around her since I can remember. Are you telling me if she wants to go out with you, you won't go?"

"No, I'm saying I didn't go after her."

"You want me to believe it was her idea?" he asks. "That's a laugh. What would she want with a block of lard like you?"

"Intelligent company, maybe?" I guess. "A chance for a few laughs?" If Brittain knew me better he wouldn't go after my physical appearance. He'd have to complete graduate work at the Harvard School of Slams to come up with a name I didn't hear a thousand times in junior high. Block of lard? Give me a break, Brittain. I pull away to go to class, but he stands in my path, swelling his chest. I'm thinking this probably isn't how Lemry would want me to do this.

I tell Mark to get out of my way. I may not be a fighter, but I do have a documented history of being able to take a punch. Ask Dale Thornton.

He doesn't budge. "If we fight," I say, "we go home for three days. My mother fixes me a glass of lemonade and a peanut butter sandwich and tells me to try to stay in school. Whaddaya s'pose your old man will do?" Brittain didn't get that tight an ass growing up with Ward and June Cleaver.

We stand toe-to-toe a few seconds more, glaring each other down as a crowd starts to gather. I push my bluff. "All that and you're going to be embarrassed, too. This ain't your day, buddy."

Mark's not quite sure about me, and his need for decorum wins out. He steps back and I turn for my class.

"She's a bitch," he blurts after me.

I stop, turning, thinking I may go ahead and try to take him out. "What?"

"Mueller. She's a bitch. A pathological liar. I only stayed with her out of pity. It's true, Calhoune. I was going to dump her, but she got to it first. She'll tell you all kinds of wild stories, but I'm telling you because she'll pull you in just like she did me. She's pretty and all that, but there's something seriously wrong with her. You'll either believe me or you'll find out for yourself."

I walk back toward him, stop inches away and say, "I'll find out for myself."

He shrugs, his feathers all nicely back in place. "Suit yourself. You should hear what she's said about you already."

I look at my watch. Less than thirty seconds to the bell. "Maybe we can make it a topic for discussion in Lemry's class."

My butt hits the seat with the sound of the bell.

Mr. Caldwell starts into yesterday's homework in detail, but I'm not paying much attention, which is too bad because I didn't do mine and if I went along with him, I could get it finished in time to hand in. That was a major encounter with Mark, and I'll bet it won't be the last. I've always thought Brittain was about a half turn of the knob from being out of control, and he's strong. In junior high I was afraid of him, but in junior high I was afraid of everybody. Now I'm not sure if it was because of his size or the fact that he always looked like he could lose it at any minute. If I have to tangle with him, it'll be a toss-up. He may whip me, but he'll get hurt doing it, because I'd wage a true holy war for Jody Mueller now that I know how he treated her. And he just showed me trump; he's a phony.

"Isn't this a bit coincidental?" Mom says, in response to my telling her I might be going out with Jody Mueller and I'd appreciate it if things looked a little better around here from now on, housekeeping-wise. Carver stands in a neutral corner of the kitchen.

"What's that?"

"That you're planning to go out with your worst enemy's girlfriend?"

"Hey, listen . . ."

"You've been scrapping back and forth with Mark Brittain for two years at least. I've never heard you say one good thing about him."

"That comes from my unwavering commitment to the truth," I say. "What's the coincidence?"

"That when you decide to start going out with someone, you choose his girl. That could appear a bit of a low blow to someone who isn't aware of your impeccable integrity."

"Funny," I say, "but Brittain said about the same thing, only you both got the order wrong. I didn't decide to start going out and then pick the girl. The girl picked me and I decided to start going out."

Mom nods, thinking. "Are you sure she's not doing it just to get even with him for something? How do you know you're not being used?"

I throw up my arms. "Use me. Use me."

"I don't know, Eric," she says. "You asked for my advice,

and I just think you should be a little careful."

Carver comes a half step forward. "May I say something?"

"Long as you're on my side," I say.

"Long as you're on my side," Mom says right behind me.

Carver's getting used to us. "I think Moby has every right to take a chance with this girl. Especially considering how long he's been attracted to her. If she's using him, it's a lesson he won't forget. If not, he's got a shot at something he's been wanting for a long time."

Mom places a flat palm against her chest. "Well, Ann Landers. When did you become an expert on affairs of the heart?"

"Well," Carver says back, "I was a teenager once, and anyone who can remember that is an expert, but more recently I've had the experience of manipulating my way to being with you."

"Manipulating?" Uh, oh. Carver's on thin ice. "How have you been manipulating anything?"

"Not in front of the boy," he says with a smile.

"Yes, in front of the boy," she says back.

"Well, who do you think sent Jack Callum out of town three weekends out of four for more than sixteen months?"

Mom glares, looking genuinely stunned.

"That's right," Carver continues. "And there was nothing

fair about it. I was his boss. There were plenty of times I could have gone myself or sent other auditors."

"But you sent Jack."

"I sent Jack."

"You were ruining my romance."

Carver nods. I'm liking him better all the time. Jack Callum was a jerk of colossal proportions.

"You were ruining my romance *intentionally*."

Carver nods again. All this time I thought he was Cream of Wheat. No way. This guy is Grape-Nuts. "Jack Callum wasn't for you," he says.

Mom is incensed, truly so; past kidding around. "I guess that was for *me* to decide."

Carver doesn't back down. "What did you decide?"

"I decided he worked away from home too much. I decided he cared more for his job than he did for me."

"He did care more for his job than you," Carver says. "He didn't complain once when I shipped him out."

"But you were doing it to keep him away from me."

"I was doing it to let myself get closer to you. Look, the guy was a bozo. He still is. I hate to say this, but I think your head was turned a little by that body. I'll admit, he has one of the best builds this side of the Mr. Olympia contest, but that body is in inverse proportion to his brain." Carver is right.

Jack Callum is *buff*, as they say in the body-building business, but he is also a poster boy for Adjustos of the Universe if I ever saw one. "I always wondered what you guys talked about over a candlelit dinner."

Mom says, "Carver, you need to know I don't like people messing in my business behind my back. This really angers me." She is quiet a minute, thinking. "In fact, this may hurt our relationship."

Carver shrugs. "If it does, so be it," he says. "I was—am— in love, babe. If Jack had been a decent guy, I'd have stayed clear. But you looked way too good to me to be hanging out with the likes of him."

Mom still glares. It isn't easy, to get under her skin, but making her look or feel tricked will do it.

"Anyway," Carver says, "the point is that Eric and this girl Jody see something they like in each other, and they ought to look into it. They're kids. There's a lot to learn about being in a relationship."

"And you're about to learn it." Her tone is softer, and I can see Mom backing off her anger a bit, though Carver's going to have to be awful nice to her for a while. What the hell, he's nice most of the time anyway. I like seeing him stand up to Mom. I wouldn't say this to her, but she can get pretty full of herself, being this big writer and all; constantly getting recognized because her picture appears next to her column in the paper.

Mom makes Carver take her out for a nice dinner, which is like throwing Brer Rabbit in the briar patch. As they're leaving she straightens him out some more, but it doesn't seem to be doing much harm, and I'm thinking there's a little piece in Mom that's glad to have someone care about her enough to get underhanded. As they disappear, I realize I haven't given Carver much of a chance. He's an okay-looking guy; spends a little time at the gym himself. He doesn't brag himself up, and he's real gentle when it comes to my mother. I should lay off the fact that he's intrigued by recreational vehicles and that he sometimes wears black socks with shorts. I think I'm so used to my mom telling me relationships don't mean anything to her that I get to seeing her boyfriends as these one-dimensional boobs who won't be around long enough to get to know me anyway. Old Carver might be different. My mother doesn't look quite so tough when her partner doesn't buy her line.

I wonder if other people use their bedrooms the same way I do. When things get packed full—like they are now for me—I retreat here. Since I was very young, Mom and I have had an agreement that my room is private as long as I don't leave anything organic here long enough to change from a solid to a liquid giving off gasses. If my clothes are within ten feet of the washing machine on wash day, they get washed. If not, they don't unless I wash them myself. That keeps her out of my room without an invite. I can't think of a time when I would have kept her out, but her respect for my private space has allowed me a true sanctuary. Which is exactly what I need right now.

After workout this afternoon, I shot up to the psych ward to see Sarah Byrnes, though we never did make contact. Her dad was there, sort of hovering. From a distance I watched him talking to her, and though he whispered, he appeared pretty worked up. I couldn't see Sarah Byrnes's face—only the very still back of her head—but I'm sure she didn't respond. Old Virgil smelled a rat, I think, because he was *intense*. He saw me, shot me a glance that felt like a fist to the chest, and went right on talking to her. The attendant watched awhile, then disappeared to get Laurel, the therapist, who watched a few seconds herself before walking over and gently laying a hand on Mr. Byrnes's shoulder.

He slapped it away. "This foolishness has gone far enough," he said. "If this little girl doesn't get herself together I'll drag her on home and let her get better there."

Laurel said he'd have to get himself under control or leave, and he sprang from the couch like a predator, crowding, towering over her. I thought he'd hit her, but Laurel didn't back down even a step.

With my heart in my throat, I moved in their direction, hoping to hell Sacred Heart had a plan for events like this, because I knew I'd have to do something if he hit her, but tangling with Virgil Byrnes wouldn't be like tying up with Mark Brittain, or even getting your butt kicked by Dale Thornton. This would be like getting your butt kicked permanently. I have newfound respect for his madness now that I know for sure what he did to my friend.

To my tremendous relief, two attendants straight from "Wrestlemania Three" reached them ahead of me, one moving behind Mr. Byrnes and the other stepping between him and Laurel. The larger one said, "Sir, I'm afraid we're going to have to ask you to leave."

"You can ask me all you want. This here's my kid and if I leave, I leave with her."

"I'm afraid that's not possible," said Schwarzenegger Number One.

"You have no right to keep her here against my wishes."

Laurel broke in. "I'm afraid that's not true. This girl is clearly in need of help. If you take her, I'll call Child Protection Services and report extreme emotional abuse and neglect. It'll get decided in a shelter care hearing, and you have a completely nonresponsive child here. "

A calmness descended over Virgil Byrnes, and when

I think back, it was the most chilling part of the whole incident. His face went blank and he nodded slightly. "Very well," he said, and turned to Sarah Byrnes. "Young lady, you get it together, or there will be hell to pay."

He turned abruptly and walked toward the exit. Unfortunately I was standing in front of it. In a voice so low it almost sounded like a growl, he said, "Something's up and you know what it is, young Calhoune. Don't make the mistake of getting mixed up in it, hear me?"

"Yes sir," crossed my lips before I could even think.

He nodded. "You're a smart boy. If my little girl is listening to you, you tell her she best get herself home. This is family business."

Then he was gone.

The staff didn't leave Sarah Byrnes and me alone long enough for any conversation after that, and I have a feeling she would have remained a statue. Words can't describe the sense of menace that man puts out.

So I'm lying here under the earphones, thinking if I had the hammer Peter, Paul, and Mary are singing about, I'd sneak up behind Virgil Byrnes and give him a whack; do what someone should have done a long time ago.

It's amazing to me how things seem always to pile up on each other. It would be enough to deal with all that's going on with Sarah Byrnes, or with Jody, or even with just trying to get my times down before Regionals. But it's all there together. All I really want to do is the right thing. But how do you ever know what that is? I mean, I know some people who could help me with Sarah Byrnes's dilemma—Lemry for one, my mother for another—but I promised not to tell. So is it right to go for help when I've promised I wouldn't, or is the right thing to keep my promise? The stakes are high. You don't have to look into Virgil Byrnes's eyes more than a second to know that.

And what about Jody? Truth is, I'm scared to death to start anything up, and not because she used to go out with Brittain. It doesn't make me proud to say this, but even with all the work I've done on the shimmering nerd I once was, there is a scared little fat boy inside me who is terrified of being seen. And I think if you're going to be with somebody, you owe it to them to show yourself. High stakes there, too. I think I've been afraid to admit how much I wanted to be with her until it became a possibility. Maybe I should have gone ahead and had some girlfriends I wasn't interested in; you know, a few tune-up bouts before the main event. I hate going into this not knowing what I'm doing, hate having to act cool when I ain't. Funny thing—this is the first time in my memory I've wished I had a dad. It pisses me off that mine left.

CHAPTER
ELEVEN

I've tried to look at Brittain from Lemry's point of view, and I really leave him alone away from the pool now, but if I had to go cold turkey—well, life wouldn't be worth living. He's been such an asshole since Jody and I have been seeing each other that today Ellerby and I decided to kill him on the two-hundreds to teach him some humility, letting him lead for seven laps before eating him up on the eighth. Twenty of 'em like that. He didn't even stay around to shower after workout, which means in an hour he'll feel like he's staked on an anthill from the residual chlorine.

Things are finally looking up for Sarah Byrnes. She's not completely out of the woods, but the cavalry is storming over the horizon. I'm glad, because I'm not strong enough or smart enough to carry this load myself.

The next time I visited Sacred Heart we couldn't talk because her dad was there. It was as if he was stalking us. After that we went outside, but he followed us to the landing at the top of the stairs where he could watch, and Sarah Byrnes couldn't talk. Finally, I took her hand. "Once for yes and twice for no. Do you think he knows you're faking it?"

She squeezed three times.

"Three? Oh, 'I don't know.' You want three to be 'I don't know.'"

Once.

"You're not going home with him, are you?"

Twice. Hard.

"Good. You want me to try to get you some help?"

Twice. Hard again.

"Wait," I said, "hear me out. What if I could work it out so you were protected? I'm not sure, and if I can't I won't do anything, but if I could, would it be okay?"

Twice.

Sarah Byrnes didn't trust anyone. She'd been "helped" before. Still, I didn't believe I could just let her dangle in the wind like this. I also knew if I betrayed her, it would be the last time.

"Look," I said. "I'm going to sneak my notebook and a

pen into your room, under your mattress. You tell me what to do, or at least tell me what you're going to do. You must have a plan. It's making me crazy to be in the dark. Okay? If I leave it, will you write in it?"

Once.

Mr. Byrnes said, "Any luck, boy?" as we passed him on the back stair, Sarah Byrnes staring straight ahead.

"No sir. I talk because they said to keep things as normal as possible, but she doesn't answer."

"This is bullshit," he said, looking past me to Sarah Byrnes. "She's hearing every word, and I'd bet you know that, Calhoune. Tell you what, if I find out it's true, there'll be hell to pay for you, too. Won't always be this hospital to protect her. Or you, either. If you know something I should know, you best spill it."

I stopped and stared directly into his eyes. "Look, Mr. Byrnes," I said, "I'm a lot more afraid of Sarah Byrnes not talking than I am of what you might do. If she was talking to me, the whole world would know it." My heart pounded *lie!* so hard I thought he would hear it, but he looked hard at my eyes and said, "Okay." *God*, he's scary.

Sarah Byrnes's room isn't off limits, so I had no trouble planting the notebook between the mattress and the box spring when Mr. Byrnes was talking at the nurse. But Mr.

Byrnes was there when I went back to get it two days later, so I had to wait. Sarah Byrnes and I walked the courtyard again under his ever-present glare. The weather was springlike, though that kind of weather never lasts long in February, and I carried my coat over my arm. "Did you write in the book?"

Once.

We walked in long, slow circles with me babbling about Lemry's class, Ellerby and Brittain, Carver and the way he stood up to my mother, whatever I could think of to wear down Mr. Byrnes's patience. But he stood at the landing atop the stairs, waiting like some bird of prey.

Then I told her about Jody, and to my surprise, I told her *all* about Jody. I told her how good I felt to be with her and to have her want to spend time with me. Before I knew it I was talking about the abortion. I had promised, but there I was, and I didn't think to try to stop myself until it was over. Tears ran down Sarah Byrnes's cheeks. I had never seen that before, and I remember thinking absently how they meandered along the scarred crevices of her face rather than in a straight line like they would on a smooth one. I didn't know why she was crying, but I stopped and I stood looking at her, and then I hugged her. She didn't hug me back, but I felt her relax a bit and fall gently against me, and more tears came. When the tears dried I took her back up the steps. Passing Mr. Byrnes I said, "Nothing," but it's a pretty safe bet he didn't believe me.

Old man Byrnes's radar was working overtime, and he bird-dogged me every step so I didn't dare go into her room for the notebook. I had to come back late the next day. Sarah Byrnes was sitting through a group therapy session, so I just told the nurse I had left a notebook with my homework in her room. These people really do treat me like I work here.

Dear Eric,

They've been telling me—in case I'm listening—to write things down ever since I got here, and now they would be satisfied, except they won't know, because if you show this to anybody I'll rip out your intestines and strangle you with them. I have never trusted anyone completely, not even you, and I don't know if I do yet. I'll find out by whether or not I give you this or just rip it up. Here goes.

I can't ever go home again. My dad is getting crazier, and like I said the other day, there's nothing too mean for him to do if he thinks he needs to. Eric, just believe that and don't get stupid and try to call the Child Protection people or the cops. They can only help after something's happened, and the threats they make don't mean anything to my dad.

I came here because I thought I was going to kill myself, and even though it seemed like a good idea, I was afraid. I needed someplace safe to decide if I could or should do it. I considered running away, but I might as well just admit it, I'm so ugly that even if I do get away from him, my life will always be like this. There's no running from what he did. For a long time I thought the trick was to make myself as mean as he was. That's what Crispy Pork Rinds was all about. I wanted to be as mean as I could to all the people who had been mean to me, and I needed my dad then, because being around him kept me feeling that way.

But then I got up here and things changed. They care about you here, and I've seen some kids that have a lot more wrong with them than I have except you can't see it. There's a boy here who was shut up in his closet when he was three years old with his puppy that his stepdad killed. He was there for at least a day but probably it was longer. And there's a girl who watched her dad kick her little brother to death from a place under the stairs where he couldn't see her, and she still hates herself for not stopping him, but she was only six. I was sitting in the group, pretending I'd been beamed up, when she told that story, and all of a sudden she was shrieking and crying and she ran across the circle and hugged me and told me not to give up and that she feels on the inside like I look on the outside, but she couldn't stand it if I gave up because the ones of us who are scarred have to stick together. I wanted to talk and tell her I would stay and fight, but I couldn't because if I talk they'll think I'm better and send me home. It hurts so much inside me I can hardly stand it, and I've thought more about killing myself, but I know I won't. I feel worse for their lives than I do for my own, except I wish I could hide my scars on the inside like them. I just want to be able to keep mine a secret some of the time.

I'm writing this because I don't have to give it to you. Anyway, ever since that girl hugged me, I know I'm not the only one in the world who hurts, or even the person who hurts the worst. If the ones who hurt the worst stay, then I can, too.

I've started having these dreams about when my mother was still around. I was pretty, Eric. I was pretty. People said that. In these dreams I see myself that way, and even though I know something was really wrong with my mother, it still feels like love when I remember it. And they aren't like real dreams, they're like memories. Our group counselor says they're important because we can hitch our new lives to them.

I remember how my mother and I used to hide after my dad beat her up and we'd hold each other in the dark, but I also remember her laughing and playing with me when he was gone. She loved me in her way, Eric. She really did. It's hard to stay mean when you remember how that feels. I forgot about it until I got here and saw these kids trying to dig out the little bits of love in their lives, and when I saw they could find them, I started to look for mine. I owe these kids a lot. Sometime before I leave I'll have to talk because I need to tell them they've made things better *for me. I also need to tell them about my life because it isn't fair that I know about them, and they don't know about me.*

And I know I have to quit remembering my mother as loving me because it hurts too much. There's only one way she can help me now, and that's to come back and tell the truth—and put that son of a bitch away.

The ink color has changed because it's the next day. It was hard to let you take this. I was relieved yesterday when you didn't get a chance to get it out of my room. But I can't let myself chicken out now; I'm out of good choices. And then there's you. When we were younger I kept you around because you were an easy friend. And it's only been since I got here, since that girl hugged me, that I figured out if I have a chance it'll be because I let somebody like me. You saved me, Eric. God, remember when you first turned out for the swim team and you started losing all that weight and got scared I'd think you were leaving me? So you ate like two pigs instead of one? When I found out you were staying fat for me, I went home and cried and cried. Nobody ever did anything like that for me. I cried again the other day when you told me about that Jody girl, and you might as well know it's because I was afraid you'll go away from me. I know I'm not pretty anymore, Eric, but I'm a girl under all this mess. I don't love you or anything—at least not like that—but it makes me afraid. I also cried because you told me she had an abortion and there've been so many times in my life I wished that's what I had been.

These kids up here, they act like the toughest kids in the world, just like me, but this is the first time I've ever seen under that toughness—in anybody else or in me. I'm really scared, because if I'm going to have a life, I'm going to have to act different, and I don't know if I can.

So there it is, and by God I'm going to give this to you and you better not give it to anybody else. And one other thing: When I start talking again don't expect me to act like this letter all the time, because I won't.

"I need to talk to you off the record," I said, standing on Lemry's porch after midnight.

"You want to stand out here and freeze," she said, pulling her robe tight, "or would you like to come in?"

In the light she saw the red rims around my eyes. "Mobe, what's the matter?"

"You sure we won't bother your husband?"

She smiled. "My husband goes to work out at five in the morning. He does not wake up for midnight callers. Now what's the matter?"

I burst into tears.

Lemry put her hand on my back, and guided me to the

couch. "Sit. Tell me what's the matter."

"God, I think my heart is going to break."

"Is this about Jody?"

I shook my head. "That would be easy."

"Tell me."

"It has to be off the record."

"I'll promise if it's at all possible I'll keep it to myself, Mobe, but if it requires outside help, I always have to consider that."

I watched her carefully.

"You'll just have to take a chance."

It boiled down to this: Somebody a whole lot smarter than me and Sarah Byrnes needs to help keep her old man off her and get a start on the life she got a glimpse of writing that letter. If I didn't do *something*, Sarah Byrnes would either get dragged back home by her dad, or she'd run away and be alone. The letter was clear: shaky as I was, I was her only friend. I'd rather have her hate my guts and be safe than love me and be alone.

I handed Lemry the letter.

She read it and tears rolled out of her eyes like big sad pearls, and I knew she'd do the right thing because she felt just like me. She read it again and said, "She's right, Mobe. Her mother's the only person who can set this straight. We better find her."

CHAPTER
TWELVE

"**M**an," Ellerby says, pausing for the cross-traffic before taking a right on the red onto Compton Street at the edge of the Edison district, "I must be getting the kind of faith my dad talks about, bringing my holy-mobile down here again." He pauses. "Lemme guess. We're not here bringing the word and the light to Dale Thornton."

"That's why I hang out with you, Ellerby. You're like a genius or something."

"So what is it we're bringing?"

"Questions."

"Make them easy ones, okay? I'd hate to see that guy get pissed."

"I'll do my best."

Ellerby pulls the Cruiser up against the cracked and broken sidewalk at the edge of the vacant lot across the street from Thornton's house, and I gaze across the icy street toward the driveway leading back to Dale's shop. The balance has obviously shifted between Dale and me since junior high, if only because I'm bigger now and not as afraid of my shadow as I once was. But I'm like Ellerby; Dale Thornton is still not a guy I want on my bad side. He has the same nothing-to-lose look, and I'll never be comfortable around that. But he's the only person to answer these questions.

"Wait here. I see his car. I should just be a minute."

Ellerby leans back into his customized bucket seat as I step out. "What if he kills you?"

"If you're sure I'm dead, drive away."

The door to Dale's shop stands ajar, and I hear the clanging of metal on metal as I approach. I knock twice before pushing my way in, still unseen by Dale, who appears to be hammering on a stuck bolt. He looks up, then back to what he's doing. When the bolt breaks loose, he straightens up and nods. "Fat Boy," he says. "What's up?"

"Hey, Dale," I say uneasily. "Need to ask you some questions."

"You with the cops?"

I laugh. "They're not that kind of questions."

He watches me.

"So," I say, "what do you think?"

"Is that the first question?"

"No. I'm just trying not to be pushy."

Dale wipes his hands with the ever-present grease rag and leans against the back of the station wagon. "This is about Scarface, right?"

"Yeah."

He replaces the grease rag. "I promised a long time ago I wouldn't talk about her. I already said too much. I ain't got much, but my word's good."

"She told me about the stove. You don't need to worry about having spilled the beans on that anymore."

Dale stared suspiciously. He'd obviously had second thoughts about breaking his word. "You know," he warned, "you do-gooders need to be careful. You think just 'cause you want to help somebody, somebody's gonna be helped."

"I'm not asking you to let any more secrets out, Dale. Honest, Sarah Byrnes told me. I came to ask if she ever said anything about her mother. Like about where she thought she went, or anything like that."

"Whaddaya want with her old lady?"

I say, "I'm not sure, but Sarah Byrnes says her dad is getting crazier and crazier, like when he burned her. Said she thinks he's getting ready to do something bad. Her mother is the only one who could blow the whistle."

"I thought Scarface wasn't talking. You said she was holed up at the crazy house, keepin' her mouth shut."

"She's still holed up there, but she's talkin' some. At least to me."

"She's crafty, that Scarface. Bet there never was nothin' wrong with her. Bet she coulda talked all along."

You don't get ahead of Dale Thornton when it comes to survival. "I'll bet you're right. So what about it? Ever hear her say anything about her mom?"

"Just that she hightailed it after her daddy burned her. Scarface never heard nothin' from her again. Said for a while she was scared her old man maybe killed her."

"Did she say where she might have gone if he didn't kill her?"

He sits back. "Only place like that woulda been Reno."

"Reno, Nevada?"

"They got a Reno somewhere else?"

"Not that I know of."

"Then Reno, Nevada. Jesus, how come everybody said you was so smart, Fat Boy?"

"I had 'em fooled. They don't say that anymore."

"I ain't surprised."

"Why Reno? What did Sarah Byrnes ever say about Reno?"

"Said her momma always wanted to be a singer or a dancer or some shit like these chicks she seen in Reno once, up on the stage at some gamblin' place. Her mom told her that's what she woulda done if she wouldn't of married her old man. Scarface told me once her mom used to talk about it all the time, like it was some kind of possession or somethin'."

"Obsession."

"Yeah, that."

"Did it sound like something she'd really do?"

"Whaddaya mean?"

"Well, was it like me wanting to grow up to be a stand-up comic, or was it something she'd really do?"

Dale shakes his head. "How the hell would I know? I never met her mom. She only talked about her once or twice. I don't know why she'd wanna be around her old lady anyway. Hell, she up an' left, right? Scarface'd been better off like me, no mom at all. I'd rather have nobody than somebody who'd do me like that."

Dale has a point. "Look," he says, walking back toward the workbench, "I'm done with this here courtroom drama. Come over here an' hold this piece so I can rethread it."

Mautz flagged me down in the hall between fourth period and lunch today, and I swear it felt just like junior high, only this time I was innocent. "Mr. Calhoune, could I talk to you for a minute?"

What am I gonna say, no? I crammed my books into my locker and walked over to him. I've grown, but he's still a monster. "Yes sir."

"Thought we might have lunch," he said. "Down in my office."

"What'd I do?"

He smiled. "Nothing. I want to talk something over with you."

I glanced over at Jody standing next to her locker. "I was going to eat with . . ."

"Come on, lover boy. One lunch away from her won't hurt you."

This was unwinnable. "Okay, I'll meet you there." I walked over to Jody. "Gonna have to stand you up."

"Lunching with the king?" She'd overheard.

"Yeah. Guess I better keep my food in my Baggies until right before I eat it. Less chance of contamination."

"I'll be outside at the tables," she said. "If you get finished early, come on out."

"Eric," Mautz said to me in his doorway. "Just like old times."

"Yeah, well, except I'm not trying to strong-arm my way into the publishing business."

"That's good."

"It was a pretty good paper," I said, smiling. "A little misdirected, maybe, but hey, the grammar was good, the writing concise."

He wasn't amused. We got away with that paper a lot longer than he would have liked. I was surprised not to feel intimidated as badly as I used to. "Well, we're not here to talk about misguided journalism," he said, directing me toward a chair across from his desk. His lunch was spread neatly before him like a still life, and I opened my paper bag, extracting a sandwich. "How's school going for you this year?"

Look in my files, I thought. I said, "Okay."

"Good. Your grades going to get you into a good college?"

I said I could go pretty much anyplace I wanted.

"Good," he said again. "Secondary education is important. Got to have a good education to get a good job."

I started to tell him it was hard to argue with that, but he went right on. "Tell me about your Contemporary American Thought class."

Be patient, and the rat will always come out of his hole. "Good class," I said. "What do you want to know about it?"

"What do you discuss in there?"

"Current problems," I said. "The students set up the curriculum at the beginning of the semester, and we divide it up so everyone's issue gets covered."

"What kinds of issues?"

"All kinds."

Mautz smiled. "Are you evading my questions, Eric?"

"What do you mean?"

"Just that. I ask what you talk about in Mrs. Lemry's class, and you beat around the bush."

"Why don't you ask Ms. Lemry?"

"Because I'm asking you."

This was starting to feel *bad*. I mean, Mautz invites me to lunch (and makes me bring my own, but who's complaining) to ask me what's going on in a class when all he has to do is ask the teacher? Come on, folks. "Tell you what, Mr. Mautz. You tell me what you want to know and why you want to know it, and if I can help you out, I will."

"You haven't changed much, have you, Eric?"

"Probably not much." I looked down at myself. "Lost a little weight, but I still don't like to be pushed around, and I still don't like to be tricked."

"How are you being tricked?"

"I *would* be tricked by answering questions about Ms. Lemry's class when you could just ask her. You're not telling me what this is about."

Mautz rocked in his chair, staring at me, his index finger

tapping his lips lightly. "Very well," he said finally. "Frankly, I've been a bit distressed by what I've heard about that class, and about you and your friend Steve Ellerby."

Wait long enough . . . "What have you heard?"

Mautz was quiet again, seemingly considering how much he wanted me to know. Finally he put up his hands. "That some important Christian values are being trashed, for one, but that's a subject for Mrs. Lemry and me. Also that you and your friend Ellerby seem to be mounting a vicious campaign to humiliate Mark Brittain."

Ah, Brittain. It was my turn to sit staring.

"What do you say about that?"

I was quiet a second longer. "Well, to tell you the truth, I haven't spent a lot of time or brain power on humiliating Mark Brittain. He does that pretty well himself. I don't mind telling you I don't like him, and if he weren't part of the swim team I wouldn't give him the time of day."

"What about his girlfriend?"

"Jody?"

Mautz nodded. "Mark tells me you've been slandering him to her."

"First, she's not his girlfriend, and second, I have better things to do than slander Mark Brittain. Like I said, why mess with what's already working?"

Mautz sat forward and memories of junior high flooded back to me. I fought hard to remember that things were different now; I had done nothing wrong. "I don't mind telling you, Mr. Calhoune, that I believe Mark Brittain is a special kind of kid. His moral values are flawless, and he doesn't bow to the temptations most kids bow to. You included. Now, I talked with his mother this morning, and she's very worried. She believes he's under a lot of stress and says he seems particularly depressed. I can't order you to leave him alone, or I would. Instead, I'm asking you to give him a little slack."

I gazed around the office, at the impeccable organization: every book in place, the top of his desk clean and shiny enough to skate on. My eyes landed on a large crucifix in the middle of his bookcase. The design at the center was identical to the one in the center of the decal in Brittain's rear window. "Do you go to the same church as Mark?"

"What difference does that make?"

"Something about this conversation just made me wonder, that's all."

"Well, it's none of your concern. But I see no problem in telling you that I do."

I sat back, breathing out.

"What does that have to do with anything?" he asked.

"Nothing. Really, I just wondered. Can I go now?"

"What about my request?"

"About Mark? I'll give Mark so much space he won't even know I'm on the same planet."

"What about his girlfriend?"

"If he gets one, I promise I won't even talk to her." Blood flooded into Mautz's face, but he retained control. "I meant Jody Mueller."

"I'll ask her to give him some space, too."

Mautz pointed his finger at me, his carotid artery swelling like a fire hose. "You're skating on thin ice, young man."

"What is it you want me to do about Jody Mueller, Mr. Mautz?"

"If you had an ounce of compassion, you'd stop seeing her. At least until things have stabilized."

"You mean until Mark Brittain is stabilized? My organ donor card will expire before Mark Brittain is stabilized. The guy needs help." I stood. "I'll leave Mark alone." I said. "But I'm not going to stop seeing Jody Mueller." I started for the door.

"You know," Mautz said, "I've always seen you as a bit misguided, Eric. That's no secret. But I've never seen you as cruel. Not before today."

I was *this* close to telling him about his favorite choirboy's response to Jody's pregnancy, but that would have been a bad move for Jody, so I said, "I don't get it, sir. How come Jody

Mueller's feelings don't carry any weight here? You think she doesn't have a right to say who she goes out with?"

"I think her head is turned because you're a clever boy," Mautz said evenly. "That's what I think. And I think the only reason you're taking her out is because she used to go with Mark Brittain. And I think that's cruel."

He's an amazing man, that Mr. Mautz.

In the pool this afternoon I didn't taunt Brittain, didn't set up any games with Ellerby to mess with his head; I just kicked his ass. Every time I thought about him crying to Mautz, I just turned up the heat. If he keeps messing with me, I could turn out to be a pretty good swimmer by the time Regionals roll around.

I hung around a bit after the rest of the team hit the showers.

"What do you need, Mobe?" Lemry asked as I followed her into her office just off the pool deck.

I told her I thought she should watch out.

"For what?"

"For Mr. Mautz. He was asking me all kinds of questions about CAT class today. Like he was trying to get something on you."

She looked at me strangely. "Like what?"

I said I didn't know, but that's how it felt. Then I told her about Mautz's and my conversation concerning Brittain.

She listened carefully, looking a bit puzzled, and annoyed. "Tell you what," she said when I finished. "You go on doing what you're doing and don't worry about it. I do agree with Mr. Mautz on one thing. It would be good for you guys to give Mark a little room. He doesn't have much of a sense of humor, and that makes things doubly tough on him. Breakups are hard under any circumstances. Everybody hurts, Mobe. Remember that."

I said I had decided to leave him alone.

"You might see if the Very Reverend Mr. Ellerby would join you in that decision."

I said I would. Then, "I might have some information about Sarah Byrnes's mother."

"Really? What kind of information?"

"Well, I talked to an old friend of hers who said her mom used to talk about going to Reno to be a card dealer and maybe learn to dance. You know, like in those shows they have."

"How reliable is that?"

I told her about Dale and how he and Sarah Byrnes became friends.

"Sounds like you believe him."

"He's not the kind of guy with a reason to lie," I said. "He doesn't have much to lose."

Lemry put her fingers to the bridge of her nose. "That would have been at least fourteen years ago."

I nodded.

"We'd be lucky to find her. That's a long time to hold a job as a dealer. Or as a dancer."

I shrugged. "All I know is what Dale said."

"Do you think Sarah Byrnes would talk to me?" she asked. "If I went to the hospital with you, do you think she'd trust me?"

Boy, who knew. Sarah Byrnes is full of surprises. I can never tell when she's going to go along with something and when she's going to take my head off. I said that.

"Well, find out."

I said I'd try, then Lemry told me to have a seat. I dropped my towel onto the cushion to keep the chair from getting wet and planted myself.

"Listen, Mobe, Sarah Byrnes has had a big impact on you, and her name comes up so often lately that I feel I know her. Sometimes the hardest thing about being a schoolteacher is having to leave the tough cases behind so you can cater to the masses. Most good teachers hate that. This girl seems to have worked her way into the part of me that doesn't let go. I really do want to help, and it seems as if the *only* help is to get her mom back here to tell the true facts. But I'm going to have to follow your lead. She trusts you if she trusts anybody.

You're going to have to make the decisions about when to tell her what. I'm willing to put some energy and even some money into helping, but she has to want that for it to make a difference. It might be that we should find her mother first, before we say anything, to see if she will have anything to do with her daughter. I don't know."

I thought of all Sarah Byrnes's and my time together, tried to picture her reactions. "I know one thing," I said finally. "Sarah Byrnes hates not knowing worse than anything. She has to okay anything we do. And the first thing I'll have to do is make it okay that I've told you everything."

"Get to it."

"You son of a bitch," Sarah Byrnes spits through gritted teeth. "She's a teacher, you dickhead. She has to tell Child Protection Services, at least."

"She said she wouldn't do that," I say, "and I believe her."

"She's a *teacher*," Sarah Byrnes says again. "There's a fine if you don't tell. Jail, you asshole."

I know Lemry wouldn't lie. "Look, I want to bring her here. We can go out into the courtyard, and you can see for yourself."

Sarah Byrnes looks at me through those slits in her scarred face as if she's going to clean my clock on the spot. "I thought I could trust you," she spits. "Shit, Eric, you of all people." She turns to walk away.

But I grab her arm. She pulls away, but I don't let go. "Look, you're starting to piss me off. You tell me all this shit, and then expect me to stand by and let whatever happens happen. Well, bullshit. Ellerby was right. Once I know something, I can't unknow it or pretend it isn't so. I'm responsible for anything I know. I was careful who I told. Lemry is safe. She is. And there are no other good choices. Shit, all you do is present me with impossibilities. You can't stay here forever, and you can't go home. Anything else I come up with won't work for some reason you think of. . . ."

She jerks hard from my grasp. "What do you know?" she screams, and the attendants look up. "What the hell do you know? You went off and got yourself okay. Lemry is a big deal hero to you because she's your goddamn swim coach. She's the one that helped you be okay. Well, look at me, Eric. Look at me! I'm never going to be okay! Never!"

I could back down; would have a couple months ago, but I've seen Sarah Byrnes's dad for what he is now, and I've seen what that might do to her, and I'm simply not willing to let it be anymore. I'm just not. If you just wait around and let things happen, then they'll happen, and likely as not you'll eat shit. "No, Sarah Byrnes, you're wrong. You're just never going to be pretty. That part's right. But that's old news. Since right after the day your dad burned you. But you are going to be okay. Goddamn it, you are! You were right. Being fat was a choice, even though I didn't know it at the time. But when I did know it I was still willing to stay that way so you wouldn't think I'd get all svelte and leave. That's how much your friendship meant. I hated being fat, but it was worth it not to lose you. And that has to make you *something*, at least to me." I stop for a breath and realize tears are streaming down both our faces. I grab her and hold her, and though she doesn't grab me back, once again she doesn't push away.

Home. My room. My bed. Simon and Garfunkel on my CD player, barely audible over the wind whistling through the trees and the hard flecks of snow snapping against the glass. So these are the best years of my life. I'm scared. I promised Sarah Byrnes I'd help—promised Lemry would, too—and I don't even know what help is. I love her, but sometimes I wish I never knew her. That doesn't make me too good a friend, but when I think of just training hard to make it to State and going out with Jody and studying the nature of the cosmos with Ellerby over a six-pack of burgers—well, that's what I long for right now. I just want it to be simple. But it won't be.

CHAPTER
THIRTEEN

For the past three days, Sarah Byrnes has been living in the apartment above Lemry's garage. She bolted from the psych ward within twenty-four hours after the attendants heard her speak. I went up to the ward to tell Laurel, her counselor, that Sarah Byrnes was okay, but that there were good reasons for her not wanting anyone to know where she was.

"It's her father, isn't it?" Laurel asked.

Sarah Byrnes had told me not to tell Laurel anything about her dad because she'd be required to report to Child Protection Services. If they started questioning her dad, he'd get cranked up and come looking for her, which he'll do anyway, but maybe with a little less zeal. I said, "I stand on the Fifth."

She smiled. "I'm just glad to know she's safe, Eric. Thanks."

Getting Sarah Byrnes to stay at Lemry's place was easier than I thought it would be—she left the psych ward still majorly pissed at me for telling Lemry about her dad. She kicked me out of the hospital right after she blew her cover but met me in the parking lot the next afternoon, less than half an hour after she called demanding that I get my ass down there, because she wasn't going to take the chance of the staff getting worried about liability and telling her father she had talked. She slammed down the phone before I could tell her my mom's car wasn't there, so I called Ellerby, but his phone was busy. I ran the mile and a half from my house to Sacred Heart, worried Sarah Byrnes would get to the parking lot, find no one waiting, and take off in a huff.

Sarah Byrnes had no sweat getting out—she simply stuffed her things into a bag, waited until no one was looking, and walked out a back way to the parking lot. I was waiting at the corner telephone booth, where I'd finally contacted Ellerby only seconds earlier. I told him to *hurry.*

"Call you a cab, ma'am?" I said.

She said, "Don't mess with me, Eric. Just get me out of here. My dad will be here in a few minutes."

"Be pissed at me if you want," I said. "I did the only thing I could do. Lemry's still in on this, and she hasn't called Child

Protection. If you can't trust that, then I don't know what."

"She can just stay the hell away from me," she said. "I've had all the help I need to last me for the next five years."

"Yeah, well, it ain't all the help you're gonna get," I said as the Cruiser rounded the corner, Ellerby sitting low in the front seat in dark glasses and a broad-brimmed hat. He pulled up beside us, glanced stealthily both ways before leaping out to open the back door. He said, "In."

Sarah Byrnes looked at him like he was crazy, then back at me. I shrugged and said, "In."

A dark car—an older model Oldsmobile with tinted windows—approached from the direction Ellerby had come, and Sarah Byrnes glanced up in panic, jumped into the back seat, and lay flat. "Drive," she said, and it didn't take an astrophysicist to know the ominous form at the wheel was Virgil Byrnes. He must not have seen me, or known Ellerby's Cruiser, because he coasted slowly, seemingly looking for a parking spot.

Ellerby dropped into the driver's seat as I slid into shotgun. "So where will I be dropping you, miss?" he asked. "The Sheraton? Marriott? Maybe the Hilton? Excuse me, what was I thinking of, we have no Hilton. Knock five dollars off my tip."

"Drive!" Sarah Byrnes said through gritted teeth.

Ellerby pulled slowly onto the street, passing within three feet of Mr. Byrnes's dark blue monstrosity. "That's an *ugly* car," he said, and gave a short honk as we passed. I turned my head away as Mr. Byrnes glanced up.

"You'll think that's real funny," Sarah Byrnes said, "when he finds out you drove the getaway car."

In the side-view mirror, I watched Mr. Byrnes walk across the parking lot toward the hospital. In a few minutes the stakes to this game would go up.

"So where to?" Ellerby asked again.

I glanced over the seat at Sarah Byrnes and said, "To Lemry's house."

I expected a protest—like maybe she'd kick the windows out—but she stared straight ahead.

"She's expecting us," I told Ellerby.

Sarah Byrnes just shook her head in disgust, holding onto her tough act, but seeing her father had rattled her.

Shortly after we arrived, Lemry sent Ellerby and me packing. "Why don't you guys go do whatever it is guys do for a few hours? We'll call if we need you."

Sarah Byrnes appeared unsure, like a cornered animal, but said nothing. I was just glad to get away from her before she got a chance to get me alone and separate my body parts.

▼ ▼ ▼

So here we sit in the middle of Lemry's class on the first day Sarah Byrnes has been with us, which is hard to figure because I would think school is the first place her dad will look—I'm surprised he hasn't already. I've had very little chance to talk with Sarah Byrnes, because Lemry told me to leave her alone until she got her bearings.

Mautz is sitting in today, uninvolved, but leaning against the wall near Lemry's desk like a sentry. I'm thinking this might be a good day to go light on my usual form of class participation. We're into the last installment of the abortion issue—Lemry gave it a few weeks' enforced rest to let people calm down—and Mark Brittain is well into the same old happy horseshit he uses to scold the world. Ellerby is following my lead of restraint because, even though he wouldn't agree to follow Mautz's edict to stay off Brittain's case, Lemry told him that when a fool and a wise man argue it's sometimes hard for those of us on the outside to tell the difference. That shut Ellerby's trap right quick.

We sit in a circle, and I'm watching Jody stare at the flat surface of her desk while Brittain rambles. Sarah Byrnes is directly across from us, shifting nervously in her seat in a way I recognize, and if Mark Brittain recognized it too, he'd shut the hell up. But Brittain's four-point-oh grade average includes no A's for insight, and he forges on like a runaway gospel train without

Ellerby and me there to throw objects onto his tracks to derail him. "It's God's law," he says, "that every human must step up and take responsibility for his actions. All life is sacred, and if a woman makes the mistake of fornication and she gets pregnant, she has the moral obligation to bring that child to term."

Bring that child to term. Jesus, Brittain, you've been watching too many doctor shows.

"Not everything is about Christianity, Mr. Brittain," Lemry says. "We've heard that argument about enough, I think. Let's go on."

"With all respect," Brittain says, "everything *is* about Christianity. It's when we believe it *isn't* that we get into trouble."

Lemry sighs. "Okay, everything is about Christianity for you, Mark. But there are other perspectives, and I want to hear them."

"Let's stay with this view just one more minute," says a soft voice, and the class looks up in unison to see that it's coming from Sarah Byrnes. Sarah Byrnes scoots her desk an inch or so forward, staring directly across the circle at Brittain. "Are you telling us *all* life is sacred? That it's all equal?"

Sarah Byrnes's intensity visibly pushes Brittain back in his seat, but he holds his ground. "That's right."

"You think my life is as sacred as Ms. Lemry's? Or Mr.

Mautz's, over there? Or yours?"

"Of course it is," Brittain says, and I detect a note of patronization. *That* is a big mistake.

Sarah Byrnes slides out of her seat and walks across the room, her Nikes as silent as moccasins on a hard dirt trail, and kneels in front of Brittain. Mark looks at the desk. Very softly she says, "Look at me."

Brittain looks up, but his sight drops immediately back to his desk top. The rest of the class, me included, fidgets.

"No," Sarah Byrnes says, as softly as before, *"keep* looking at me."

Brittain lifts his gaze, and I think I see a drop of sweat form on his forehead. Mautz looks at Lemry, but Lemry doesn't move a muscle.

"Are you saying," Sarah Byrnes continues, "that if you knew you were married to someone who would do this to your baby," and she touches her face, "you should have that baby anyway?"

Brittain looks confused; he doesn't know the real story behind Sarah Byrnes's condition.

She pushes. "Is that what you're saying?"

"I think . . . Yeah, that's what I'm saying."

Sarah Byrnes sits back on her haunches and sort of smiles, looking across the room at Mr. Mautz. Then she leans forward again and puts her hands on Mark's desk. "I'll give you one more chance," she says. "Are you telling me that a woman who's married to a man she *knows* will disfigure or kill her baby, and who knows she doesn't have the guts to get away from him, should have that baby anyway?"

Brittain has regained some composure. "We can't make predictions like that," he says. "All life is sacred. Everyone deserves a chance."

"Think you'd like to have my chance?" Sarah Byrnes asks, pointing to her face.

"It's not something I'd *choose*," Brittain says, "but . . ."

"It's not something I'd choose, either," Sarah Byrnes says quickly. She stands up to walk back to her seat, then turns in the middle of the room. "You and Mr. Mautz go to the same church, don't you?" she asks.

Brittain glances at Mautz, who nods imperceptibly. "Yeah," Brittain says. "What's that got to do with . . ."

"Do all the people in that church think all life is sacred?"

Brittain says, "They certainly do."

"And do they treat people's lives as if they're sacred?"

Brittain feels safe here. "Of course they do."

Sarah Byrnes moves a couple more steps toward her desk. I swear to God she's going to grow up to be a crispy version of Perry Mason. She whirls and faces Brittain. "Mark Brittain,

I've been in the same class as you from first grade on, and I could count the number of times you've spoken to me on an amputee's fingers. I can't even get you to look me in the eye. Are you telling me my life is as sacred to you as Jody Mueller's? I mean, up until Eric the Great aced you out?"

Brittain opens his mouth, but Sarah Byrnes whirls, and all of a sudden she's running it down Mautz's throat. "And this man, who goes to the same church you go to, you know how many decent words—hell, *any* kind of words—he's uttered to me in the past six years? Zip. Zero. I have a three-point-six grade point average, for God's sake; had a straight four-oh in junior high, and the best he's been able to do in all that time is to chew out *my friend* for an underground newspaper that was so bizarre it didn't deserve a minute of his time. He didn't even respect me enough to show me his disgust. He told *Eric* what to say to me."

Mautz starts to speak, but she whirls back to Brittain. "How come you people care so much for the unborn when you don't give even a little bit of a shit for the born?"

Now Mautz breaks in. "Mrs. Lemry, don't you think this has gone far enough? I would expect you to have a little better control of your class."

"She seems in control to me," Lemry says. "You ought to be here on a bad day."

But Brittain is wounded now, and I think we're about to have a bad day. His face is red, his neck pushing against his collar. "Crybabies," he says. "Nobody wants to take on the tough stuff. You've been pulling all kinds of stuff since you were a little kid and hiding behind the fact that you were disfigured. I'm tired of all the excuses! Tired of them, you hear? You step up and take your medicine! You should be damn glad you're alive and that God loves you!"

"Jeez, Brittain," Ellerby says, "get a grip. Tap your helmet, man."

"Go to hell, Ellerby! Just go to hell! You're the perfect example of what's wrong. You're worse than she is. You're even worse than Calhoune! You are evil!"

Lemry looks over to Mautz. "*Now* it's out of hand," she says quietly. "Okay, class, let's give it a rest. . . ."

Brittain turns to fire on her, but Jody steps in as he opens his mouth and says, "Mark Brittain, shut your mouth." Brittain stops in midsentence like somebody filled his mouth with a bomb. "I've heard your self-righteous BS for the last time. I really believed that you were special for a while there, but you just make me sick."

"You better . . ."

"Shut up!" She turns to the rest of the class. "Man is known by his works. I've heard that out of Mark Brittain's mouth so many times I thought he made it up. Well, let me tell you about Mark Brittain's works. A little less than a year ago, I had a six-week-old fetus inside me. Mark Brittain's and my works." Tears form at the edges of her eyes.

I move my chair close to Jody's, and she takes my hand. "I wanted to keep it. He said no. I said I'd go away to have it. That's how desperate I was, how awful I felt about what I'd done. And you know what he said? You *know* what he said? He said he could never do the work he needed to do in the world with an illegitimate child hanging over his head. He said I'd have to get rid of it."

"That's a lie!" Brittain yells. "You . . . you bitch, Mueller. I knew you'd try to slander me when I dumped you."

Jody doesn't miss a beat. "I asked him about the church's stand on abortion, and he told me that what he had to say to the world was more important than one error in judgment. An error in judgment. That's what he called it. He said making love to someone who didn't have the common sense to protect herself was nothing more than that. He didn't call it fornication then, he called it an error in judgment.

"And you know what I did? I had the abortion. That's how screwed up I was. And I had it alone, because Mark Brittain couldn't be seen at the clinic. I had to cross lines *I'd marched in* to have an abortion *alone*." She turns to Mark. "I don't know right or wrong about sacred life, Mark Brittain, but I know this. You don't talk to Sarah Byrnes that way. You just don't. And you don't talk to me that way, either. Not ever again."

Having gathered his books, Brittain stops at the door. "What you all just heard out of Jody Mueller's mouth is a filthy lie. It's just one more example of what happens when you try to take the high road. You can believe it if you want to, but it's a filthy lie."

"Well," Ellerby says, "I won't be doing my report on shame. I could never top *that*."

CHAPTER
FOURTEEN

Boy, today the stakes went up. Mautz barged into Lemry's class to say Mark Brittain tried to kill himself last night. Mautz looked directly at Lemry, then me, then Ellerby, and finally Jody, as if to let us know where he considered the blame to lie.

"I'm not pleased with what I saw in here yesterday," he said after his announcement, "nor with what I've heard about what goes on in here. A sensitive boy . . ."

"Stop!" Lemry said, with such force that Mautz backed off immediately. "I'm not interested in your personal thoughts about suicide, sir, and you have no right to imply that the responsibility for Mark Brittain's decision lay with members of this class."

"Mrs. Lemry," Mautz said right back, "maybe you don't know how serious this is. Mark Brittain is lying in Sacred Heart Hospital on the edge of a coma as a result of a drug overdose. This wasn't some adolescent cry for attention."

"I feel as badly about that as you do," Lemry said. "Maybe you've forgotten that Mark is a member of my swimming team, and I respect him as a student. But you are out of line in this classroom, and if you don't leave, I'll lodge a formal complaint with the Washington Education Association."

Mautz's eyes blazed. "Mrs. Lemry, I'm the vice-principal at this school. I . . ."

"That's right," Lemry said. "You're the *vice*-principal. The vice-principal in charge of discipline. If I'm having a discipline problem, I'll call you. Right now, I'd like you to leave, or I'll go to the principal's office and bring Mr. Patterson back here to straighten this out. If you'd like to talk to me during my break, that's third period."

"You could be getting yourself into serious trouble," Mautz said, but he looked uneasy, as if Lemry had scored.

"I want you out of my classroom," she repeated, and Mautz turned to leave.

The guy must be unconscious. He never noticed how the class sat stunned at the news of Mark, how the breath blasted out of the room as if we'd been kicked in the collective stomach.

"I'm sorry you had to hear that," Lemry said the moment the door closed behind Mautz. We stared blankly back at her. "Looks like this is a good time to talk about suicide."

She gave us a minute, then said, softly, "Let's talk."

"Oh, God." Jody burst into tears. "He really meant to do it. I know Mark. He really meant to do it. This is my fault." She dropped her head to her desk, and I tried to take her hand, but she pulled it away.

"Let her be," Lemry said. Then, "I know you think it's your fault, and I know that hurts. And it's going to hurt, there's no stopping that. But it's *not* your fault. Mark Brittain himself said we're all responsible for our own actions, and this was his, Jody, not yours."

"But if I'd been more careful. I knew what he was like. I knew . . ."

Ellerby stepped in. "If you're going to assign guilt," he said, "you can't assign it all to yourself. I've been badgering Mark Brittain for more than two years."

"Maybe," Jody said through more tears, "but I humiliated him. That's what he couldn't stand, to be humiliated. I went with him for two and a half years and I knew that."

A flood of anger welled in my throat, and I thought for

a minute I'd actually choke on it: *Mark Brittain humiliated himself.* Screw Mark Brittain. He'd been cramming his philosophy down our throats as long as I could remember and now that his true colors had been uncovered, *we* were supposed to feel shitty.

Lemry slowly paced the outer edge of our circle. "Listen, a person attempting to take his own life is a tragic thing. I'm sure everyone here can think of something they wish they'd said to Mark, but none of us knew. Obviously Mr. Mautz thinks I should take responsibility because of what I let us talk about as a class. But I want no misunderstandings. I'm not to blame for Mark's decision and neither are any of you. Suicide is *personal,* and I refuse to have anyone walk out of here today without understanding that. Mark Brittain needs help; hopefully this will help him get it. He'll need understanding from all of you. He'll need to not be abandoned. But your guilt will only give him the mistaken belief that his actions were not of his own doing."

Lemry stopped pacing. "I don't want to sound harsh, and I know I'm probably getting ahead of your feelings, but we don't have time to process everyone's pain before the class is over. We do have time to put it in perspective."

Sally Eaton, the girl who pickets the abortion clinic at Deaconess regularly and who thinks Mark Brittain is the cleverest thing since remote control, raised her hand. "Ms.

Lemry, I've known Mark for a long time, and he's somebody who stands up for what he believes. I think he's too sensitive for the callous way this class looks at things. Some cruel and untrue things have been said, and I think he's been treated unfairly by all of you—and this is the result."

Lemry cut her off. "You can have your thoughts about that, Sally, but I repeat: No one is responsible for Mark Brittain's decisions but Mark Brittain. I agree we can all learn something about how fragile the human psyche is, but the lesson here is to look at our own thoughts about life and death, not take the blame for someone else's."

Sally started to protest, but Lemry continued quickly. "You're entitled to your feelings, Sally, and I'll be happy to talk with you after class, but I won't have *anyone* blaming anyone for this in my classroom. That's final."

Sally stood and gathered her books, bursting into tears. "That's fine. I'm dropping this class. You can flunk me if you want. This class is *mean! That's* why Mark Brittain is in the hospital!"

I thought Lemry would stop her, but she walked to the classroom phone and called the office to let them know Sally was out of class and very distressed. She said she thought Mautz might be able to help her. At her desk she heaved a sigh. "Anyone else?"

Silence.

"One of the worst things schools do is give you the idea that they can take responsibility for other people. We want the best athletes and students and debaters to be role models—to set examples for the other kids. We pressure many of you to do that all the time. We ask for perfection—no, for a *show* of perfection. Then we're disappointed when you let us down, and even if we're not, you are. Well, I want to go on record as saying the sooner you learn you're your own life's accountant, the sooner you'll have tools to hammer out a decent life. Mark Brittain is in the hospital because he tried to poison his body. He felt bad because of *his* responses to the world, not yours. Other people may try to tell you differently, but don't let them. You won't be helping yourself, and you won't be helping Mark Brittain."

We sat in silence, absorbing Lemry's words. That silence was interrupted by Mautz's booming voice over the intercom: "Mrs. Lemry, could you come to the office immediately, please? Thank you."

When the bell rang, ending class, Lemry hadn't returned.

Workout felt strange today; Brittain wasn't leading his circle pattern, and there was no one to go after, though Ellerby and I gave each other good challenges playing games with the clock. When Brittain's group knelt to pray before the first set of two-hundreds I found myself looking away, a bit ashamed. I *could* have laid off him a little.

I meant to ask Lemry why she didn't get back before the bell, but I never got the chance.

At home, Mom said pretty much what Lemry said, but a little voice nags at me, saying I should be more careful. None of that is at Jody's expense, though. I don't think I should have stayed away from her, and I'm not going to start. Brittain did what he did at the abortion clinic, and trying to take himself out on drugs doesn't buy him any sympathy from me in that regard. I *could* do with a little less confusion.

I got a bit of a kick start from Carver, Mom's boyfriend. He listened quietly to our conversation—Jody was here for dinner—then followed Jody and me out into the garage. I was on the stepladder, pulling down some canned goods Mom keeps stored in the high cupboards, when he said it. "My father killed himself."

"Excuse me?"

"My dad. He killed himself."

I glanced over at Jody, then back at him. "God, man, I'm sorry."

He smiled. "I didn't say it for sympathy, Eric. It was a long time ago, I was eight. I thought it had to be my fault; he was always mad at me—you know, because of things I couldn't do.

I was halfway through a week's grounding for my grades when he killed himself. He put a gun in his mouth."

I was off the ladder now, standing with an armload of cans, speechless.

"I was thirty-five when I finally came to the conclusion that it wasn't my fault. I'd gotten very depressed, and a guy I worked with talked me into seeing someone—a therapist who talked me into tracking down family members who could tell me about Dad. Turned out no one was all that surprised. Seems he was one of those guys who just felt bad all his life and decided to get out. His brother took me on a long camping trip into the Idaho primitive area. Three days we hiked in—I was so lost I couldn't have found my way out in an airplane—and Uncle Ned wouldn't bring me out until he was convinced I knew everything about my dad he could teach me, and until he was convinced I knew Dad wrote the end to his own story.

"Your teacher was right, guys. Taking on someone else's monsters will kill you." He turned and walked back into the house.

"Thank you," Jody said as the door closed, then turned to me. "He's a good one, Eric."

I knocked on Lemry's door tonight sometime after ten-thirty, after dropping Jody off. "You guys still up?"

"Yup. Some of us."

"Is everything okay?"

"You from Blockwatch?"

"No, I mean at school."

"Come on in, Mobe," she said, and I kicked the snow off my shoes and stepped in, handing her my letter jacket. She hung it on the coat stand and we walked into the living room where Sarah Byrnes sat in her pajamas and a robe, drinking hot chocolate.

"Ms. Byrnes and I are having a discussion on risk-taking," Lemry said.

Sarah Byrnes looked up at me, a bit sheepishly, I thought. "We're going to try to find my mother; give her one chance to do the right thing."

That Lemry is some kind of genius. No way I could have figured she'd pull off an alliance with the orneriest kid north of the equator.

"We've been reevaluating our lives," she said with a smile. "If we don't start taking some chances, we're both going to make the same mistakes over so many times we'll rot."

I understood about Sarah Byrnes, but why Lemry?

She went on. "I'm trying to decide whether to rip out Mr. Mautz's heart, hold it a second for him to get a good look, then give him a loud round of applause."

I flinched. "What for?"

"Mr. Patterson went out of town this afternoon, which makes Mautz acting principal for three days. He's suspended CAT class because Mark Brittain's father came to the school to complain, charging I was irresponsible in my handling of 'sensitive material,' leading to Mark's suicide attempt."

"To hell with Mautz," I said. "Let's have class anyway. We'll organize a protest."

Lemry smiled. "Thanks but no thanks, Mobe. That would be a protest orchestrated by you and Ellerby; sort of like a picnic organized by ants, no offense. Actually, I'm going to take three days' sick leave. Ms. Byrnes and I are going to Reno to try out a blackjack system she heard about in her math class."

Reno. "What're we gonna do for CAT? What about swimming?"

"Study hall for CAT—that couldn't hurt anyone—and John Billings for workouts. I've already written up the workouts and called John. He's willing to drive the bus to the meet on Friday, too."

Sarah Byrnes smiled like a little kid and shrugged. "You said I could trust her," she said. "Swim fast. We'll see you on Monday." I had never seen her calm.

I pulled out a quarter and flipped it to her. "Put it all on seventeen black."

I got home after midnight, and all the lights were out except in the hallway leading to my room. A note was tacked to my door: *A man called looking for Sarah Byrnes. I said I didn't know where she is, but he left a number for you to call, no matter how late you got home—482-4366. Mom.*

Shit.

I took the note at its word and dialed the number.

"Yeah?"

"Hello. This is Eric Calhoune. I had a message to call you. It said I should call . . ."

"Yeah. Well, young Calhoune, do you know who this is?"

"Yes," I said. "I mean, I assume it's Mr. Byrnes. Sarah Byrnes's dad."

"Well, you assume correct."

We were both silent a minute, until I said, "Uh, why did you want me to call?"

"Why do you think?"

I was scared to death, but unwilling to say anything he didn't know. "I don't know, sir. I just got home and there was this note. . . ."

"Don't mess around with me, boy!"

I held to it. "I'm not messing around, sir. Why did you want me to call?"

He was quiet another second. Then in a low, dangerous

voice he said, "Now you listen, and you listen good. I know you know where my daughter is, and you best be telling me before you hang up that phone, or I'll skin you alive, and that ain't just a figure of speech. I want no more of your nonsense. Tell me where the girl is."

My heart hammered in my throat, my voice shaky, as if a vibrator were poised on my Adam's apple. "I don't know where she is," I said. "I haven't seen her since right before she left the hospital. She was mad at me."

"Did you hear me say I wanted no more of your nonsense?"

"Yes sir. This isn't nonsense."

His low laugh chilled my spine. "I can smell your fear clear across town," he said. "I'll give you one more chance, then I'm hanging up. If that happens, you better be on the watch for me every minute. Next time you and me talk, it'll be up close. I'll hurt you, boy. Believe that."

"I'm not denying I'm scared," I said. "But I don't know where Sarah Byrnes is. If you're threatening me, I'll call the cops."

The same laugh. "Be my guest."

The line went dead.

CHAPTER
FIFTEEN

So don't think *that* doesn't give me a reason to forget my homework and my newfound girlfriend and my five-hundred-yard freestyle times. Someday, when we're all looking back on this and laughing—a time I hope comes *very* soon—the quick minds will say I should have called Lemry and told my mother and notified the police and sent up a bat signal. But there's a method behind the madness of keeping my mouth shut. If Lemry and Sarah Byrnes get lucky in Reno, they could come back with Sarah Byrnes's mother, and if she puts the finger on old Virgil, that'll end it.

See, in court, as she has reminded me a number of times, Sarah Byrnes would be trying to recall an incident that happened when she was three years old, *in the courtroom with her father,* knowing if he got off, her life wouldn't be worth a plugged nickel. The defense attorney would ask scores of questions about other things that happened when she was three, things she couldn't remember or would surely get mixed up about; things her father could remember and wouldn't be a bit mixed up about. He has had no run-ins with the law on record, not even a parking ticket. He is a mean man—a smart, wicked man—who has kept totally to himself. Reasonable doubt would be on his side. If he got off, so long Sarah Byrnes. Only Sarah Byrnes's mom can set the record straight.

So why should that stop me from telling about his threat to me? Because if it's brought out that I know her dad burned her, then he's got more reason to want to do me harm. Plus Sarah Byrnes would never tolerate someone else being threatened by him. She'd do something stupid like go back home, or run away and be left with those horrible scars and no one who loved her. I might be missing something, but it doesn't seem so. What I intend to do, at least until the Maverick sisters are back from Reno, is lay the hell low and never be out alone. For some reason, Mr. Byrnes doesn't come to school or he would have already, so I feel safe there. This might be a good time to see whether or not terror creates a faster distance swimmer.

Ellerby and I stopped by Lemry's house on my way to

school today to be sure there wasn't a mass murder overnight. Lemry and Sarah Byrnes were loading the car.

"We'll drive straight through," Sarah Byrnes said, and I noticed how alive she looked. Her scars were the same and I still couldn't imagine anyone laying eyes on her for the first time without flinching, but something seemed different.

I dragged her off to one side. "Tell me how this happened."

"What?"

"You and Lemry. A few days ago you couldn't say her name without spitting it into the dirt."

"Jealous?"

"I don't think so. I'm just thinking that a few days ago I risked teeth to get you over here, and now you guys are Butch and Sundance."

"She didn't bullshit me."

"Huh?"

"She didn't say everything was going to be all right, or that my face wasn't really ugly, or that there were other kinds of beauty than physical."

"What *did* she say?"

"She said it looked like my life had been pretty hard."

Lemry called from the car, and Sarah Byrnes put her hand on my elbow, for the first time ever that I remember. "Thanks, Eric. You really are a good friend."

During study hall, which should have been CAT class, a call comes over the intercom for me and Ellerby to report to the office immediately.

"This *has* to be about Brittain," Ellerby says quietly as we walk side by side down the empty hall.

I agree. "What do you think we should do?"

"I don't know," he says, and he sets his jaw, "but I'm getting pretty tired of this crap."

"Have a seat, gentlemen," Mautz says as we appear in his open doorway. A man in a dark business suit sits erect in a chair across from Mautz's desk. He's bald save for the short-cropped semicircle of brown hair stretching from ear to ear like a fat equator, and he looks *very* solemn. "Boys, this is Cal Brittain. Mark Brittain's father."

Ellerby says, "Pleased to meet you."

When we're seated, Mautz says, "Mr. Brittain has something to say to the two of you."

We're silent.

Mr. Brittain clears his throat, staring sternly at us. "I came to tell you boys I don't hold you responsible for my son's unfortunate actions."

I don't know about Ellerby, but I could sit three or four hours and not know how to respond. The silence is quite uncomfortable.

Finally Mautz says, "What do you boys have to say to that?"

Ellerby pinches the bridge of his nose, closing his eyes. "Will you be calling the rest of the students in, two by two, to tell them the same thing?"

Mr. Brittain looks confused. "Of course not. I . . ."

"Then why are you talking to us?"

Mautz breaks in. "Mr. Ellerby. I'll caution you *one time* to show respect. "

Ellerby looks right at him. "I don't have any to show."

"You're getting yourself into deep water, young man. Let me recommend . . ."

"No deal," Ellerby interrupts. "I don't need forgiveness for something I had nothing to do with." He turns to Mr. Brittain. "I'm really sorry Mark tried to kill himself," he says. "I really am. But you guys calling us in here to let us off the hook is just a way to tell us we're on the hook."

Mautz's neck is swelling, his eyes blazing, and I learn something from Ellerby right this minute that I'll use against bullies for the rest of my life: Call in the goddamn cavalry as quick as you can.

Mautz says, "As much as it may have been lost on you boys, Mark Brittain is an exemplary . . ."

Ellerby says, "Could I use the phone?"

"What?"

"The phone. Could I use it?"

"For what?"

"To make a phone call." Without Mautz's response, Ellerby reaches across his desk and punches out seven quick digits. "Dad? Hi, this is Steve. Look, could you come over to the school? I'm in a bunch of trouble and if I were these people I'd want you in on it. No, right now if you can . . . Thanks." He drops the receiver into its cradle, looks up at Mautz, and says, "He'll be right over. Until he gets here, my friend Eric and I are standing on the Fifth."

Ah, the Fifth. *There's* a piece of legal artistry I'll bet Mautz wishes had never been penned.

Reverend Ellerby is an impressive guy. He's big and handsome, and he looks more like a movie star than he does an Episcopal minister, except he wears one of those stiff white collars you normally associate with a Catholic priest. I see him moving through the outer office, smiling at the secretary, before he raps lightly on the open door.

Mautz says, "Please come in."

Mr. Ellerby introduces himself, gives Steve a playful punch on the arm, and sits between us. He gives Mr. Brittain a nod of recognition and says he's sorry about the unfortunate experience he's been through with his son. Mr. Brittain nods back.

"So," he says, "Steve tells me he's in a bit of trouble. Somebody want to tell me about it?"

Mautz appears uneasy. He's bigger than Mr. Ellerby, but definitely outmatched in *presence*. "Actually," he says, "I'm not sure it was necessary that you come. That was your son's idea. We're trying to sort out what we feel is the problem with Mr. Brittain's son, and we believe your son and Mr. Calhoune could shed some light on it."

Mr. Ellerby turns to Steve. "That doesn't sound like 'a bunch of trouble' to me, Steve."

"I guess I should have said I was *about* to get into a bunch of trouble," Ellerby says. "Mr. Mautz thinks Mark's problems started in CAT class—you know, the one Ms. Lemry teaches— and that Mobe and I tried to push Mark over the edge. In other words, I get the distinct feeling, though I admit no one has actually said it, that we're being blamed for Mark gobbling downers."

Mr. Ellerby looks perplexed and turns immediately to Mautz. "Is that true?" You can tell he knows more than he's letting on, that he and Steve discussed this earlier.

"Of course not," Mautz says, a bit defensively, I thought. "No one is being blamed, actually . . ."

Mr. Brittain breaks in. "Reverend, I've worked hard to

bring Mark up as a God-fearing citizen. I know there are some major theological differences between your beliefs and mine, but I'm sure you can appreciate what I've tried to do with my son. I talked with Mark extensively after his suicide attempt, and he's been quite repentant. But he's also been adamant that he felt driven to it by your son and Eric Calhoune. They have constantly taunted him in public and generally treated him with disrespect. My son is quite a serious boy, with high expectations of himself. He's in a vulnerable part of his life, as I'm sure you must know. Frankly, I'm asking that you get control of your boy. I'm already making some moves to get limits put on this so-called CAT class."

Mr. Ellerby nods. He looks Mr. Brittain square in the eye and says, "I'm truly sorry about your son's misfortune, and I think it's probably been helpful for my son to hear how you feel. He and I will talk about that." He stands and offers Mr. Brittain his hand. "Now if it's all right with you, I'd like to have a word with Mr. Mautz alone."

I don't think Mr. Brittain is ready to leave, but the power of Mr. Ellerby's dismissal leaves him with nothing to do but get up and go anyway. At the door, he turns to Mautz. "I'll talk with you later by phone."

Mautz nods. "That will be fine."

Steve and I rise to leave, but Mr. Ellerby motions us to

stay. "You two hang in for a minute," he says, and turns again to Mautz. "Tell me the real purpose of all this."

Mautz says, "I'm not sure what you mean."

"I mean my son doesn't call me in on anything unless he thinks it's out of hand. So far a lot hasn't been said. I want it all said."

Mautz seems knocked off center. "Well, Reverend, your son may have jumped the gun a bit. Mr. Brittain came with some concerns about Steve and Eric, and I thought we could get to the bottom of them if we just brought it all into the open."

"I'm assuming you agree with Mr. Brittain about Steve's and Eric's responsibility."

"Actually, to some degree I do."

"To what degree?"

"To the degree that Mark Brittain is trying to do some very difficult things—exemplary things—with his life. . . ."

"*Christian* things?"

"Yes," Mautz says. "I'm sure you can appreciate that. At any rate, he is running into some very stiff resistance, even attempts at humiliation, from these boys. I believe the pressure on him was just too much. I'm sure you'll agree suicide is very grave business."

"No pun intended, I'll bet," Mr. Ellerby says. He really

said that. "And you believe that Eric and Steve, combined with this Contemporary American Thought class, drove him over the edge?"

Mautz nods. "I'm sure there are other factors, but I do believe that is the major part."

"Other factors," Mr. Ellerby says quietly. "Could some of those other factors include the kind of pressure this boy feels to perform? The kind of thinking that allows no mistakes? Pressure from home and church to *never* let his guard drop?" He leans forward. "Mr. Mautz, do you know why our constitution advocates a division between church and state?"

Mautz is smart enough to wait.

"Because the two don't belong together."

"In my mind," Mautz says, "maybe they belong more together than we've allowed them to be in the past couple of decades."

Mr. Ellerby shakes his head vigorously. "In your mind, that's fine. But you work for a school district that I support financially, and you have a responsibility to the law. Sir, I'm a *preacher* and I don't believe the church should get into the state's business. They have different functions. I have an educated guess about you and Mr. Brittain getting your heads together to decide this suicide thing was the result of some kind of religious persecution. But we aren't talking about religion here, Mr. Mautz, we're talking about rigid thinking. The kind of thinking that doesn't allow anyone else's ideas, and which also doesn't allow a person any room for error. What's wrong with Mark Brittain is that he can't allow himself to make mistakes. That makes humiliation his worst and constant enemy. Somebody needs to back off that kid."

Mr. Ellerby must have hit a soft spot, because Mautz comes out firing. "With all due respect," he says through tightly constricted vocal cords, "I don't think a man who advocates for women on the pulpit, or equal rights for homosexuals, or sexual information to children too young to handle it, should be in this office telling me what's best for one of my students. . . ."

"*That's* what I wanted to hear," Mr. Ellerby says, smiling. "Now, for your own good, hear this: The one of your students I'm interested in is my son. I'm pretty sure, after what he's heard today, he won't be bothering Mark Brittain anymore. But you've crossed a line, my friend"—and he points to Steve and me—"in front of witnesses. I'm guessing this all came to a head today because Mr. Patterson is out of town. When Mr. Patterson is *in* town, we're going to have this conversation again. Until then, I'll be watching to see that neither my son nor his friend is harassed." With that, he stands.

Steve and I get up with him, but Mautz says, "I need to see you about a different matter, Eric."

Mr. Ellerby squeezes my shoulder, and he and Steve walk out together. Wow. There are some all-right adults around. Unfortunately, the one I'm stuck in this office with isn't among them.

I stand silently while Mautz puts himself together. He's been wounded, and there's no sense in me collecting the fallout for Mr. Ellerby's direct hit.

Mautz straightens his desk, as if it needs it, then walks to the door of a small inner waiting room behind his desk. He opens it and says, "Mr. Byrnes, you can come in now."

Shit.

"Have a seat," Mautz says, and Mr. Byrnes settles only a few feet from me. He glares.

"Eric, Mr. Byrnes is here because his daughter has left home. He could have made a scene coming here to remove her, but he chose not to because he thinks you know where she's staying, and this could all take place more privately."

I say, "I don't know where she's staying."

"Mr. Byrnes doesn't believe that's true."

Now what I'd like to do is streak out and grab Mr. Ellerby to come back and tell Mautz that not only is it unconstitutional to mix church and state, it's also unconstitutional to mix the devil and state. But I am frozen to my spot. I've said this before—not more than a million times: Mr. Byrnes is a scary, scary man. "Well," I say, "it is true. I don't know where she is."

"Young Calhoune," Mr. Byrnes says, his voice barely audible, "you've known my daughter since grade school, been friends with her close to six years. Except for that Thornton kid, you're the only friend she's ever had. Now I don't know what keeps you around, ugly as she is, but I do know she was talking to you in the hospital when she wasn't talking to *anybody* else. It doesn't follow that you don't know where she is, so I'd appreciate it if you'd cut the nonsense and get on with it. She's confused, and I want to help her. It isn't easy going through life looking the way she does." He turns to Mautz. "I would think, you being the man in charge, that you could help me out."

"I have to agree with Mr. Byrnes on this one, Eric," Mautz says. "It really doesn't make sense that you don't know where Sarah is."

Surprise of surprises. Mautz agrees with the adult. "Well then, it doesn't make sense," I say. "But I don't." It occurs to me that Lemry hasn't even told any teachers Sarah Byrnes is at her place. If she had, Mautz would know it.

"Mr. Calhoune," Mautz says evenly, "how is it you've been at the center of all the trouble around here in the past few weeks? I have a man here worried about his daughter. A handicapped daughter at that. You know where she is. Are you *ever* going to grow up and take responsibility for yourself, or are you going to spend the rest of your life at the center of everybody's trouble?"

Something about watching Mautz in the face of Mr. Ellerby's barrage, along with my sheer terror of Mr. Byrnes, lets me take him on. I raise my palms. "Okay," I say. "You got me. I know where she's staying."

"And where is that?" Mautz asks.

"I'm not telling you. Mr. Mautz, this man has threatened me to my face and over the telephone. You don't have any idea what he's capable of doing. But I do, and he knows I do." I turn to face Mr. Byrnes. "I do, Mr. Byrnes. And if something happens to me, *everyone* will know. I don't know how you fooled Mr. Mautz, but I'll bet it wasn't hard. I'm not fooled, though. And what you better do is leave me alone and leave Sarah Byrnes alone and hope we keep our mouths shut. She's not coming back to your place. Ever."

Mr. Byrnes barely has a reaction, but I feel an actual physical blast of cold from his stare, and I know instantly I've made a big mistake. Mr. Byrnes is not a man to threaten. But I'm in so far there's no way out but all the way through. I turn to Mautz. "So either I'm suspended for not cooperating or I'm going back to class, but I'm through in here."

Mautz stands. "Maybe you'd better take the rest of the day off, Eric. Go home and think about it."

"If that's an offer, I decline," I say. "If it's an order, I'd like it in writing, please. My mom will need to know your side of the story. I'm liable to just tell her you're crazy."

I can tell Mautz is pissed, but he's dealt with my mother before when she thought her little dumpling was wronged, and I think the threat of her coming in on the heels of Mr. Ellerby might be too much for him. "Get back to your class," he says, and I'm headed for the door, sweating so bad I could be doing breaststroke.

CHAPTER
SIXTEEN

It's well after ten at night, and Ellerby and I are replenishing the juices we lost in practice with a half rack of Gatorade. Lemry may be gone, but her memory lives on through precise and voluminous workout notes, and Mr. Billings was up to the task of carrying them out to the letter.

"Guess we ought to lay off Brittain, huh?" I say.

"Yeah. Until my dad said it, I didn't think about what it's like to be Mark. You know, all the pressure to be godlike and stuff."

"Speaking of which," I say, twisting the cap off another Gatorade, "that was pretty heavy shit today between your dad and Mautz."

Ellerby smiles and takes the bottle, nearly draining it. "My old man's a heavy dude. He doesn't believe butt time on Planet Earth necessarily makes you wise. Guys like Mautz always hate my dad."

"No shit."

"Mautz really brought old man Byrnes down on you after we left?"

"Really did. Man, if I hadn't crapped my drawers with glee a few seconds earlier, watching your dad dismantle him, I'd have sure crapped them with astonishment when old Freddy Krueger stepped into the room."

Ellerby shakes his head. "Guess we better not be goin' over to Lemry's anymore, not without covering our tracks. All Byrnes would have to do is follow us around for a while."

"Yeah. It's a long shot, but it would sure be nice if Lemry and Sarah Byrnes found her mom. Then everything would come into the open."

Ellerby switches on the ignition. "I wonder why he didn't just snatch her someplace close to school. That's what I'd have done."

"Maybe he thought he could make it look legitimate. Hell, Mautz is still convinced it was just a little family trouble."

We talk awhile longer, polishing off two more Gatorades before I tell Ellerby to take me back to his place to get my mom's car because I'm so tired I can't keep my eyes open and my arms are rags from all the butterfly Lemry left for us to do. All through workout, I pictured her and Sarah Byrnes driving down the highway, laughing their asses off at the workout she left for us. I even entertained the idea that Lemry let Sarah Byrnes make it up.

I'm on cruise control, gliding across town on Washington Street, timing the lights perfectly. I've driven this so many times, I could do it in my sleep, which is a pretty good description of what I am doing. My head is actually bobbing, and I pop the radio on and punch a button tuned to K-101 Oldies, cranking it to near full blast. The biggest hits from the fifties and sixties. I have no trouble finding the button; they're all tuned to 101.

"Turn that down."

A shout blasts out of me at the voice coming low out of the back seat.

"You should use your rearview mirror."

I whirl around, face to face with Virgil Byrnes, then whip my eyes back to the road. Suddenly I am in adrenaline overdrive. "Get out of my car! That's against the law. I can get you arrested!"

"The door wasn't locked," he says. "I didn't know it was your car."

"What do you want?"

"You know what I want."

"I told you, I'm not telling. . . ."

The sharp cold point of a knife indents my cheek like a pencil on a fresh tablet, and Virgil Byrnes's voice goes stone cold. "I told you not to mess with me, boy."

"Okay," I say back. "I believe you."

"Then you better come clean. You played a few too many cards today in your principal's office." Again I wish I hadn't said I knew what he did to Sarah Byrnes.

I don't answer.

"Pull into the park. Take the first left, and we'll find a place to talk."

I brake and we glide easily into the entrance of Manito Park.

"Past the lights," he says, and I drive slowly past the duck pond, toward the upper, undeveloped area. My terror is truly unimaginable, but somehow I hold myself together, and slowly the mercury vapor lights fade in my rearview mirror, and then it's just me and Mr. Byrnes and the dark. All heroic thoughts of what I might do if I ever got alone with him have vanished like warm breath on a cold night, and all I want to do is live.

"You better not do anything to me," I warn meekly.

"People will know. Sarah Byrnes will know. So will Le . . . so will other people."

"So will *who*?"

"Nobody."

The knife sinks deeper into my cheek, and warm blood trickles toward my chin. The son of a bitch is cutting me.

"Ellerby," I say. "My friend Ellerby. He'll know."

"You got a regular band of merry men," he says. "Where's my daughter?"

"I can't tell you that."

The burn in my cheek spreads and blood flows freely. Jesus! He's cutting my face! "I don't have time for this," he says. "Before this night's over I'm going to have my daughter and be gone. Now you'll either be hurt real bad—maybe dead—or not, but I'll have her one way or the other. Nobody's got a right to take a man's family. No one. I don't care about your friend Ellerby or your principal or your momma or nobody. I care about getting my baby and disappearing. Now tell me where she is, boy, or you'll be tasting this knife on your tongue."

Oh, Jesus. He's going to shove it through my cheek! I stomp the gas pedal to the floor and the blade slices back toward my neck as Byrnes falls hard against the back seat. I'm screaming, "Go ahead! Go ahead! Kill me! You're coming, too, goddamn it, you're coming, too!"

We're pushing fifty when we reach the exit to the park, and I'm sure we take the corner out onto the deserted street on two wheels. If no one tries to stop me, I'll hit a tree. The speedometer pushes seventy.

"Stop this car, you little shit," he says, "or I'll drive this knife into the back of your neck."

"Go ahead!" I scream again. "Go ahead! You're a dead man with me, asshole!" It's as if I can keep my nerve through my screams. "Go ahead! Go ahead! Kill me! Kill me!"

I see him coming over the seat on the passenger's side, and I know he'll get control of the car, so I slam on the brakes, throwing him against the windshield, then bash the door open with my shoulder and sprint back into darkness to hide, and go for the cops when he's gone. He stuck me with a knife! *That's* good for jail time.

I dive off the road into the underbrush on the edge of a large stand of lodgepoles, watching Byrnes flip a U-turn back in my direction. If he goes past, I'll run out the way he came and work my way through the neighborhoods downtown to the police station. I touch the stinging flap of skin on my cheek with a strange sense of satisfaction. When the cops see that, there'll be no doubt.

Byrnes stops less than twenty feet from me, headlights illuminating the trees. I hold my breath and hug the ground like a flat rock, shuddering as the melting snow soaks through my flimsy jacket.

Mr. Byrnes slips out of the car, peering into the shadows around me. The headlights aim high and to the right of me, and I have no way of knowing whether I'm visible. He moves carefully in my direction, and I truly believe my heartbeat will drive a dent into the cold ground beneath me. He's ten feet away now, and though he gives no indication of spotting me, I can't contain the panic, and I push myself up, venting a guttural animal yowl, and hightail it for the trees and the park exit beyond.

A dusky strobe from his headlights passes through the trees while the car turns toward the road through the park. Then it's black again, and I slow to dodge the black silhouettes of the trees, which seem to spring from nowhere. Near the park exit, I crouch, peering back into the darkness, then east, where I catch broken glimpses of the headlights as the car circles the perimeter, moving toward the exit. I sprint, hoping I can beat him and disappear into the neighborhood, but he rounds the last turn as I break onto the street, and though I cross safely, I'm dead sure he saw me.

The headlights cast my eerie blurred shadow in front of me as I push my exhausted frame down the middle of the street before cutting to the sidewalk. I glance desperately around for an alley, any place I can cut into the neighborhood to get off the street; see nothing, and run straight down the sidewalk with one eye on the driver's-side door, knowing if he jumps out, I'll leave him in the dust. If he doesn't drive up on the sidewalk to pick me off, I'll be safe until I get downtown.

As I think it, it's real. The car cuts sharply toward me, jumping the curb, and I dive over a three-foot chain-link fence, roll twice, pick myself up, and race to the next yard, screaming with the renewed energy only an adrenaline blast can create. I cut behind the house to find an alley and double back, hoping to give myself time while he figures what I'll do next.

But old man Byrnes didn't become the chilling menace he is being duped by the likes of me. Twice I reach the entrance of the alley—once on each end—only to see my mother's car idling quietly within twenty-five feet. Each time I dart back to hide among the garbage cans and clotheslines, wondering if he's some sort of spook, if maybe he can read my mind. I know that can't be true, but when I steal across several lawns to an adjacent alley two blocks away and creep into the intersection only to find the car waiting, I'm *rattled*.

I consider pounding on someone's door, but a lot could go wrong—there wouldn't be much time if no one answered—and I still hope I can get downtown before he catches me. To actually get his hands on me, he'll have to get out of the car, and that evens things up.

Moving down off the south hill now, into middle and poorer sections of town, I realize my chances of rousting someone out are gone. Loud yelling and nighttime violence are more common here, and people lock their doors when they hear it. But if I can get through the Edison district, I'll be only a few blocks from the police station.

I haven't spotted him for three blocks now, so I may have lost him in the maze of backyard swing sets and garages and old cars that dot the alleyways. I won't go back out onto the street until the downtown lights are in sight. Then I'll run for it.

Behind me, a cat bounces off a loose garbage-can lid, and a muffled shriek escapes my throat. I crouch to catch my breath. I don't know the area well, but I have some sense of it from having visited Dale Thornton.

Dale Thornton! That's it! Byrnes is keeping up with me because he knows I'm going for the cops. That's got to be it. But Dale Thornton lives near the middle of the Edison district, the opposite direction from the station. If I can get to his house, I'll be safe. Dale's not in love with me, but he's got to hate old man Byrnes. Dale's the only person beside me and Lemry who knows what he did.

I start moving in that direction when steel fingers grip my

shoulder. "Messed up big, boy. What'd you think, I was going to stay in the car while you raced up and down the alleys? Not too hard to figure why you kids don't score higher on your SATs." His grip is so tight my arm numbs. I pull away, but he tightens it until I'm on my knees. "Told you I was done messin' with you," he says in a raspy whisper, and suddenly the cold edge of his blade rests on my throat. "Now you've had a taste of your own blood, and I'd be more than happy to give you a wide smile."

I close my eyes.

"Don't think for a second I won't do it, boy. Now just tell me where my daughter is and let this be over."

"How do I know you won't hurt me after I tell?"

He laughs. "You only know I will hurt you if you don't." The pressure of the blade creases my throat. "The next words out of your mouth better be the whereabouts of my girl."

"Reno."

I think I feel the blade cut.

"The truth," he rasps.

"Reno," I say again.

His free hand goes to my hair as he pulls my head back so hard I feel whiplash. "How'd she get there?"

"Lemry." In this state I would do anything: turn on my friend, murder innocent babies, *anything.* Later I will feel shame, but now I feel only terror in its purest form.

"Who's that?"

"Teacher."

His grip relaxes, and I roll away hard, actually hearing hair tear out of the front of my scalp, and I'm up and screaming down the block fast and loud, seconds before searing pain bursts into my left shoulder blade. My shrieks increase as I storm toward the lights. Behind me a car starts and I leap a back fence, cutting across another lawn for a lighted street, screaming, screaming, screaming.

I'm back in an alley, and the pain in my shoulder blade is dulling a bit, but the terror is not. I rumble across two more streets, two more alleys, toward the heart of the Edison district, until something looks familiar in the dim light. I think it's Dale's street. I cut across another yard, unsure whether to turn right or left, and now the pain in my shoulder returns with such intensity I think I'll vomit. I reach for the source with my right hand but I can't get to it. It has to be his knife, but I can't reach it. My left arm is completely numb. I have to stay conscious.

It's late. After midnight. Anything I see moving will be him. Liquid warmth trickles down my back, and I'm suddenly glad I couldn't get to the knife. I'm like a punctured tire: Don't take the nail out until you get to a service station.

I have to take a chance on the direction. Without landmarks, I'm geographically dyslexic. It is absolute fact that in unfamiliar surroundings, I have a better than fifty percent chance of going the wrong way by following my instincts. I've seen Dale's house, but only from the front street, and from here I recognize little. My instincts say go right. I turn left and begin to jog, praying my disability will be true to me.

"Jesus Christ, Fat Boy; what're you doin' here? What the hell time is it? Shit, you're lucky you didn't wake my old man! He'd think nothin' of kickin' your ass all the way back to your house. What the hell you doin' here? Man, I wouldn' be runnin' around this neighborhood at night. Someone'll kick your ass an' take your stuff. Hey, what happened to your face? Jesus. Here, follow me out to the garage. Man, you're lucky you didn't wake up my old man. You know what time it is? What'd you do to your face?"

Dale leads me down the dirt driveway to the garage, unlocks the monster Master padlock and steps in, feeling for the light switch. I haven't spoken and I'm fighting to stay with him. The overhead fluorescents flicker, and I turn my back to him.

"Jesus Christ. What's that? What the hell is that? Shit, you got a knife stickin' outta ya. Oh, Jesus Christ. How the hell you get a knife stuck in you?"

"Byrnes," I say, and suddenly I'm struggling for air, dropping to my knees.

"Oh, shit," Dale says. "Want me to take it out? Want me to pull that sucker outta there?"

For the first time, I know I might really be in trouble, that I could die. I shake my head weakly. "911." I pitch forward onto my good arm and ease myself to the cold concrete floor. Dale is screaming for his dad.

I don't know whether I passed out or fell asleep, but reflections of red and blue lights chase each other around the garage walls when my eyes open again, and I'm being hustled into the back of a blue-and-white van. I'm on my back; the knife must be out. Prickly pain dances in my left hand, and I watch with strange detachment as the medic inserts a needle attached to a tube into my forearm. Everything is fuzzy. Gauzy. A policeman's lips are moving just above me, but I can't hear a word. Hey, man, these guys have this all under control. I'm outta here.

CHAPTER
SEVENTEEN

You know, actually this isn't so bad. The last time I got this much media attention I won the sixteen-and-under fifteen-hundred-meter freestyle at the Spokane Summer Games two summers ago. ORCA SWAMPS COMPETITION, the headline read. They didn't know I already had my marine moniker. The radio and TV stations also did the story from the "weight angle." Summer is slow for sports coverage.

But this is better, because lying in a hospital bed, my size is not an issue. Hell, that could be anything under those covers. For all they know I'm in a body cast. And I'm the victim of a major crime; *headlines* for the Regional section. Ellerby said he'd consider letting someone stick a knife in him for the kind of attention I've been getting. I suggested he let that someone be me.

I've told my story probably seven hundred times so far, and it gets better with age. I need to work on the part where I karate-kicked the knife out of his hand and it landed in my shoulder, but the rest stands up pretty well. Dale Thornton is getting a kick out of his supporting role, and his dad has told several reporters he's camping out near the main entrance and will personally see Virgil Byrnes die a slow death before he gets within a mile of my room. The Thorntons like me a lot better as a two-bit TV star than they did as a one-bit smartass.

That's all very clever, and as long as my mom and Carver and the media and the police and medical folk keep parading through the room, I'm feeling pretty cocky. But when I'm alone, what I feel is lucky to be alive and pretty scared. Old man Byrnes has disappeared, and that makes me plenty nervous. But the real danger is to Sarah Byrnes. The cops are hunting her and Lemry down in Reno, but the hotel they were supposed to stay at hasn't heard of them. Lemry was supposed to call her husband when they arrived in Reno, but he missed her call, so the city cops have their place staked out, and highway patrols in three states have been notified to be on the lookout. I just don't want them driving into town not knowing old man Byrnes is on the loose.

And hey, I'm thinking of becoming a drug addict. Whatever they're giving me for the pain in my shoulder is *not* bad.

"Hey, man."

Mark Brittain stands in my doorway. I'll be gone to hell.

"Hey, man," I say back.

"You're kind of famous."

"Guess so." I reach down to the side of the bed to find the button that raises my head. "So, how you feelin'?"

"Okay, I guess," he says. "Kind of stupid."

I don't know what to say. I can feel that he wants to explain himself, and I don't have it in me to hold him in contempt. I've had time to think: The wound I have is just a hole; *his* wound is humiliation. I've felt both, and they don't compare. I think all this—feel some connection—without Mark having said but one sentence. Feeling kind of stupid.

I say, "We keep this up, there won't be much of a team for Regionals."

He nods toward my shoulder. "You out of it?"

"Looks that way. Doctor says it'll take a while to repair the muscle damage. Needs time, mostly."

Mark looks at the floor. "I've been watching the news. I heard what Mr. Byrnes did to his daughter. He must be a pretty scary guy."

"Off the charts scary."

"What I said in class . . ."

I raise my good hand. "Don't worry about . . ."

"All that stuff about responsibility." He shakes his head. "I've been working with a guy up here. A counselor." He laughs. "A *therapist*. He's not a counselor. I need a therapist. Anyway, I've been thinking wrong." His lower lip quivers, but he smiles through it. "I've got a lot of work to do. . . . My dad . . . Listen, tell Jody . . ." and he closes his eyes. "Just tell her I'm sorry, okay? About the abortion and all. I lied, Mobe. You know, right before I took the pills . . ." He stops. "Jesus, I lied."

I start to tell him I understand, though I probably don't completely, but he's gone.

When my eyes open again, a shadowy figure fills the doorway, but I can't focus. These painkillers kill more than pain. I smile and wave and close my eyes. Either a couple of minutes or three days later when I open them again, the shadowy figure ain't shadowy and has moved to the side of my bed. Lemry says, "Rough weekend?"

"Worst on record."

Lemry puts her hand on my bad arm. "This doesn't bode well for your swimming career."

"Yeah, I don't think I can qualify for the relay. You guys have any luck?"

"We found her."

"No shit?" I say. "You found Sarah Byrnes's mom?"

My excitement isn't matched. "We found her within the first twenty-four hours," she says. "Only had to walk through the casinos looking. She didn't look much different from the picture Sarah Byrnes had."

My enthusiasm crashed. They found her, but . . . "So what happened?"

"Well," Lemry says, "we got down there just before midnight, and got a room at Harrah's, which is one of the big hotel casinos. I was beat, but your friend wanted to get on with it, so we spent the next few hours wandering through casinos. We asked around, showed some of the dealers and floor people the picture, but they weren't helpful. I think a lot of people hide out there.

"I finally talked Sarah Byrnes into crashing for all of forty-five minutes. We checked around in the same random way for a few hours before breakfast back at Harrah's.

"The hostess at the restaurant kind of started when she saw her, but of course, as Sarah Byrnes has told me a number of times, that's not unusual. Then I noticed she couldn't take her eyes off Sarah Byrnes, and she looked very distressed. So

I asked to see the picture again, and I looked at it and I looked at the hostess and by God, except for the hairdo and a few wrinkles, they looked alarmingly alike. I told Sarah Byrnes to compare it, and before I knew it she was out of her seat headed toward her. The woman saw her coming and jumped up and walked toward the door. Sarah Byrnes hurried, but she walked faster and faster until she was almost running, and Sarah Byrnes yelled, 'Mom!' and the woman broke into a sprint and was through the main entrance and out into the street. By then I was running to catch them.

"So now Sarah Byrnes's mom has thrown off her high heels and is running full bore down the sidewalk, panicked and not about to be caught. So I kick it into high gear and shoot past Sarah Byrnes to get her mom before she can reach the end of the block, because I'm afraid she'll run out right into the street." She sighs and closes her eyes. "God, all the poor woman wanted to do was get away from us."

I'm so drawn into the story the pain is gone. "What happened? You caught her, right?"

Lemry laughs. "Did I catch her? Was I or was I not the Iowa state eight hundred meter champion in high school?"

I stare, surprised.

"I was. You think swimming is the only sport I know?"

"Not anymore," I say. "What did she say?"

"She screamed, 'Let me go! Let me go!' but I held on to her arm, trying to calm her and hoping I wasn't going to spend the night in a Reno jail for attempted kidnapping. I told her it was all right, that we just needed to talk, and I called her by name and she didn't dispute me, so I was certain who she was. Then a police car rounded the corner down the block, and she shut up like someone had pulled her plug.

"By then Sarah Byrnes had caught up with us. Julie— that's her mother's name—didn't want police involvement, so she agreed to go with us, and we took her back to our room, where she called down to the restaurant to say she'd become ill and had to get to an emergency room, and I guess someone covered for her."

"So it was really her?" I ask. "God, what are the chances of that?"

"Not good," Lemry says.

"So what happened?"

Lemry sighs. "It got ugly. First her mother tried to deny who she was, even after all we'd just been through. Then she said she'd split with her husband *before* Sarah Byrnes was injured, I think hoping Sarah Byrnes didn't remember. Sarah Byrnes got steamed and called her a lying bitch, and they screamed at each other for close to fifteen minutes before Julie broke into sobs and Sarah Byrnes said she hoped she choked to death on her tears. I tried to get control, but it was like trying to stop a dogfight. Sarah Byrnes kept yelling, 'Look at me! Look at me, Mother! How could you leave me? How could you do that?' while her mother just sobbed and said how sorry she was."

I can see Lemry is moved. She's telling the story as if it's still happening, and her chin quivers.

"Finally I called a truce, and we agreed to meet that night back at our room. I was afraid Julie would skip out, but there was no way to get any further until they got apart and had time to think. We just had to take the chance, though I spent most of the time between preparing Sarah Byrnes for the possibility that she'd split. But seven o'clock rolled around, and sure enough, she knocked on the door. It was better this time because Sarah Byrnes had agreed to be civil long enough to find out what she needed to know."

"What did her mom say?"

"She said she knew she'd burn in hell for leaving, but it couldn't be worse than what she'd gone through for the past fourteen years. She said she had made a number of suicide attempts at first, but even messed those up; that leaving her daughter was bad enough, but not protecting her in the first place was unforgivable. She said she'd known Virgil was crazy since before they got married, but couldn't break away from him."

"Jesus, if she knew he was crazy, why not?"

"One of the eternal mysteries of men and women, Mobe. When a person feels worthless, nothing he or she does is surprising."

"So how'd it end? She didn't come back with you, did she?" I wasn't asking. I knew.

Lemry shakes her head. "She didn't come back with us. Sarah Byrnes begged her to, told her she could make up for everything by coming back and telling what happened; how crazy her dad was getting and about the hospital. But her mother said no. She didn't believe she could live through the humiliation of a court hearing—that she wanted to, but just couldn't. She said the next thing Sarah Byrnes would have to deal with would be her suicide."

That pisses me off. "What a spineless . . ."

"Not so fast. She was telling the truth. You have to give her credit for that. This is not a strong woman, Mobe. The courage to pull this off is nowhere in her."

"God, what did Sarah Byrnes do then?"

"She got quiet. She was very polite, and we ended it. She climbed into bed and went to sleep." Lemry laughed. "*She* went to sleep. I was dead sure she'd try to disappear or hurt herself, so I sat up all night, but she slept until morning, got up and said, 'Let's go,' and we came home."

That scares me. I've seen Sarah Byrnes quiet like that. Lemry reads my mind. "It made me nervous, too, Mobe," she says. "It was as if she gave up on the spot, and I was really afraid of what might happen when we got home. I still am. I just hope she's able to put it together in a way that works for her. But I have to tell you, this kind of loss is out of my league."

I think she's finished, but then she puts her hand on my arm again and gives me a look into her life. I wish adults could know how important that is to us sometimes. She said, "I grew up in a little town in Iowa called Cradle Rock. The big thing there was Little League. Boys and girls played on the same teams, not because the feminist movement was fifteen years ahead of its time, but because there weren't enough boys in town to make up the eight teams.

"My first team was the Phillips Junior Oilers. The local Phillips 66 station sponsored us. I remember picking up that green T-shirt with the gold lettering across the chest, and the cap with a golden P. I was so proud. I wore that cap everywhere. You couldn't wear the shirt anywhere but to games, but you could wear the hat anytime.

"I was a skinny little girl, not at all pretty, and I knew that. Kids told me all the time. All my life I hadn't fit, couldn't think of the clever things to say. I didn't have any possessions anyone wanted, and it seemed I didn't have anything inside me anyone wanted, either. Sometimes I look at pictures of me back then, and I can't believe the monumental sadness in those eyes. It's as if that's another little girl altogether."

Lemry gazes toward the side wall, and I see surface tension holding a tear.

"We didn't have much money," she says. "Almost no one in town did. But my parents and my grandmother saved enough extra to buy a really nice glove. It was a Warren Spahn autograph model, so I suppose it was a glove for a pitcher, but I didn't care. I only remember the cool leather against my face. And the smell. God, that smell *meant* baseball. I oiled it every day with neat's-foot oil and tied a baseball into the webbing each night to break it in and create the pocket I dreamed would cradle a million fly balls, scoop up a million grounders, pluck a million screaming line drives out of the air. That mitt, even more than the hat, was the symbol of my belonging on the team."

Lemry strokes my arm lightly, and I am quiet, in the hands of a true storyteller telling a true story.

"When I got to the field for our first game, I was so excited I thought I would throw up. I hadn't slept a wink the night before and spent the entire day throwing my baseball against the side of the garage, grossly exaggerating the speed of the grounders dribbling back as I snapped them into the merciless trap of my glove and threw the runner out.

"I didn't catch one ball in warm-ups. They dropped to the right of me. They dropped to the left of me. They hit my arms and fell harmlessly to the grass. But I was just so happy to be there, to belong with these other kids with 'Junior Oilers' across their chests, that it didn't matter.

"When coach called us into a huddle before the umpire yelled, 'Batter up!' he went over our positions and the batting order one last time, but he didn't need to for my sake because I had memorized those things from the first practice. I batted ninth. I played right field. I knew what that meant. I knew I was the very worst hitter on the team and the very worst fielder. But I didn't care, because I had a new glove and a green-and-gold uniform and I belonged.

"We were the home team and batted the bottom half of the inning, so we touched our gloves together in the middle of the huddle and yelled, 'Go Oilers!' and broke to take our positions. I was so proud. But before I got even to the baseline, Coach's hand was on my shoulder, and when I turned around, Ronnie Callendar stood next to him. And he said, 'I want you to give Ronnie your glove.'

"I said, 'What for?'

"He said, 'He doesn't have one.'

"Coach watched my face fall—I know he did—and I think he knew how I felt because he was very kind, but he said,

'Cindy, if we're going to win this, Ronnie has to have a mitt. A shortstop has to have a mitt, that's just all there is to it.' I looked at the glove on my hand; I bit my lower lip while I read Warren Spahn's name, and I handed it over. Coach told me to play as far back in right field as I could so no balls could get over my head—that I could run faster forward than backward—and sent me on my way. I walked so far back I almost disappeared into the playground swings beyond the field.

"Just that quick I *didn't* belong, and I remember thinking something always has to spoil it. I was hurt and embarrassed and I wanted to go back to being invisible me again, but I couldn't because I had on the green shirt and cap, and all of a sudden that uniform was my enemy. I remember hating Ronnie Callendar for being poor, and I hoped his father never got a job and they'd have to move away.

"Every game after that was miserable. I couldn't quit because we would have only eight players and all the kids would hate me. Coach didn't always take my glove; in fact, I don't know that he ever took it again. But each time I walked down that hot, dusty summer road toward the playing field, I knew he *might*, that I didn't really belong because they could take my glove."

Lemry looks down at me, returning to the room from her story. "That's what I thought about all the way back from Reno. I remembered how I truly wanted to die. And all I lost was a baseball glove. Sarah Byrnes lost the one thing she's been holding on to."

Lemry's story is the story of my fat little life; life before swimming, before Ellerby. Before Jody. "You're worried," I say. "You're afraid Sarah Byrnes has lost too much."

She chuckles, but there is no humor. "I am worried," she says. "But I'll tell you, Mobe, the sadness of this weekend has hit me hard, and I'll fight to the death to keep the things I'm worried about from happening.

"When the Nevada highway patrol pulled us over to tell us about what happened here with you and her dad, I saw a flash of the girl I drove down there with. I think it gave her energy to fight, but I don't know. It's a close call. At any rate, she agreed to tell me before doing anything rash, and I believe she will. That is one amazing kid, Mobe. I see why you've always liked her. She's what courage is about. And she's certainly changed the way I look at my own life. Anyway, she's over at the house now, with my husband, who is happy as a pig in shit because all my arguments about why he shouldn't have guns in the house just went down the toilet. Cops have the place staked out, too, so at least she's safe."

God, the one person who could save Sarah Byrnes won't do it. When my mother comes tonight to visit, I'm going to hug her till she breaks.

CHAPTER
EIGHTEEN

Life is turning into a play. The theater is this hospital room, and mine is the finest seat in the house. Mark Brittain entered stage center again late last night after Lemry left. I was watching a rerun of "Taxi," and I don't know how long he stood there before I noticed and invited him in. He's getting out tomorrow and was freaked about facing everyone.

"What would you do, Mobe?" he said. "No offense, but you used to be the reigning prince of fools. I mean, let's face it, you ate a lot of shit. You and your friend Sarah Byrnes."

I punched MUTE on the remote and rolled over to take pressure off my shoulder. The man had a point. If Sarah Byrnes and I had saved it instead of eating it, we'd have the beginnings of a fertilizer dynasty today. I really did want to help Mark—if for no other reason than it's nice to be the expert on something, even if it is the ingestion of foul foreign substances emanating from deep in the bowels of my enemies. I wanted to say things would return to normal for him as soon as he got settled in school. But the time for bullshit has passed. I don't know how close my brush with death was, but it *seemed* close. The time for bullshit has passed.

"You know, Mark, people call me Moby because I'm a chunko swimmer. I could get pissed; you know, threaten to go after anyone who calls me that. I'm not a fighter, but I could get up for it if I thought I needed to. I wouldn't always win, but you'd have to want to mix it up to take the chance. I truly believe I could get people to quit calling me Moby, but I could never stop what they think when they see me in a tank suit, and I couldn't stop what they'd say about me if I went around with a chip on my shoulder. Hey man, the sun comes up, the sun goes down; winter turns to spring, spring turns to summer, and Eric Calhoune is a barrel-chested, no-waisted hulkster. Besides, folks calling me Moby is pretty funny, don't you think?"

He shrugged. "I won't call you that anymore."

"That's not the point. I don't mind it anymore. In fact I like it. It's who I am. I'm Moby. The point is, if you go around making things look different than what they are—and what everyone *knows* they are—nobody's going to want to get close to you because they know you don't tell the truth. You just have to tell, the truth in a way people recognize."

Brittain looked toward the window, watched his reflection in the pitch black of the night outside. His chin quivered, "How do I tell the truth about what I've done? How do I say I sent Jody to get an abortion by herself when I knew how scared and confused she was? How do I tell people that? I mean, what words do I say?"

"You say you fucked up. You say you were wrong."

Mark was quiet. Then he said, "Could you do it?"

"I don't know. I really don't. But if I were in your shoes, I *should*."

He was quiet again. Then, "You know who came and saw me today?"

"Who?"

"Steve Ellerby's dad."

"No shit. What did he want?"

Mark smiled. "He said if I was interested, he'd be willing to spend some time with me looking at some different perspectives on Christianity."

"That's a good offer," I said. "He's a smart man."

He smiled again. "Yeah, well, I told him my dad might

not look too kindly on that, and he said, 'Mark, you're only seventeen years old, and you've already tried to take your own life. I'd say that means something's not working. If you need more information to make things work, I'd get busy with it.' So I guess I might. No reason I have to tell my dad everything." He looked at his watch. "Look, I gotta go. Just thought I'd check in before I got out." He turned to leave.

I said, "Hey, Mark," and he stopped. "I'll bet if you called Jody and talked about this, it'd go down easier at school."

He considered a minute. "I'll think about that."

Act II opened when I blinked awake to one of those half-hour advertisements for a surefire way to stop male pattern balding in its ugly tracks, and Sarah Byrnes stood in her coat beside my bed, shaking me gently. It was after hours, so I knew she had sneaked in.

"I'm leaving, Eric," she said. "I stopped to say good-bye."

"Leaving? Where are you going?"

"Away."

An empty pit expanded in my stomach. You can't talk Sarah Byrnes out of anything. "Jesus," I said. "Don't leave. Please don't."

"I have to."

"Why? God, Sarah Byrnes, this is the best things have ever been. I mean, you have a *place*. You're safe."

"I'm not safe as long as my dad's out there," she said. "If I'm gone, and nobody knows where I am, then everyone will be safer. As long as he knows I'm around, you won't be safe and neither will Lemry. But he won't try to get revenge. He just wants me. He's crazy, but he's simple crazy. He would have killed you that night, but not to be mean. He'd have killed you to get to his 'family.' That's me. And he'd kill me before he'd let anyone else have me. I just have to get away."

"Where would you go?"

"There's this place I know about in the Midwest—Kansas, I think. It's a group home where they take care of handicapped kids, kids with terminal illnesses and permanent disfigurement—stuff like that. I read about it five years ago in *Life* magazine, and I always thought I might go there and work someday. I was smart even back then; never let my dad see the magazine. He won't find me in a million years."

"But you won't even have a high school diploma if you leave now. At least wait until graduation."

She shook her head, and that old look of disgust popped up. "Getting stabbed didn't make you any smarter, did it? You think my dad's going to wait until graduation to come for me? I thought I heard him in the backyard *tonight*. Look, Eric, don't argue with me. I came because I might never see you again. All our lives I've been pretty tough on you." She smiled and I watched her scars crease and stretch in that old familiar way. "I keep remembering how you stuffed yourself to the brim every day after you started swimming; staying fat for me. Jesus, Eric, you were such a dork." She touched my hand. "But see, I didn't want to be so mean. It's just how I survived. Lemry helped me see that, just by being nice to me. When we were on our way to Reno, I felt like a regular person for the first time since I got burned. We laughed and told jokes and stopped to eat in these greasy little restaurants in towns that nobody's ever heard of, and for a little while I felt like I'd stepped outside my prison."

"But you can stay with Lemry," I pleaded. "You can have more times like that."

"If it wasn't for my dad, I would," she said. "I really would. I want you to tell Lemry that, okay?"

The panic that had been crawling up my throat began choking me. "Listen, Sarah Byrnes, maybe this is just selfish, but I don't know how I can stand the thought of you being out there and me not knowing where."

"Eric, I can take care of myself."

"I know. But I don't know if I can. I can't remember a time when there was no you. And I can't imagine a time like that now."

"You're just going to have to learn to be tough," she said,

and the cold crept in. "Look, I've been thinking a lot, and the only way I've held on was by hooking onto memories of my mother; fantasies of my mother, actually. I really thought someday I'd get back with her and find out there was a place for me. When my dad was at his worst—and you can't even imagine it, Eric—I would just go away in my head and think of my mother. I'd remember all those times she dressed me up and took me downtown and played with me in the park and read me stories. I knew I'd never be pretty again, but I'd have someplace to *be*. And even when I had to give all that up, I still hung on for the day she'd come back and put my dad away for good. Well, that ended in Reno. My mother is gutless. It's over." She was quiet a second while I desperately tried to think of something to stop her.

"Listen, I got a bus to catch, okay? Just let me do it. Let those newspaper people know I've disappeared. That way Dad will know." Then Sarah Byrnes bent over and hugged me, and I felt the wet stickiness of her craggy face for what I believed was the last time.

Tell you what. I've had enough of this shit. I've had enough of not being able to get anything to turn out my way. It's two in the morning, and I'm standing in my doorway waiting for the hall to clear so I can get out of here the back way. My clothes were in that little closet by the door, so at least I don't have to go into the freezing night with my fat butt hanging out the back of a hospital gown. I called Lemry and told her to pick me up in the parking lot, then hung up real quick so she couldn't try to talk sense into me. Her curiosity will get her there. I'll call Mom from the phone booth in the parking lot to tell her not to panic when the hospital reports me missing.

Lemry's tires crunch to a halt on the frozen snow as I hang up the phone in the booth. Carver answered, so I told him to take the phone off the hook so the hospital can't call my mother and scare her. Carver is getting better all the time. He made sure I wasn't about to tangle with old man Byrnes again, then told me to take care of whatever needed it, and after that we'll all sit down and make a plan. I'm sure he'll wake Mom and tell her, but he'll also keep her from getting crazy. I've got a sling and a thick pad over my shoulder blade, so if I'm careful I won't cause myself additional injury; it'll just hurt.

"What're you doing, Mobe?" Lemry says as I slide into the seat. "What's going on?"

I tell her what Sarah Byrnes said and point her toward the Greyhound station. "We've got a little time," I say. "I called and the next bus doesn't leave until three-fifteen." Lemry's tires spin in the snow as we fishtail onto the street.

By three, we've been standing next to the storage lockers,

out of sight and directly across from the ticket counter, for more than a half hour, and there is no sign of Sarah Byrnes. My shoulder aches like a hot bowling ball is lodged inside, and sweat pours off me like a watershed, but I keep my mouth shut and my eyes peeled.

"Are you sure she's taking the bus?" Lemry asks.

"She said, 'I got a bus to catch,'" I answer. "Her exact words."

"She *told* you she had a bus to catch," Lemry says, more to herself than to me. "That means she probably doesn't. If she wants to get away clean, she's not going to tell you how. Not with your big mouth."

In seconds we're back on the street, shooting down the unplowed street toward Amtrak, which is ten or twelve blocks from the bus station. "I hope we're right," Lemry says. "God, I hope we're right."

We're right. Sarah Byrnes sits on a long bench in the brightly lit cavernous hall, her feet propped up on her raggedy suitcase, scarred face hidden deep in a book. She's famous now, and though her picture was never in the paper, anyone who sees her knows exactly who she is.

She glances up as we approach and leaps to her feet, but Lemry is on her like a gentle bulldogger, wrestling her to a halt, then sinking with her to the floor.

"Just let me go," Sarah Byrnes says quietly. "Please, Ms. Lemry, let me go."

"No can do," Lemry says back, and I scoot over to grab Sarah Byrnes's bag.

"The only way this will be over is if I leave," Sarah Byrnes tells her. "You don't know my dad. Nobody knows my dad."

Lemry rises to her feet, pulling Sarah Byrnes with her. She grasps her shoulders firmly in both hands and looks her straight in the eye. "I don't give a good goddamn about your dad. I've heard enough about your dad. He . . ."

"He used to tie me up. He wouldn't let me eat. He locked me up sometimes. He's bad, Ms. Lemry."

"Then he'll go to jail," Lemry says without flinching. "I'm taking over here. That's it. You're out of the pilot's seat."

Sarah Byrnes starts to protest, but Lemry tightens her grip, and Sarah Byrnes folds, falling into her. Lemry says, "That's better."

Shit. This was too easy.

CHAPTER
NINETEEN

Boy, ain't it a trip where heroes come from.

Sarah Byrnes went home with Lemry, and I got out of the hospital officially a day and a half later. It took Brittain a couple days to get up the courage to come back to school, which is two or three days before *I'd* have made it, so we showed up together. Two TV trucks set up at the edge of the parking lot to tape my return, but Mr. Patterson ordered them off the grounds and all they got were pictures of me and Ellerby driving into the parking lot. Ellerby had the Cruiser washed and waxed so it shone like it really was from heaven, and he gave them a couple of blasts of Mahalia Jackson belting out "Bless This House" on the speaker system before he shut her down. I believe Ellerby may have the power to bring Mahalia back, or at least bring on some righteous letters to the editor.

I caught Brittain watching me several times in class and a couple of times in the hall, and finally I walked up to him and asked if I could help.

"Gotta do this on my own," he said.

CAT class was still a study hall, with Mautz monitoring, because Mr. Brittain lodged a formal protest, and even though Mr. Patterson told Lemry he could lodge all the protests he wanted and CAT class would roll on, Lemry was on paid leave. She was home with Sarah Byrnes in a kind of protective custody until the cops figured out what Mr. Byrnes's next move might be. It seemed smart to not place his targets in the middle of fifteen hundred kids. So Patterson didn't need to worry about taking Mr. Brittain on until Lemry got back.

About fifteen minutes into study hall, Mark Brittain raised his hand and asked Mr. Mautz if he could speak to the class.

I think Mautz thought the fat kid with his arm in a sling or the handsome renegade preacher's kid might turn study hall into a verbal free-for-all if Brittain said the wrong thing, but the part of him that thought all kids should hear Mark Brittain won over. "Sure, Mark. You can talk."

Mark stood and cleared his throat while everyone turned in their seats. You could hear his heart beating from across the room. "I need to clear some things up," he said, "or I'm not going to be able to show my face for the rest of the year."

We stared in silence.

"I'm a liar," Mark said. "I think the last words I said to this class were that Jody Mueller was a liar. Not so. Jody got an abortion just like she said. It was my baby. I was too scared to face what I'd done and too ready to protect myself, so I let her go up to the clinic alone and get an abortion alone and go home alone. Then I tricked her into thinking it was her fault. On one of Jody's good days, I couldn't have done that, but after her abortion she didn't have any good days. Everything she's said about me is true."

Mark took a deep breath. Then his voice cracked and tears ran down his cheeks, and he turned to Jody. "I'm sorry, Jody. I'm *so* sorry." He turned back to us. "I don't know what this does to my feelings about abortion or about God or about myself, but I'm going to find out." He looked at Mautz. "And now I'm going home, because I don't feel like talking anymore or being around anybody. I'll be back tomorrow."

Mautz started to protest, but Mark said, "If it means detention, it means detention. Somebody should have put me in detention a long time ago." If I don't remember another thing about that moment, I'll remember how relieved he seemed.

For a moment, there was only the sound of Mark Brittain's heels against the hardwood as he tucked his books under his arm and walked toward the door. Then there was the sound of Jody's heels following him.

Ain't it a trip where heroes come from.

Carver wasn't spending many waking hours at our house. He's an accountant by trade and the tax season had him by the short ones, as he put it. He came over late to sleep with my mother so she wouldn't fret about Mr. Bogeyman Byrnes sneaking in and nabbing her dumpling, and a couple of nights we all stayed up and drank hot chocolate and talked about what it must have been like for Sarah Byrnes to grow up the way she did. When I talked about the burning, or the horrible restraints, Carver seemed edgy, and when I said no one believed Sarah Byrnes when she tried to tell, he got so quiet Mom changed the subject.

One night he told Mom he had to go out of town on a week-long audit for a company over in Moses Lake.

"You're just tired of being under siege," she said. "You want a vacation."

"If I wanted a vacation, would I go to Moses Lake?"

That settled, he was on his way.

The next time I saw him was on Channel Six. A cop protected Carver's head with his hand as he bent into the back of a police car. His hands were cuffed behind him.

Wayne Haverly, live and on the scene, announced that in a strange twist in the Virgil Byrnes case, a local accountant had gained entry to Mr. Byrnes's home, where he lay in wait and subdued him. Byrnes was in serious condition at Sacred Heart with multiple fractures, his face so badly beaten as to be unrecognizable.

Mom visited Carver several times in the next couple of days, but said surprisingly little and never invited me along. Mr. Byrnes recovered steadily in the hospital as more and more charges were heaped on him. There is no statute of limitations on his kind of indecency. Sarah Byrnes stayed out of sight, as did Lemry. It was all very bizarre.

The next time I saw Carver was also on television, in an exclusive interview with Elaine Murphy, taped at the county jail. Carver was dressed in slacks and an open white shirt, his sleeves rolled up as if ready to dig into an audit.

Elaine introduced Carver and gave a summary of the case. Then she said, "Mr. Middleton, the prosecutor's office is considering charging you with assault with intent to commit bodily harm. What is your response?"

Carver sat back, looking cool and calm. Mom sat beside me, her fingers absently playing along my good arm. "Well," Carver said. "I assaulted him, though I certainly didn't intend to commit bodily harm—not at the outset. Everything I did after our initial confrontation was in self-defense. I realize I hurt him, but I foolishly didn't have a weapon, and I truly believe he'd have killed me if I hadn't put him out."

"So how will you plead?"

"Well, I gained unlawful entry, so I have no problem pleading guilty to breaking and entering. Beyond that I only did what I had to do to stay alive."

"So you would plead guilty to breaking and entering?"

"I am guilty of breaking and entering."

Elaine Murphy nodded. "Mr. Middleton . . ."

"Please call me Carver."

"Okay. Carver, why do you think the prosecutor's office is so vigorously pursuing more serious charges against you? You did, after all, apprehend a dangerous criminal."

"They've told my lawyer they intend to prevent any further such vigilante activity; that a clear statement has to be made to the public."

"How do you respond to that?"

"I have no problem with it. Virgil Byrnes is out of the way. That's all I care about. "

Elaine Murphy pauses, checking her notes. Then, "Carver, research into your background indicates you spent two tours of duty in Vietnam. Is that correct?"

"That's correct."

Mom lurched forward. "I didn't know that," she said. "He never said a word to me. That's strange. I did an article on athletes who fought in Vietnam once, and he never said a word." She sounded betrayed.

"And is it true," Elaine Murphy continued, "that you were part of a Special Forces unit engaged in top secret duty? And that on three separate occasions your unit suffered greater than seventy-five percent casualties?"

"Yeah," Carver said. "That's all correct."

"I understand you're quite a decorated soldier." Carver nodded, his expression unchanged. "That was a long time ago, Ms. Murphy."

She nodded. "I see. Isn't it possible, Carver, that you could use your war history, and the possible trauma that came from it, to mount your defense?"

Carver smiled. "Ms. Murphy, my participation in the Vietnam War makes me sad. It doesn't make me crazy."

I watched my mother's head in her hands, and watched her gently shake as tears leaked between her fingers.

Elaine Murphy was silent a moment before breaking for

a commercial. The Eveready Rabbit kept truckin' while I held my mother, then Elaine Murphy began the second segment: "Carver, can you tell us how you tracked Virgil Byrnes? The local police mounted a massive dragnet, all of the principals were under close surveillance, yet there was no sign of him. You found him at his home."

"I found him *in* his house," Carver said. "There was no evidence of his coming or going that the police could have seen from their vantage point. An old potato cellar leads into Byrnes's basement from underground. The cellar itself looks like nothing more than a mound of dirt at the edge of the backyard. You have to understand that the police are severely limited by manpower, and their main focus was protection of those principals you mentioned. I had no considerations but to find him. I knew he wouldn't leave town because of things his daughter had said about him, and I knew he had no friends and certainly didn't know the street network. He had to eat. He had to sleep. He had to do those things at home. I simply went in through a basement window and waited. Had I known about the underground entrance, there'd have been no violence. He took me by surprise."

"Did you wait long?"

"About nine hours."

"And your intent," Elaine Murphy went on, "was simply

to apprehend him and let the law take its course?"

Carver was quiet a moment, then leaned forward, placing his elbows on the simple gray metal table between himself and his interviewer. "Yes, that was my intent. But when that didn't work out, when I saw the power of his instincts, I have to admit I wanted to hurt him. And I want everyone out there to know that under normal circumstances, I would never, never advocate for that. But I sat by for several months, watching the fallout from this man's actions. His daughter, who is severely scarred for life, was in the psychiatric unit at Sacred Heart, completely shut down. My girlfriend's son was in a constant state of hopeless turmoil, trying to repair what was beyond repair. That was before Mr. Byrnes stabbed him with a hunting knife—with intent to inflict bodily injury, by the way. People were falling in his wake like flies. An attorney friend of mine estimated he might spend seven years in prison.

"But Virgil Byrnes is nothing if not patient. He didn't commit any of his crimes out of greed or any kind of personal gain. He committed them because that's the way he is. In seven years he will still be the way he is, and people I love and care about will have to worry about him all over again. So I didn't let up once we were locked in combat."

"Wait, Carver," Elaine said, putting up her hands. "You

need to know you may be hurting your case . . ."

Carver put up his own hand. "I'm on a roll here. You asked about Vietnam. I fought in Vietnam because of other people's beliefs. I joined the service when I was twenty-one years old and the first protester hadn't burned the first flag. I participated in operations I'm convinced cost the lives of hundreds of innocent people. Mothers and children, grandfathers and grandmothers. Yeah, and some soldiers, too.

"And I didn't go just once, I went twice. And then all hell broke loose over here and I discovered I'd been a warrior for nothing more than stubborn men's beliefs. All that cost to Vietnam, all that cost to America. All that cost to me.

"Well, this time I was a warrior for my own beliefs. I did not intend to lay a hand on Mr. Byrnes if he merely came with me, but I'd be lying to say there was no sense of satisfaction in rendering him harmless once he did come at me. I'm not asking for acquittal, or even leniency, but I am asking for fairness. I did what I did and I knew the possible consequences. In the eyes of the law, I was wrong. And make no mistake about it, I *believe* in the law, and I expect to be punished by it. It could cost me irreplaceable time with the woman I love and time away from her son, whom I would give anything to know better and to gain his respect. But sometimes sacrifices have to be made. This seemed like a good place to make mine." With that Carver stood, put his hand out to Elaine Murphy, who took it in surprise, probably wondering how she was going to fill up the rest of the half hour, and disappeared from the camera's view.

I looked over at Mom's tear-streaked face and took her hand. "Use my college money to get him a lawyer," I said. "He's got all the respect I have."

Boy, ain't it a trip where heroes come from.

EPILOGUE

Local Teen Adopted

Finds Adoptive Family Within 24 Hours of 18th Birthday

The final chapter of a family tragedy was written yesterday at the county courthouse when Cynthia and Tom Lemry signed formal adoption papers, gaining custody of Sarah Byrnes less than 24 hours before her 18th birthday. Local readers will remember Ms. Byrnes as the youngster whose face and hands were purposely burned on a hot wood stove by her father 15 years ago. The incident came to light this past February after Virgil Byrnes assaulted another teenager, 18-year-old Eric Calhoune, with a hunting knife.

"Better late than never," said Cynthia Lemry, a local high school teacher and swimming coach, in a statement to the press. "If someone had stepped up for this young lady a long time ago, years of heartache could have been avoided. She's a remarkable human being, and we're honored to have her in our family."

"I guess they're just in the nick of time to pay my college tuition," the new Sarah Lemry said with a smile.

Also attending the ceremony were Eric Calhoune, the victim of Virgil Byrnes's attack; Sandy Calhoune, the boy's mother and a frequent columnist for this newspaper; Carver Middleton, who served time on an assault charge against Virgil Byrnes in a related incident; the Reverend John Ellerby, controversial Episcopalian minister whose support of female clergy and full homosexual rights has frequently focused a spotlight on him in his 15-year stay at St. Mark's; and his son, Steve Ellerby, who describes himself as "a controversial Episcopalian preacher's kid."

Sarah Lemry confirmed that following the burning 15 years ago, her father refused her opportunities for reconstructive surgery, saying her condition would teach her to "be tough." She refused comment on further torturous physical abuse allegations, for which, among other charges, Byrnes has been found guilty in superior court and sentenced to more than 20 years in the state penitentiary at Walla Walla.

When asked if she would now seek the reconstructive surgery she was so long denied, Sarah Lemry again smiled and said, "I don't know. It'd be a shame to change just when I'm getting used to it."

In moving remarks before signing the papers, Judge Katheleen O'Conner said, "In all my years as a commissioner and as a judge, I have seldom been prouder—of my job or of the people here before me. I truly believe there is enough courage standing right here in this room to make our country great again."

The ceremony was reportedly followed by a celebration with Sarah Lemry's family and friends.

So there it is. I think I feel good about the way things turned out. The pizza was great.

I didn't get back in the water this year, had to go to Regionals and State as team manager. (That hacked Mautz off because it meant the school had to pay my expenses without exacting their pound of flesh—or in my case, ten pounds.) Ellerby won the hundred fly and Brittain placed third in the hundred free. I like to think I could have placed in the top six in the five hundred, but I'll just dream on. I got a scholarship to swim at a small NAIA school over on the coast, so I've got another four years of cramming the barrel of my body into a tank suit and stepping onto the blocks to the chant of Mo-*by*! Mo-*by*! When I visited the campus, the coach told me he'd have me down to sprinting weight after the first four weeks. I said, "Yes sir." Better men have tried—and she was a woman.

Ellerby's going to the U, so we'll be on the same side of the state and should be able to keep in touch, but I know our lives will go the way they go, and we'll end up friendly strangers. Sarah Byrnes will live with the Lemrys and go to the community college for at least a year until she decides what to do with her life. That means she'll be taken care of better than she could be anywhere else in the world, and she'll be here every time I come home. She's still fascinated by that group home she read about in *Life,* and that makes me feel good because it means she still has dreams. God, I love her.

Carver was sentenced to six months on work release, which basically meant he spent nights and weekends in the county jail for a little while. He pleaded guilty to a lesser assault charge, and the judge gave him the full sentence allowed by the law, along with a severe tongue-lashing about vigilante justice, then suspended most of that time due to the fact that too many lives had already been tragically affected and he wasn't about to add to that. The judge got both heavy criticism and loud support in the press, but I think he couldn't have cared less. Carver's going to be on parole for a while, but that's no big deal, he's never even had a parking ticket. I told my mother I was sorry I ever called him Boo Radley, and that from now on I'd call him Dad, whether she has the guts to marry him or not.

She just cried and said that was nice. If I told her cronies down at the paper what a Class A wimp she's getting to be they'd take her off the sports page and put her on the Food section.

Jody and I had a good spring, and I think we'll have a great summer. She's going to school on this side of the state, so we'll just have to play things by ear. One of the toughest things in the book—in my mind—is to test a relationship by splitting up, but it's probably as good a test as there is. Except for Lemry and her husband—and I don't know a lot about them—I don't have many models for how men and women are supposed to be together, and I figure I better take my time finding out for myself. One thing I do know: Families can get pretty messed up while they're looking pretty good. Look at the Brittains. If I'm ever going to have a family, I'd like to avoid that.

It's a scary thing, moving on. Part of me wishes life were more predictable and part of me is excited that it's not. I think it's impossible to tell the good things from the bad things while they're happening. Once I thought being a fat kid was the worst thing that could possibly be, but if I hadn't been fat I would never have known Sarah Byrnes—I mean Sarah—and that would have been a true tragedy in my life. And what is a worse thing than living like she lived for all those years? Nothing I can think of, but someday some kid in a group home somewhere in Kansas—chronicled in *Life* magazine more than five years ago—may be touched by her courage, and I guarantee that will change his or her. life forever.

So I'm outta here. My thing for this summer is leisure. Ellerby's coming by with Jody and Sarah in a few minutes, and we're headed for the lake in the Cruiser with a few tons of junk food, to sit out on Jody's houseboat and get into some major ingestion. I've gotta bulk up; give my new swim coach something to work off me.

STAYING FAT
FOR SARAH BYRNES

Most people who have heard me talk about *Staying Fat for Sarah Byrnes* know the idea came from a real event much like the one depicted in the story. I knew of the event but had no connection with the people involved, so the personalities needed to come from my imagination. They weren't hard to find, really; my own life as a teenager provided some, my years as an educator offered up more, my life as a therapist provided even more, and my life as a human being resulted in the rest. In other words, I get my characters from the same places nearly all writers do.

But the texture of any story is in the details; personality quirks, even coincidences, questions asked and answered, questions asked and not answered.

I created the CAT class out of boredom; not boredom from writing the book, but rather remembered boredom as a high school student. Back then I *longed* to engage in a subject that affected me personally, one that might answer questions pertinent to me in real time. I had questions about religion, sexuality, romance, morality. I wanted to be able to envision a future away from a logging town of less than a thousand people where everyone knew everyone else's business, or thought they did.

My first job in education was as teacher/coordinator/director of a very small alternative high school in Kennewick, Washington. It was an experimental program, created under "vocational education" to provide a safety net for kids who'd been expelled from the Kennewick public high schools for behavior or for falling so far behind that they couldn't catch up quickly enough to graduate within a year of their appointed date. Instruction for the basic Three Rs skills was required, but of course the problem was the same as it is today with reluctant students; that of "making it worth it."

I was fresh out of college with a sketchy high school history of my own, and with these kids the "tried and true" methods I'd studied in my ed courses had been tried and found *not* true. Contracting with them for proficiency in basic skills wasn't that difficult; hell, they'd agree to anything to avoid having to participate in creating their own educational goals (getting them to accomplish those goals was a whole different thing). But the tough part was creating an atmosphere wherein they might give a damn about showing up regularly and take some pride in our little enterprise. By the time the class had grown to about fifteen, I called a meeting to come up with a name for our school, and maybe a mascot. It was loosely modeled after a more established program in neighboring Pasco called Operation Motivation. My premier student—premier in the sense that he'd been the first enrollee—was a Golden Gloves boxer who had neglected to put on his golden gloves before roughing up a rival suitor for his would-be girlfriend. He raised his hand and said, "It's a dropout school. Let's call it *Dropout School*."

The name passed unanimously. I overruled the first ten mascots they came up with just because I refused to say them out loud in the main office, and we finally agreed to "Hooker Headers" (exhaust headers being an accessory for improving a car engine's performance; these particular headers being manufactured by the Hooker company). You can imagine the mascots I turned down.

But the meeting was the most successful thing we'd done as a group, and it gave me the idea for the forerunner to Sarah Byrnes's CAT class. "We're gonna start every day with a conversation," I said. "It's going to last the entire first period. We're going to talk about things that are important to you."

"How are you gonna know what's important to us?"

"Because you're going to provide the issues we talk about."

"What if we don't come in with anything?"

"Then I will come in with something and I can almost guarantee it will Bore. You. To. Death. You will bring in issues out of self-defense."

"Do we get a grade?"

"Yup."

"What grade?"

"We're pass/fail, so if you show up on time and you keep your eyes open, for starters, you'll get credit."

"We can't sleep?"

"You can't sleep."

"Shit."

"Uh-huh."

I was blessed with very few natural teaching skills other than a sense of humor, and was painfully ignorant of quality curriculum resources, but this one class got our program off the ground. The kids had never had their own issues considered important, and after I kept my promise of boring them to death during the first couple of sessions with subject matter of my own, they began to respond. Those discussions turned into essay and poetry themes. I'd stay up till three in the morning creating basic math "story problems" based on their interests. Sometimes it was a reach, but any discussion that had anything to do with *rules* turned into a social studies issue.

I'm sure if I could go back and relive it all, there were more sputtering starts than smooth takeoffs, but when I started writing *Staying Fat for Sarah Byrnes,* my imagination went straight to my initial days as an educator, such as it was, back in the very early seventies, to create the CAT class that then guided me into some of the major themes for my novel.

Different kids, different times, different backstories; but pretty good CAT glue.

CHRIS CRUTCHER

1. You've written fifteen books thus far. Do you have a favorite?

Not really. There are several I could make a case for, but as most authors will tell you, it's like trying to pick a favorite child; you love each for different reasons. Twice a year I have a definite favorite; when my royalty statement comes. Apart from that all my books represent where I was at the time I wrote them, so in short: No. No favorite.

2. And how about characters. You've written some incredibly memorable ones—is there a character whom you feel especially close to?

There are a number. I'd have to say the character I feel

closest to would be the main character in *King of the Mild Frontier*; it's an autobiography, so that character is . . . me. But I'm guessing you're asking about *fictional* characters. Probably the character's voice I feel closest to is T. J. from *Whale Talk*. He's smart and oppositional and fierce. Those are characteristics I happen to respect—most of the time— and they're interesting to me. The character that was easiest to write, and arguably the most fun, was Angus, from "A Brief Moment in the Life of Angus Bethune," a short story in *Athletic Shorts*. For whatever reason Angus exploded into my head fully developed. It was almost as if I were channeling him. For adult characters I'd have to go with Coach Lemry from *Staying Fat for Sarah Byrnes*, and Mr. Nak from *Ironman*.

3. You've always been known as a strong defender of the First Amendment and you are a past free speech defender honoree by the National Coalition Against Censorship. Why should young people care about the First Amendment?

That's a really good question, because the First Amendment—the *reason* for it—tends to be misunderstood these days. Usually when I'm called to defend it, the situation involves someone trying to ban one of my books in their school or in their curriculum. Young people normally come down on my side in that conflict because for the most part they don't like outsiders deciding what's good or not good for them; they'd rather do that for themselves, and in an overwhelming number of situations, they do just fine. But so many letters and emails I get from those young people tell me why *my* books shouldn't be censored or banned. What they may not understand is that it's easy to defend something you like. The First Amendment requires that we also defend what we *don't* like, and maybe even hate. If *one* book is banned, *all* books fall into the crosshairs. What may be more important are the other freedoms the First Amendment affords; the right to speak out against injustice, even if it negatively affects those in power; the right of the free press to cover the affairs of those in power, so our government or our corporations don't feel free to operate in secrecy, or force their will through illegal means. The scary thing about having this all-encompassing freedom is how easy it is to take for granted. Young people are "next up," so it becomes incumbent upon them to be well informed. Democracy is a fragile flower and untended, will die.

4. You've often joked that you didn't read as a kid, and anyone who has read *King of the Mild Frontier* knows you didn't do any homework. Who are the authors and books you admire now?

First, I should say it was a mistake for me to shun

reading as a teenager. Somehow I got the idea that it would be cool to get through junior high and high school doing as little as possible. As much as it made me feel good to be a smartass and to "get over" on my teachers, what it did was put me behind. When I look back I'm pretty sure I would have written my first novel before the age of thirty-five had I known more about how novels were written; and the only way to find *that* out is to read them.

That said, I wish I had been exposed to more of the literature I'm familiar with now. I think Sherman Alexie's *The Absolutely True Diary of a Part-Time Indian* is as good a young adult novel as has been written in the past thirty years. Laurie Halse Anderson and Matt de la Peña have yet to write a book that doesn't draw me in. Walter Dean Myers's *Monster* and *Fallen Angels* sit at the top of my list along with Christopher Paul Curtis's *The Watsons Go to Birmingham—1963* and *Bud, Not Buddy*. Tim O'Brien flooded my heart with jealousy with *The Things They Carried*. I can find no better examples of master storytelling than Stephen King's *11/22/63* and *It*. *The Shining* scared me big-time, and I don't scare easily. I read Lois Lowry's *The Giver* again and again, wondering how she did it. And if there hadn't been books like Robert Lipsyte's *The Contender*, my books might never have been published. The hard part of a question like this is that if you ask it on a different day, I'd give you a whole bunch of different, or a whole bunch *more,* books and authors.

5. Any advice for young writers on how to work on craft?

My best advice is to read a lot . . . pretty funny coming from me if you read the answer above. But believe me, if you want to write you have to read. When I read a book that I *really* like, I read it twice; once for the pure pleasure of reading and again to see how the author did it. I want to know how I was fooled, how I was set up, why I liked certain characters so much and had such contempt for others. I pay a *lot* of attention to the little details in that second reading, because those are what make a story *real.*

Learn the *mechanics* of the language. Writing a story is like building a house; you don't take a hammer and some nails and a bunch of wood and throw one up. Without the right tools and materials, you won't get it done. Same with writing. And make *word choice* a priority. If you're an "approximate writer"—one who uses *almost* the right word, you're going to have a lot of manuscripts in a desk drawer and none between covers. The more you pick the exact word you need, the fewer modifiers you'll need, which will make your writing seem less self-conscious.

Most important—and this may or not speak directly to

craft—*never* let anyone say you can't do it. There will be all kinds of people telling you how hard it is to get published and how your chances of getting noticed are so slim. Well, it *is* hard. But if you think it's impossible to get published, run down to your local independent bookstore, or to a Barnes & Noble. Look around. There are a *lot* of books, and many of them are written by people who are still alive; and quite a few are first novels or memoirs. *Somebody's* getting published. Guaranteed, it's somebody who has kept at it.

6. What's next? What are you working on now?

Just finished a new novel called *Losers Bracket* about a foster kid who lives in conflict, as she longs for the biological family who can't take care of her, and lives with the one that can but isn't her flesh and blood. That one's scheduled for publication, so its fate will soon be in the hands of the reading public. I have a completed first draft of another novel. That one is about an unorthodox young man who shows up in a community eleven years after a horrific mall shooting in which a number of kindergarten and first grade students were gunned down, and it confronts the struggles of the survivors of that shooting as they graduate from high school. Recent incidents require that I do a lot of editing to bring it current. A third project, which I'm five chapters into, is a much lighter, humorous book about an arts camp, called *Camp Infinity*. I'm using younger characters and my eye looks toward *zany*.

Sounds like a lot, but I've recently come upon some solutions for the ADHD that has haunted me all my life, and I'm zoned in. Hey, I'm seventy-one. I probably have only another thirty or forty years to write.

Chris Crutcher was raised in Cascade, Idaho, a lumber and cattle ranch town located in the central Idaho Rockies, a two-hour drive over a treacherous two-lane to the nearest movie theater and a good forty minutes to the nearest bowling alley. In high school he played football and basketball and ran track not because he was a stellar athlete, but because in a place so isolated, every able-bodied male was heavily recruited. "If you didn't show up on the first day of football practice your freshman year," he says, "they just came to your house and got you. And your parents let them in."

Chris Crutcher's years as teacher, then director, of a K-12 alternative school in Oakland, California, throughout the nineteen-seventies, and his subsequent twenty-odd years as a therapist specializing in child abuse and neglect, inform his writing. "I have forever been intrigued by the extremes of the human condition," he says, "the remarkable juxtaposition of the ghastly and the glorious. As Eric 'Moby' Calhoun tells us at the conclusion of *Staying Fat for Sarah Byrnes*, 'Ain't it a trip where heroes come from.'"

Chris Crutcher has also written what he calls an ill-advised autobiography titled *King of the Mild Frontier*, which was designated by *Publishers Weekly* as "the YA book most adults would have read if they knew it existed."

The author has received a number of coveted awards, from his high school designation as "Most Likely to Plagiarize" to the American Library Association's Margaret A. Edwards Lifetime Achievement Award. His favorites are his two intellectual freedom awards, one from the National Council for Teachers of English and the other from the National Coalition Against Censorship.

Chris Crutcher lives in Spokane, Washington.

www.chriscrutcher.com

LOSERS BRACKET
By the author of *Staying Fat for Sarah Byrnes*
CHRIS CRUTCHER

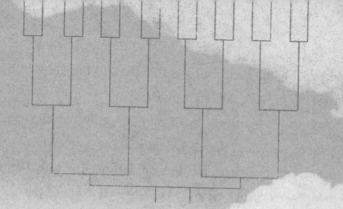

CHAPTER
ONE

The fact that life's not fair doesn't bother me. If the universe had distributed the IQ points allotted to my bio family evenly, we'd all dwell at the extreme low end of the range. But it made me "gifted" and the rest of them . . . not so much. That might sound like bragging but it's . . . yeah, bragging; but hey, this is *my* story. If they see it differently, let *them* tell it.

So, anyway . . . the universe also made me super coordinated and quick. Nobody in the rest of my family can juggle, like, *one ball*, though I have to leave open the possibility that Nancy—who contributed half my DNA—ate and drank and snorted away her athleticism. I hear my sis, Sheila, is a pretty good athlete in bed. Hard to believe we're sisters. My bio dad, Rance, is this ghost Nancy keeps at the edge of her life just so she can berate him.

I now live with another family altogether, which should be good news, but there's *something* about *real* family; you're connected, and that's it. Most times when I'm with Nancy or my sister Sheila, we fight like hungry pit bulls over table scraps, but when we're apart there's this crazy pull to get back, so historically I've done crazy stuff to make that happen. If the foster system really worked, it would have put Nancy with us in foster care. That way the person who needed help most would have gotten it.

But that didn't happen and Nancy lost three of us; there's an older brother, Luke, somewhere. Sheila was in and out like a ping-pong ball for most of her first ten years before social services stuck her in residential treatment. They took *me* before I dried off; no mother's milk for *this* future point guard, for which I should be grateful because God knows what all it would have been fortified with. *But*, no permanent home early on because if Nancy was better at anything than picking bad boyfriends, it was tricking social workers into thinking she was working on her "issues."

Service providers? I've known a few. Bet I could give you the first names of enough public health nurses to populate a softball team. FRS workers? Too many to name. FRS stands for Family Reconciliation Services. That's where your caseworker sends in a parent educator to help your mom deal with issues that arise when you've been sent back home for one more last chance. Issues like, should I duct tape my two-year-old daughter to the toilet seat in response to her shooting out nuclear *tag poop*. It's called that when you crap so much volume with so much force that it runs all the way up to the tag in the neck of your filthy Dora the Explorer T-shirt.

Issues like, can this nice man I met at a "cocktail lounge" last night live in the basement to help with rent? No? He *seems* nice. Is a level-three sex offender better or worse than a level-one sex offender? Doesn't matter? I promise I won't leave Annie alone with him.

So here I'd be, living with well-to-do people who provided for me and funded all my passions: youth basketball, parks and rec cross-country, and track. They kept me in the finest Nike gear and Nike runners, gave me my own room with a walk-in closet and separate bathroom. And they bought me *books*. Then Nancy would save up enough drug money for some shyster lawyer to petition juvenile court to send me back for that one more last try and there I'd be again, in her three-room shack that smelled like the bottom of an ashtray, waiting every morning outside the one bathroom—while her new boyfriend sat on the throne reading the *entire* paper after he'd used all the hot water—so I could get in to run a comb through my ratty hair and brush my teeth, and then be late for school where my counselor could give me the third degree about why my attitude, and my appearance, had taken this unexpected downturn.

You don't tell her it's because you're back with your mom.

But here's the deal: if Nancy had been serious; if she'd stopped with the drugs and the creepy brand-new best friends, I'd have aired out that hovel and lived with her till I turned eighteen—wrapped myself in athletic gear from Play It Again Sports, walked to all my practices, and complained not a second. Because in the end, blood is thicker than good sense.

But the bouncing back and forth makes you crazy.

So what you do—or at least what *I* do—is figure a way to get as much bio-family time as possible while living in the lap of relative luxury. This does not necessarily sit well with your bios, because when you get together you're the one with the fancy clothes, the iPhone with the Bluetooth headphones, and the superior attitude.

It also grates on your foster family, because they notice a serious behavioral downturn after your day with anyone with the surname Boots. Pop Howard says it's like I've been hanging out so far up the holler I can't see the sun. In fact, once Nancy's parental rights were terminated, Pop put grave restrictions on my time with her and my evil sis. Like, none.

Which turned me into a liar.

For someone continuing to get the benefit of extreme doubt, Nancy was a master at getting on the bad side of social workers. See, if you choose the life of a social worker you're not going to make a lot of money, and people your age who majored in business and make four times your salary building websites and inventing software that lets you download free books and music snicker behind your back while they're telling you how much they admire your selflessness. Social workers don't so much get exasperated because five or six years of college has left them among the working poor, but if you don't cooperate with their do-gooding, it makes their career choice look ill-thought-out. At least that's the gospel according to my good friend and long-suffering caseworker, Mr. Novotny.

It was a whirlwind ending. I'm in fourth grade, nine years old, back at Nancy's because she peed clean for a month, which means she snuck somebody else's pee into the bottle. I'm trying to stay home from school to spend as much time with her as possible because this *never* lasts. I play sick but that doesn't work, because Nancy wants to look like a good parent and if I don't look sicker than she does when she's cold turkey, I'm not sick enough to stay home. I abandon that plan and tell her my teacher doesn't like me and lets the other kids bully me on purpose. Hey, I'm nine.

Next minute we're in the car headed for school, and from Nancy's raving I know I'm about to have some serious explaining to do. We shoot past the VISITORS PLEASE CHECK IN AT THE FRONT OFFICE sign so fast she couldn't possibly read it even if she could read, and head straight for my classroom, which I lead her directly to due to the pressure on the back of my neck. She kicks the door open so hard it breaks the doorstop and screams, "How dare you not like my Annie!" loud enough that three kids dive under their desks. "She's the sweetest girl in the world and she has a hard life! Her father is a no-good, two-timing drug dealer (like there are *good* two-timing drug dealers?) and her mother just ain't always done her best!" She jabs her thumb into her colossal chest.

Mrs. Granger puts a hand up to calm the kids, who stare at me like I just brought a giant python for show-and-tell, and walks calmly toward us.

"Get back!" Nancy says, raising an arm in defense. "I'll kick your ass!"

Mrs. Granger tells me to go to my desk and asks Nancy to step into the hall so they can discuss this away from her students.

"We'll discuss it right by-God *here,*" Nancy bellows. I don't go to my desk because I can't break free.

"I like Annie just fine," Mrs. Granger says. "I like all my kids."

"That ain't what my Annie tells me an' my Annie don't lie!"

Mrs. Granger raises her eyebrows at me, because she's caught me in plenty of lies, and Nancy takes that as a sign she thinks I'm a devil child. "This little girl been through hell," she says. "She been left by her daddy and treated like a little piece of shit by me!"

Somebody laughs because we don't hear language like that in our classroom—from adults, anyway—but Nancy looks toward the sound like a pissed-off vampire and silence reigns.

Mrs. Granger tries to guide her gently into the hall, but that is not happening.

"Don't you *even* think yur gonna duck this humiliation, stickin' me out in the hall! I spent half my schoolin' in the hall!" Nancy's eyes narrow like a gunfighter's. "Raise yur hand if this woman don't like *you*, either."

No hands go up.

"RAISE YUR GODDAM HANDS!" and three shoot up involuntarily. I figure I am in about as much trouble as I can get into with this little effort.

Mrs. Granger quietly tells Nancy if she can't get herself under control, she'll have to call security, which has already heard the commotion and is on the way. Good luck. Two skinny security guys trying to get a five-foot five-inch, two-hundred-fifty-pound woman out a regular-sized door while she's grabbing desks and whiteboards and the globe, then going deadweight . . . again, not happening.

One of the guards is on loan from the city police force, so with help from the vice principal they're finally able to wrestle Nancy to a patrol car, and I am stuck with no credible explanation as to why my mother thinks my teacher doesn't like me. Luckily Mrs. Granger isn't like that and she just motions me toward my seat.

That was the end of the one-more-last-chances. Rance, my aforementioned sperm donor, hadn't participated in *any* services, so terminating on him was a no-brainer and by the end of the day I was back at the Howards' for good, oddly proud of my mother for her messed-up way of standing up for me.

June 29—Session # Who's Counting?
ANNIE BOOTS

Looking healthy in jock gear; got her basketball; mood seems fine. Got started a little late because of a crisis with the preceding client. Annie let me know right off she had to leave at the assigned time anyway. Typical Annie.

Annie: Nothing personal. I've got a shoot-around with my Hoopfest team.

Me: Going up the losers bracket again, I assume.

Annie: (nods in the affirmative)

Me: Do your teammates know what's behind that?

Annie: Leah does. I tell Leah everything. The other girls don't need to know.

Me: You tell Leah everything? That's new.

Annie: Well, you know, everything you can tell out in the real world. I tell you everything.

Me: What do you want to talk about today? I'm assuming you don't want my take on your losers bracket one more time.

Annie: You are an astute assumer.

Me: So . . .

Annie: Do you remember the last time I got removed?

Me: Like it was yesterday. You broke a vase; said your removal was all my fault. Said your caseworker and I and all the teachers at your school made a secret plan to trick Nancy. Pretty rough language for a nine-year-old, if I remember.

Annie: Do you remember what really happened?

Me: I sure do. You lit your mother's fuse by lying about your teacher; thought you'd get to stay home from school, but instead of no people going to school, two people went to school.

Annie: Do you think it was my fault I got taken? Like if I hadn't said that about my teacher . . .

Me: I think it was your doing that you got taken on that particular day, but that incident was the very small straw that broke the camel's back. Nancy and Rance had already piled up an impressive stack. Why? What's bugging you? More dreams?

Annie: (big sigh) Yeah, I just keep seeing the look on Nancy's face when they told her at the next supervised visit that it was all over.

Me: I was told that "look" was a gunslinger's stare, followed by an impressive meltdown.

Annie: Yeah, but there was a second right before that. She was whipped.

Me: I don't know, Annie. You can see that look, you can dream that look, you can believe it was all on you. We both know how hard it is to outthink your feelings, but we also know there was no way Nancy was going to get it together to be your mom. You just got a bad draw, honey. What else you got?

Annie: You know, war with Pop.

Me: I thought we decided that's a battle, not a war. Come on, Annie, one year and you're on your own. Off to college, calling your own shots. Just hold it together.

Impression: Conflicted, which I see as normal for her age and time of life. The intensity comes from her history. Her swagger and trepidation will both get tested.

Emily Palmer, M.A.

WHALE
TALK

By the author of *Staying Fat for Sarah Byrnes*

CHRIS CRUTCHER

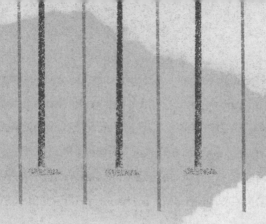

CHAPTER
ONE

In the end, write it down. Back up and find the story. Mr. Simet, my English and journalism teacher, says the best way to write a story, be it fact or fiction, is to believe aliens will find it someday and make a movie, and you don't want them making *Ishtar*. The trick is to dig out the people and events that connect, and connect them. No need to worry about who's wearing Nike and who's wearing Reebok, or anybody's hat size or percentage of body fat. Like Jack Webb on the *Dragnet* series on Nick at Nite says, "Just the facts, ma'am. Just the facts."

The facts. I'm black. And Japanese. And white. Politically correct would be African-American, Japanese-American and what? Northern European-American? God, by the time I wrote all that on a job application the position would be filled. Besides, I've never been to Africa, never been to Japan, and don't even know which countries make up Northern Europe. Plus, I know next to nothing about the individuals who contributed all that exotic DNA, so it's hard to carve out a cultural identity in my mind. So: Mixed. Blended. Pureed. Potpourri.

Adopted.

Big deal; so was Superman.

And like Superman, I was adopted by great people. The woman I call Mom—who *is* Mom—Abby Jones, was in the hospital following her fourth miscarriage (and final attempt at the miracle of birth) where she met my biological mother, Glenda, right after my presumed bio-dad, Stephan, had assisted in my natural childbirth only to come eyeball-to-eyeball with the aforementioned UNICEF poster boy. A second-generation German-American married to a woman of Swiss-Norwegian descent, he was a goner before my toes cleared the wet stuff. Any way he matched up the fruit flies, he couldn't come up with *me*. Because my mom is one of those magic people with the natural capacity to make folks in shitty circumstances feel less shitty, she consoled Glenda and even brought her home until she could get her feet on the ground. Evidently Glenda was as surprised as Stephan;

she'd had a one-night stand with my sperm donor to get even for a good thumping and had no idea the tall black-Japanese poet's squiggly swimmer was the one in a billion to crash through to the promised land.

Things sped rapidly downhill for Glenda as a single mother, and two years later, when she brought Child Protection Services crashing down on herself, getting heavily into crack and crank and heavily out of taking care of me, she remembered Mom's kindness, tracked her down and begged her to take me. Mom and Dad didn't blink—almost as if they were expecting me, to hear them tell it—and all of a sudden I was the rainbow-coalition kid of two white, upwardly mobile ex-children of the sixties.

Actually, only Mom was upwardly mobile. She's a lawyer, working for the assistant attorney general's office, mostly on child-abuse cases. Dad likes motorcycles; he's just mobile.

We never did hear from Glenda again, Mom says probably because the separation was too painful, and shameful. Sometimes I find myself longing for her, just to see or talk with her, discover more about the unsettledness within me; but most of the time that ache sits in a shaded corner of my mind, a vague reminder of what it is not to be wanted. At the same time all that seems out of place, because I remember nothing about her, not what she looked like or the sound of her voice or even the touch of her hand. I do admit to having a few laughs imagining how history rewrote itself inside Stephan's head when my shiny brown head popped out.

It's interesting being "of color" in a part of the country where Mark Fuhrman has his own radio talk show. My parents have always encouraged me to be loud when I run into racism, but I can't count on racism being loud when it runs into me. Very few people come out and say they don't like you because you aren't white; when you're younger it comes at a birthday party you learn about after the fact, or later, having a girl say yes to a date only to come back after discussing it with her parents, having suddenly remembered she has another engagement that night. Not much to do about that but let it register and don't forget it. I learned in grade school that the color of a person's skin has to do only with where their way-long-ago ancestors originated, so my mind tells me all racists are either ignorant or so down on themselves they need somebody to be better than. Most of the time telling myself that works. Once in a while my gut pulls rank on my mind, and I'm compelled to get ugly.

I called "All News All Talk Radio" a couple of days after the first time I heard the spectacularly racially sensitive ex-L.A. detective giving Spokane and the rest of the Inland

Empire the hot poop on big-time crime fighting. The talk show I called had featured the mayors of an eastern Washington and a north Idaho town declaring that the racist label put on this region is undeserved, blown out of proportion due to the presence of the Aryan Nations fort over in Hayden Lake, Idaho, and the existence of several small militias spread out between central Washington and eastern Montana.

The mayors had departed when the talk-jock finally said, "We're talking with T. J. from Cutter, about fifty miles outside our great city."

I said, "So this racist label, it's undeserved?"

"I believe it is," he said. "An entire region can't be held responsible for the ignorant actions of a few. Certainly you can't argue with that."

"You're right," I said. "I can't. But if the racist label is about perceptions, and in this case, *undeserved* perceptions, why would you guys have the Mark Fuhrman show?"

"Have you tuned in to Mark's show?"

"Not purposely," I said, "but I was scanning the stations and landed right on him."

"How long did you listen?"

"Long enough to convince myself it was really him, that you guys weren't just pulling my chain."

"Then you heard a man who knows a lot about crime

prevention and an accomplished professional radio man."

I said, "His voice was okay."

The jock said, "What's your point, T. J.?"

"That if you guys are running the most powerful AM station in the region and you're worried about people's perceptions of that region as racist, you might think twice before you give one of the true *icons* of racism in this country two hours of drive-time radio every week."

"We didn't hire Mark to talk about race relations. We hired him to talk about criminals and the criminal mind, and about the intricacies of police work. He's written books on the subject, you know."

"You didn't hire him because of his famous name?"

"No, sir, we did not."

"So when you decided your listeners needed to learn about Spokane, Washington, police work, you figured you'd get better expertise from a dishonored ex-L.A. cop rather than some retired veteran Spokane cop who might have covered Spokane's streets for twenty-five or thirty years?"

He said, "How old are you?"

"What does that matter?"

"You sound like a kid."

"You tell me why that matters, and I'll tell you how old I am."

"It matters because if you're too young, you might lack the experience to carry on this conversation intelligently."

"I'm a fifty-six-year-old retired Spokane policeman," I said, and paused a moment. "Guess I don't have the voice for it." I hung up.

I'm really not bothered by the race thing most of the time; at least I can say I don't bring it up first. And I've never wanted to be anyone else, and I don't want to be any other color. My bio-daddy must have had a pretty good brain because I have a big-time I.Q. and, Simet says, monster talent in articulation, plus I'm almost six-two and just a little under two hundred pounds. I can stuff a basketball from a standstill, and I've been clocked in a little more than ten-point-four seconds for a hundred meters. When I was thirteen, I qualified for the Junior Olympics in two swimming events, and I'm even a pretty fair cowboy, having spent parts of three summers at Little Britches Rodeo Camp. That's a pretty fair résumé for a guy who, until this year, never participated in one second of organized high school sports.

And I'm not hard to look at. Mr. Simet says I look like Tiger Woods on steroids, so I get plenty of chances to socialize. For every girl whose parents are terrified of a muddied gene pool, there's a girl who would use me as a threat to do just that. And there are plenty of girls who don't care one way or the other.

The truly unique thing about me isn't my racial heritage, or my brain or my size or my athletic abilities. Momma Glenda didn't leave me with much to remember her by, but she certainly left me with the all-time moniker. A lot of kids whose parents grew up in the hippie generation have names like Autumn or Somber or Twilight or Destiny. Who knows what their parents were smoking to name them after seasons or moods or times of day, but good old Glenda went them one better, naming me in her "spiritual" period. She may have been a little too "spiritual" on mood-altering funstuff to imagine my first day in kindergarten.

"Tell everyone your first name when your turn comes," Mrs. Herrick said, nodding to the pencil-necked, tow-headed kid next to me. The kid said, "Roger."

I said, "The."

"Excuse me?"

"The." She should have said, "Tell everyone what people call you."

The other kids giggled. My fists clenched, blood rushing into my head.

Mrs. Herrick said, "Uh, do you have a middle name?"

"Tao," I said, pronouncing it correctly as "Dow."

"Your name is The Tao? What kind of name is that?"

I shrugged. "Mine."

To her credit, Mrs. Herrick glanced at her class roster to see if I was telling the truth and moved on, but as you might guess, that wasn't the end of it.

"It's a book," I told Sue Eldridge and Ronnie Blackburn later, my back against the jackets hanging on hooks at the rear of the room. I was as yet unaware it is also an entire philosophy.

"Why did your mother give you the same name as a book?" Sue asked.

"Just did." I wanted to explain that my *real* mother, Abby, didn't do that; that it was my buy-O mother, but I hadn't been real successful articulating that in the past.

Ronnie laughed and turned to the rest of the class, who were pulling on their coats for recess. "His mom gave him the same name as a book!" he yelled to them. Then a light clicked above his head. "Hey," he said, "me, too. My mom gave me the same name as a book, too. I'm Curious George!" He squealed in delight, falling to the floor between giggles, scratching under his arms like an ape.

Suddenly he was struggling to push my knee off his chest.

"Stop!" Mrs. Herrick yelled, but I punched Ronnie Blackburn in the nose anyway. It was the beginning of a series of unplanned three-day vacations that would dot my educational career like chicken pox.

But there's worse news about my handle, and if you've been paying attention, you know what it is: My health dictates the health of the nation's economy.

"How's your son doing, Mr. Jones!"

"The Tao's up today, sir."

"That's good news. Try to keep him happy."

Think I don't get carried away with those? To avoid confusion, and raucous laughter whenever my name is mentioned, I'm called T. J.

It's over now. I'm at the end of the summer following my senior year in high school; I have my diploma in a lockbox and the advantage of hindsight. But I want to tell it without that advantage—tell it as it unfolded—Mr. Simet says any story is only true in the moment.

My father always said there are no coincidences; that when two seemingly related events occur, they *are* related and should be treated that way. My father had very good reasons to try to understand how the universe works, which I'm sure I'll get into later.

The seemingly related things that I believe kick this story off happen on the second day of school. Coaches have tried to get me to turn out for sports since junior high. Sometimes they're insistent and sometimes downright nasty, accusing me of lacking the high school equivalent of patriotism, even to the point of calling me a traitor. But I've always eluded them. I'll play basketball three or four hours nonstop on open gym night, and I've always taken a couple of guys to Hoopfest in Spokane, which is the largest three-on-three street-basketball tournament in the country, and my team has won its division every time. I think I could have been a pretty fair football player; I'm sure not afraid to take a hit or to put a good lick on a guy, but something inside me recoils at being told what to do, and that doesn't sit well with most coaches, who are paid to do exactly that. I don't blame them; I know it's me. But the better you know yourself, the better chance you have of staying clear of trouble, and I'm pretty sure I'd never have lasted a full season of football with Coach Benson or basketball with Coach Roundtree. At one point or another in the heat of a game, Benson and Roundtree retreat to the time-tested and highly grating tool of public humiliation as a motivator, and that particular tool brings me back in your face faster than a yo-yo on a bungee cord, at which time I immediately suspend the notion of giving a shit.

So why was I considering joining a swim team that didn't exist before this year when I haven't been competitive in the water since fourteen, except for trying to beat Dad into the shower every morning? It's Simet. He catches me after third-period English and says, "Jones, didn't you used to be a pretty good swimmer?"

"I'm still a pretty good swimmer," I say. "Wanna try me?" Simet and I enjoy a longstanding rivalry wherein one of us challenges the other to some athletic contest. We handicap it based on our abilities (he lies like a student with a term paper due to get an advantage) and then make a friendly wager, say my English grade against some unsavory task he needs done, like stirring his compost heap when the temperature rises above eighty, or washing and waxing his Humvee, which looks better dirty.

He says, "I want to try you, but not against me."

"Who?"

"Someone different every week."

Visions of age-group swimming pop up: permanently chlorinated hair and eyes, clogged sinuses, ear infections. "This has a familiar ring."

"What do you think?"

"That you generally give me less information than I need to make an informed decision."

He gathers his books and nods toward the parking lot. "Hop into my babe-mobile and I'll buy you a milk shake. Maybe a pizza. We'll talk."

I follow him down the hall. "Make it a steak. Something is sick and wrong here."

"Let's hope it takes you a while to figure out what it is."

At Solomon's Pizza, Simet tells me that Mr. Morgan, the principal, asked him to replace Mr. Packenbush as assistant wrestling coach, who's resigning due to reasons of health. In a burst of panic, Simet told Morgan he's been trying to get a swimming team going, since Cutter is one of only three high schools in the conference without one.

I say, "Morgan, of course, pointed out that we don't have a pool."

"Way ahead of him," he says back. "I told him I could get free workout time at All Night Fitness, which I'm praying will actually be true."

"The pool at All Night is twenty yards," I remind him, "with an underwater ledge at the shallow end that will give you a subdural hematoma if you flip your turn." A subdural hematoma is what happens to your brain if you get whacked on the head hard enough to bounce it off the inside of your skull. I hear that term a lot when my mom is trying a child-abuse case.

Simet says I'm mucking things up with details—

"With only four lanes—"

—making it more difficult than it had to be.

"—and a ladder smack in the middle of one of them."

I should think of it as a challenge.

"Every meet would be away," I tell him. "No teams would come here to swim. In a twenty-yard pool, records don't count."

"All part of what makes an insurmountable obstacle interesting," he says. "A perennial road team. Mermen without a pond."

"You're forgetting something else. Nobody I swam with in age-group swimming lives here. There can't be three real swimmers in this entire school."

He considers that a minute, takes a bite of pizza and a long swallow on his beer. "I'm going off the record here," he says. "Educators are supposed to stick together and not bad-mouth one another, so we can collectively stay ahead of the educatees. But do you know Coach Murphy?"

Murphy is sixty-eight years old, having received divine dispensation to teach till two days after he dies, and I have judiciously avoided taking PE or health classes from him for four years. He tolerates zero bullshit or less. "Yeah, I know Coach Murphy."

"Then you know what my life would be like as his assistant." He leans forward. "I have my ways, Jones. If I go down, you go with me, which is to say if I coach wrestling, you wrestle. You have completed six semesters of English. You need eight. Think how easy it would be for me to misplace your records a week before graduation or remove a leg from one of your A's. You'd be caught at Cutter High School like a rat in a Twilight Zone cage."

"They're really willing to let you have this team? No facility, no swimmers?"

"One swimmer," he says.

"One used-to-be swimmer," I say back.

"T. J., I've looked at some of your old times. You were phenomenal. And I've coached some big-time swimmers, guys headed for the trials. Tell you what, I can whip you into good-enough shape to get us points at State, which would elevate Cutter in the overall all-sport state championship."

"Spock, are you out of your Vulcan mind?" I ask in my best William Shatner, which isn't all that bad.

Simet fixes his gaze on the table. "Actually, that's why they agreed. I told them you were a lock. If I don't come through, they'll sue for malpractice."

"You mean if *I* don't come through, they'll sue for malpractice."

"Same thing."

"If it's the same thing, you swim."

He nods at the remaining slice of pizza and says, "Go

ahead and eat that," which means he is desperate. He glances at his watch as I snap it up. "You don't have to answer tonight. I'll give you twelve hours."

It could be worse. Simet is a guy who always teaches you something, and it's not always about English or journalism. He *was* a hell of a swimmer himself in his younger years, when dinosaurs roamed the planet, and he seldom lets his classes forget what a spiritual experience it is to test yourself against that particular element. And though I burned out on it back then, I remember what amazing solace I felt working out. Up until I started swimming in grade school, half my teachers wanted me medicated and the other half wanted me in reform school. It helped me focus, beveled the edges on my boundless, uncontrolled energy, dulled my rage. All things considered, it is enough to make me consider Simet's proposal.

And here comes the kicker, the thing my father would say couldn't be a coincidence. I'm walking out of Simet's room the next day, thinking if I go along with him, I'll be breaking a career-long rule banning myself from organized sports while playing as many disorganized sports as time in my life allows. I mean, I *love* athletics. When I'm gliding to the hoop in a pickup game, or gunning some guy down at home plate from center field in a summer vacant-lot game, or falling into a perfect pace five miles out on a run, I feel downright godlike. But those things I do on my own. Cutter is *such* a jock school; they pray before games and cajole you to play out of obligation, and fans scream obscenities at one another from the stands, actually creating rivalries between *towns,* which has always seemed crazy to me. I remember my freshman year when the entire town was actually happy because the stud running back from Jackson Quarry became ineligible because of grades. Our *educational* community got giddy because some kid they didn't know tanked his math class. I mean, fifteen seconds after I finish a three-on-three game at Hoopfest, I'm sitting on the curb sharing Gatorade with the guys on the other team, talking about moves they put on me, and vice versa. Why would anyone want his opponent not to be at his best?

I'm on a roll there, but the point is that athletics has become such a big thing here that our administration begins each year figuring ways to pile up points for this all-sport state championship. And the symbol, the Shroud of Turin for Cutter High athletes, is the letter jacket. A block *C* on a blue-and-gold leather-and-wool jacket at Cutter High School is worth a whole bunch of second chances in the front office, of which I'm still waiting for my first. Those who don't own one of those jackets can easily become victims of our zero-tolerance policy. Well, in the eyes of The Tao Jones, nothing is true without its opposite, and it has been my minor quest to make sure that the finest athlete at Cutter High School did his very best to never earn that jacket. I should also say I'm not *totally* righteous in my quest for athletic purity. When I was an age-group swimmer I was *driven*. It consumed me, and I get uneasy thinking of becoming that focused on it again.

Variation on the theme. I'm moving catlike through the halls toward my locker minutes after Simet has challenged me to become the Mark Spitz of the desert (we don't have a *swimming pool)* and run into Mike Barbour—linebacker extraordinaire and student most likely to graduate with multiple felonies—jacking up Chris Coughlin against the lockers by the drinking fountain because Chris is wearing his dead brother's letter jacket.

Chris Coughlin is big-time special ed. He's main-streamed into PE and industrial arts, but spends most of his time in Resource Room improving his reading skills enough to read traffic signs and memorizing the intricacies of basic addition and subtraction. Everyone knows Chris's story: born addicted to crack cocaine, then got a double dose of shit just after his first birthday when his mother's boyfriend wrapped his face in Saran Wrap to make him stop crying. At his sentencing the boyfriend said he only wanted to make Chris pass out, not cause permanent brain damage. Oops.

Anyway, Chris's aunt and uncle took him and did all they could to make it up to him, but they couldn't regenerate brain cells. Chris's older half-brother, Brian, was raised by his own biological father and is something of a legend around Cutter from four or five years ago for having gained more yards in football and for hitting more home runs in baseball than any Cutter Wolverine before or since, and for being drafted into the Cincinnati Reds farm system out of high school. He was destined to have a street or a small park named after him someday, but was killed in a freak rock-climbing accident in the spring of his senior year. That about did poor old Chris in. He didn't have much, but he had a famous big brother. Brian was a real class act: good student, good athlete, great guy. The only times I remember seeing Chris smile were when he rode behind Brian on his dirt bike, or later, after Brian was gone, when he'd brag to anyone who would listen every time he passed Brian's picture in the trophy case. They didn't live together, but Brian sure let everyone know Chris was his brother, and if you messed with Chris back in those days—he was an easy mark—you could expect a visit from Brian.

So Barbour has the jacket buttoned at the bottom and pulled

down around Chris's shoulders so he can't move his arms, and his nose is about an inch from Chris's. I can't hear what he's saying, but tears squirt out of Chris's terrified eyes and his entire body trembles. I hustle over and insert myself between them, put an arm over Chris's shoulder, and say, "What's the matter, buddy? You look like you've been staring into a giant asshole," and move him a few steps down the hall, adjusting the jacket. Chris is hyperventilating, barely able to breathe.

"When you see one of those," I tell him, loud enough for Barbour to hear, "you gotta close your eyes and pretend it's not there. 'Course it helps if you also hold your breath."

Barbour's hand clamps onto my shoulder, and I turn in mock surprise. "Barbour! 'Sup, man?"

"I was talking to him, shithead."

"That's Mister Shithead to you. You were talking to my buddy Chris? He has to get to class. I run his complaint department, though, right, Chris?"

Still speechless, Chris nods.

Barbour says, "Fine. I'll tell you. Next time I see him in this jacket, I'll take it off him and burn it. You earn one of these if you're gonna wear it at this school, something you're too chickenshit to know anything about. It's an honor to wear these colors. You don't put on the jacket your brother earned. That's an athletic department rule."

I say, "Doesn't apply. Chris isn't *in* the athletic department," and Barbour says, "Yeah, well, in this school an athletic department rule is a school rule."

"Guess that wasn't in my orientation packet," I say. "What's the matter with you, Barbour? You know the deal with Coughlin's brother. Is this *prick* thing habitual, or do you work at it?"

"One of these days you're going to find out, Jones."

"I lie awake nights, waiting for that day."

Barbour says, "I'll save my energy for a white man."

"Because of your limited I.Q. I'll give you one of those, my friend. One more will get us both a three-day suspension." Barbour's family is famous for their send-all-the-Japs-back-to-Japan-with-a-nigger-under-each-arm attitude, so I feel like I have to hold my own.

We stand facing each other a few seconds, and finally Barbour reiterates the athletic department's zero-tolerance position on letter jackets and walks away. I pat Chris's shoulder and tell him not to worry about it and start for class, but look back to see him stuffing the jacket into his locker, trying in vain to cram it behind his books.

I walk back, pull the jacket out, and hand it to him. "Chris, you can wear it. It's okay."

"He said it was a rule."

"He lied. You can wear it anytime you want."

"He said the athletic department gots a rule."

"It belonged to your brother, Chris. You wear it. If Barbour gives you any more trouble, you come tell me, okay?"

Chris stares at me.

"Okay?"

"Okay." He says it without conviction.

As I turn the corner for class, I glance back again, and Coughlin is frantically stuffing the jacket back into the locker.

I stay in the afternoon to catch up on an article for the school paper, and catch a flash of blue and gold as I pass the janitor emptying the day's leavings into the Dumpster. I wait until he moves back inside and take a look, and sure enough, drag a Cutter High letter jacket out, with COUGHLIN lettered across the back.

Later I drive over to All Night Fitness to see if there is *any* possibility I can train in that pool. We have a family membership, so I spend time there already, but almost never in the water. Since it's the only indoor pool in town, All Night rents it out for parties and YMCA swim lessons and women's and seniors' water aerobics classes. I hope to swim a few laps to get a feel, but a sign on the entrance says PRIVATE GROUP. I push the swinging door open and stand just inside.

A young man and woman in Y T-shirts stand with lifeguard poles at either side of the pool, and Y staff people are spread out through the crowd like Secret Service at the White House Easter Egg Roll. Political correctness aside, the water and deck are filled with kids who look like they'll be getting the very best parking places for the rest of their lives. In the far lane Chris Coughlin helps a little girl with shriveled arms on a kickboard. The girl locks her gnarled elbows over the Styrofoam board and kicks while Chris pulls her along. The noise is deafening, but I watch him patiently help her extend her feet, toes pointed inward to propel herself properly, then release the board long enough to let her move under her own power for a few kicks until she becomes still in the water. Then he pulls her a little farther. I am struck with how completely comfortable he seems in the water.

His brother's jacket is still in my car, and I intend to go get it, but when I yell to get his attention he glances up, then quickly away, and I know my presence embarrasses him, so I just wave. He looks ashamed. How messed up is that? You get treated like shit, then have to be ashamed that you're the kind of person people treat like shit.

I stay a few minutes, imagining myself trying to get a decent workout in that abbreviated pool. It doesn't look promising. But as I drive through the quiet dusky streets of the uncharacteristically warm Cutter fall, Chris's ease in the water flashes before me and suddenly the mathematics—the *relativity*—of it all hits me. If it kills Barbour to see a guy as far out of the mainstream as Chris is, wearing a letter jacket that doesn't belong to him, how far up his nose will it get when he sees him wearing one that *does* belong to him? And suddenly I hear the voice the universe—and Simet—wants me to hear. It says, "Swim."

Also by
CHRIS CRUTCHER

Running Loose

Stotan!

The Crazy Horse Electric Game

Chinese Handcuffs

Athletic Shorts: Six Short Stories

The Deep End

Ironman

Whale Talk

King of the Mild Frontier

The Sledding Hill

Deadline

Angry Management

Period 8

Losers Bracket